0.N̄

ONYXIS STONE PRESS, First Print Edition, February 2017

Cover Font: More Perfect DOS VGA by Zeh Fernando & Adam C. "LÆMEUR" Moore

www.bryanperkinsauthor.com

0.N̄

Bryan Perkins

ONYXIS STONE PRESS

For you.

Table of Contents

LXIV. Haley

In that sordid, gray kitchen it was a torture to cook second breakfast. Hell, it was torture to cook any meal anywhere, even if cooking only took pressing a button and telling a printer what she wanted. But even after freeing herself from servitude to that fat, pompous Mr. Walker, Haley was still being forced to cook.

She sighed, pressed the printer's little red button, and said, "Salmon and salad with a glass of water." then waited the eternity it took for the slow machine to process her order, fulfill it, and let her get on with her day—long enough for her to imagine a million, billion other things she'd rather be doing. She lifted the plate of steaming, disgusting food out of the printer's arched mouth and opened the kitchen door to reveal the office where Lord Douglas always took his meals, too busy to stop working long enough to eat the vomit-inducing food he insisted on consuming *for appearance's sake*.

Lord Douglas was there, in his huge, filigrous office, as expected, but for once he wasn't working, instead watching TV on the 3D projector in the room's ceiling.

"*Haley*," he said, standing to take the plate from her and guide her to a seat. "Now no need to curtsy today," he said, sitting back in his own seat and starting in on his food even as he talked. "Not until we're at the Christmas Feast, at least."

Haley was a bit confused, considering she had no intention of curtsying anyway, but she just sat there and watched the TV show— some action flick about an android uprising—while Lord Douglas went on speaking and eating at the same time.

"And what are you doing here, anyway?" he said through his chewing. "I thought I gave you the day off."

"You never really give me anything," Haley said with a shrug.

Lord Douglas ignored her, though—because he certainly heard it, she spoke loud and clear—saying, "You know what. Could you actually get me a hamburger instead today? It *is* Christmas, after all."

"I thought you just gave me the day off," Haley said.

"Until the Christmas Feast," Lord Douglas replied, nodding in earnest. "But I'm asking you now as my friend—not as my secretary—could you please get me a hamburger, fries, and milk shake from the printer so I don't miss the premiere of my Christmas commercial? If you hurry, you might not miss it yourself."

"*Ugh.*" Haley groaned, standing and marching toward the kitchen. "*Fine.* Whatever. But it's definitely as your employee. You can't be my boss and my friend at the same time."

Haley ordered a hamburger, fries, and milkshake from the printer, and while she waited for the machine to do its work, Mr. Kitty meowed behind her.

"Hey there, Mr. Kitty," Haley said, surprised, patting the cat's butt and scratching around his ears and chin to the sound of ragged purrs. "Nice collar, by the way. Red really is your color."

The black cat, Mr. Kitty, meowed his agreement.

"You thirsty? Let me get you some water." Haley turned the faucet on a dribble and Mr. Kitty went on lapping it up.

"There you are," Haley said. "Now wait here for me. I'll be right back. I have to deliver this stupid hamburger to the stupid Lord first, but I do want to talk to you. So don't go anywhere."

She hurried back through the door, into Lord Douglas's office, and set the tray of food in front of him then tried to scurry back out of the room to catch Mr. Kitty, but Lord Douglas stopped her before she could get anywhere.

"Haley, wait," he said, smiling wide and standing to physically sit her in a chair. "You're just in time. Look."

Projected perfectly into her eyes, thanks to the highest tech projector system in existence, was the three-dimensional image of Lord Douglas—wearing the same too tall top hat, monocle, and tuxedo that he always wore, including then as they watched the commercial. He stood at the head of a board meeting of the Fortune 5, giving out orders to the owners around him and getting only eager faced servility in return. The camera zoomed out and out and out of Douglas Towers entirely until it zoomed so far away as to show that Douglas Towers was only the lead cog—and the largest one at that— in a much larger machine. As the camera zoomed out, a voiceover narrator said, "Lord Douglas, your Christmas Feast Head. Not only the richest owner in the worlds, he's the Owner's Owner." Then the video cut to charts and graphs, not only of Lord Douglas's net worth, but of the overall increased efficiency of the entire market ever since he had been dubbed Lord.

"Well, what do you think?" Lord Douglas asked, smiling and proud of himself, taking a big bite out of his hamburger before he went on through a full mouth. "It was pretty good, wasn't it?"

"*Uh*. Yeah. I guess," Haley said. She didn't really know, though. Even since she had been freed from working for Mr. Walker, she still didn't have much experience with TV, so she didn't know one way or the other what made a commercial good or bad.

"*I* think it was great," Lord Douglas said, smiling wider. "I came up with that slogan myself, too, you know. *The Owner's Owner*. It was all my idea."

"That's pretty good." Haley shrugged. Again, she didn't have any experience with slogans, commercials, or any of that, and she really didn't care.

"I'd say so," Lord Douglas went on anyway. "It's better than my first idea was, that's for sure. The *economy's* owner. That just sends the wrong message. We want to show that I'm the best at planning and controlling the economy, not the other way around. The economy doesn't control us anymore, we control it. And that's the message I want to send. Did you get that from the commercial?"

"*Uh, sure*," Haley said, uninterested. "Honestly, though. I really don't care. It seems pretty boring."

"Boring? *Huh*. That's not what you said—or *Haley* said, rather. *My Haley*, that is. The real one. *Hand*. I can't believe I'm still getting you two confused. Are you sure there's no other name you'd rather go by? It would be a lot easier for me if you did."

"Why should I be the one to change my name?" Haley asked. "Just come up with something else to call your girlfriend."

"*She's not my girlfriend*," Lord Douglas snapped. "Not yet, at least. I haven't even been in her presence now for… *Wow*. I can't even remember. It must be decades by now."

"Then you shouldn't have any trouble telling us apart," Haley said, hoping to end the conversation with that. "Haley is my name, and I'm not going to change it for anyone."

"Alright, alright. You don't have to get so defensive," Lord Douglas said, getting defensive himself.

"*Right*…" Haley said. "So, do you have anything else for me to do, or can I take the rest of my morning off, as you just promised?"

"Until the Christmas Feast. Yes," Lord Douglas said, but as Haley was about to leave, he stopped her again. "Oh, *wait*. Actually, there is just one more little thing. If you don't mind."

"*Ugh*. Mind what?" Haley asked.

"I need you to take this letter to Rosalind," he said, pulling a blank sealed envelope out of the inside pocket of his tuxedo jacket and holding it out to Haley. "*Please*. No one over there takes my communications anymore. This is the only way I can be sure they get the message before the Feast—even when they inevitably fail to respond. What do you say? As a friend?"

"Again, *no*." Haley sighed. "This is not at all as your friend. We are not friends. You're my employer. *But*: Before you pout and complain. *Yes*. I will bring it over there because I was planning on visiting Haley anyway. That's who the letter's really about, isn't it?'

"The letter is a private affair," Lord Douglas snapped. "And I would appreciate it if you left my private affairs just that: *private*."

"*Ptuh*. Privacy went right out the window when you made me your secretary, *Lord* Douglas. You realize that I have access to all your communications for scheduling, preference mapping, and other customization purposes, don't you? There is no privacy between us, *Lord*. So stop playing make believe and hand me the envelope. I'll deliver your little love letter, and I won't tell your precious Haley any more about your personal communications than I already have in my long time working for you—which is absolutely nothing. Trust me, we have much more interesting things to discuss than you, *Lord*." She snatched the envelope out of his hand.

"Like what? Since when?" Lord Douglas demanded, seriously getting flustered. "You never told me you had such a close relationship with Haley."

"That's because I don't share our personal conversations with you, either, *my Lord*."

"I— *But*—"

"What did you expect me to do with my free time? Stay in that closet you left for me like all the other good secretaries? I'm sorry, but no. That's not me. That's not *your* Haley, either. In case you were wondering. So I wouldn't go getting my hopes up if I were you."

"I— But…" Lord Douglas stammered again.

"No, sir. No buts. Now. It's supposed to be my morning off. I'm gonna go deliver this letter and spend the rest of my free time however I want to spend it. I'll see you at Feast time."

She didn't wait for a response, instead exiting the room into the short hall that led her to the elevator and pressing the button to call it. When she got on, she said, "Take me to Rosalind, please." and the floor fell out from underneath her.

߷   ✂   ♋

Rosalind was in her own office when Haley found her, an office which was much smaller than the one that Lord Douglas used. Rosalind's office had just enough room for a desk—that was pressed all the way up against the back wall, looking out through a window onto an ocean view—and two short stools. Rosalind sat on one of the stools, using her computer to do calculations that she could have done faster in her head. "Goddamn it! Not again," Rosalind complained after another batch of failed calculations.

"God?" Haley was taken aback.

"Yes, *God*," Rosalind said, standing from her desk so quickly that she knocked her stool over with the motion. "I don't really believe in the powers of our Creator now that she's dead, so I thought I might try to update my vocabulary with my new belief system."

"Does that mean you believe in the humans' concept of a God now?" Haley couldn't believe that.

"*Psssht. No.* Of course not." Rosalind crossed her arms. "I don't know. What even is the human concept of God anyway? Who cares?" She shrugged.

"*Ptuh.*" Haley laughed. "Not me, that's for sure. But it sounds like you do."

"Well, I don't." Rosalind huffed. "The only thing I'm concerned with right now are these stupid calculations. God, our Creator, and everything else in the worlds are nothing compared to this."

"Well, in that case," Haley said, "here's a letter from no one about nothing. I'll give you three guesses what it says, and I haven't even read it myself."

"I'm sure that I don't need to read it, either. The answer's no. Not for as long as he's undercover, and even still for a long time after that."

"Is that what you want me to tell him?"

"Yes. Please, do."

"Alright," Haley said. "If you say so. But not right now. On the way to the Feast tonight. In the meantime, it's my day off, and I'm gonna use it to see Haley."

"Take your time," Rosalind said. "Huey's the only one who's in a hurry. But before you go, do you mind if I ask you one question?"

"Shoot."

"Why is it that you still work for that asshole, anyway?"

ও ✄ ৶

Apparently, Haley wasn't going to get to take the rest of the morning off after all. Haley was busy doing something with that Pidgeon guy she was always spending time with, so Haley had gone back to the office to wait, and of course, Lord Douglas was there, practically begging her to make him lunch—*as a friend*—so he didn't have to miss a rerun of his commercial. Haley reminded him that they weren't friends, that she didn't have a choice as to whether or not she did his biddings—did she though?—and then she went to get his lunch for him, as commanded.

"Thank you so much, Haley, dear," Lord Douglas said, taking the plate of food. "Everyone watches the numbers before they go to the Feast, so the run right before is always the most important for any Christmas commercial. All the others are mini focus groups if you know what you're doing. You understand, don't you?"

"*Sure*," Haley said, but she didn't care enough to even try to understand. The world of Inland was supremely boring to her.

"Great... *Good*." Lord Douglas smiled. "Then perhaps you won't mind if I ask you a few more small favors—*as a friend*—on this, your morning off."

"I'm not your frien—"

"Yes, yes," Lord Douglas cut her off. "I know how you feel about the matter, but rest assured, I feel quite the opposite. I look at you as one of my closest friends—besides Mr. Kitty, Pidgeon, and *my* Haley, of course—and I truly hope that one day you'll feel the same way about me."

"*Ptuh*." Haley scoffed. "As long as you're my Lord and boss, I wouldn't hold my breath."

"Luckily, I'm no human, and I'm capable of holding my own

breath for as long as you are of holding yours. I'll turn you around yet. But in the meantime, there are those few little favors I'd still like to ask."

"*Jobs*," Haley reminder him. "Not favors."

"Yes, well, if you'll just set out my best tuxedo and top hat, then ensure that the electric limo is charged and detailed in preparation for tonight, I'd feel much more prepared."

"Charge the limo? Can't we just take the elevator like civilized human beings?"

"Of course we could," Lord Douglas said. "And I usually do. But the limo doesn't use that much electricity, this is my twenty fifth year in a row as Christmas Feast Head, and I deserve a treat, even if it's something as small as a short car ride. Besides, as I often remind you—"

"*Image is everything. A wealthy facade leads to a wealthy wallet*," Haley recited for him.

"*Exactly*. You got it. So, does that mean you'll do me these favors?"

"It means I don't have any other option."

She laid Mr. Douglas's most expensive tuxedo and tallest top hat out on his bed, ensuring there were no wrinkles or lint in sight, then sat in the already—and always—charged limo to wait for Lord Douglas. She didn't have anything better to do until the Feast anyway.

When Lord Douglas finally came out to the garage, dressed and ready to leave, Haley got out of the car, opened his door to let him in the back seat, then returned to the driver's seat herself, despite Lord Douglas's insistence that she sit in the back with him. She didn't want to give him any reason to think that she was his friend, even if his delusions had already led him to the false assumption.

They rode the limo to the Feast Hall parking garage, Haley let Lord Douglas out of the back seat, and it wasn't until they had made it all the way into the Feast Hall lobby that Lord Douglas said, "Aw, crap. You know what. I left my hat in the car. Can you be a doll and go get it for me?"

"*Ugh*." Haley groaned, and of course, she could. She worked for him. She could do anything he asked her to do, *or else*. Haley never was certain what that "or else" actually meant, but she never felt the need to find out, either.

She ran back to the limo to get Lord Douglas's stupid hat, and as she sprinted to return it to him, she ran straight into Rosalind and fell to the ground on top of her.

"*Ugh*. I'm sorry," Haley said, helping Rosalind up and brushing herself off. "I wasn't paying attention."

"Me neither," Rosalind said, holding Lord Douglas's top hat out to Haley. "My mind's a bit preoccupied."

"Tell me about it." Haley groaned. "Stupid fucking bosses." She held up the hat as evidence. "Speaking of which, I better go before he gets pissed."

"Owners and their phallic hats," Rosalind scoffed, shaking her head, as Haley ran off to the Feast Hall lobby to deliver Lord Douglas's phallus to him.

Of course, he wasn't alone, though. The Feast Hall lobby was mostly empty—all the other owners already in the hall because they didn't have the need to maintain the fashionably late image of a Lord—but there, talking to Lord Douglas, was the second richest—and first fattest—owner in all the worlds, Mr. Walker himself, who was once Lord and even for a while there Haley's boss.

"*Ah*, Haley," Mr. Walker said, interrupting whatever Lord Douglas was saying as soon as he saw her—some argument about Mr. Walker's deliberately shoddy protector work, from the snippet Haley had heard on the way in.

"*My Haley*," Lord Douglas insisted, contradicting what he had earlier told Haley about which person with the same name was *his* Haley.

"Yes, but first she was mine." Mr. Walker chuckled. "You only get sloppy seconds, sir."

"I'm sure any seconds coming from your direction would be sloppy," Lord Douglas said. "Which is why I would never eat them. But right now, I'd like to make an appearance at this Feast, so if you'll excuse me, ol' Walky Talky." Lord Douglas gave a half bow and made his way around Mr. Walker's girth to enter the Feast Hall proper.

Haley started to follow Lord Douglas, but Mr. Walker mumbled something under his breath, and for some reason, she wanted to know what he had said. "Excuse me, sir," she said, stopping to wait for his answer. "What was that?"

"I said, How lovely to see you, dear," Mr. Walker said, bowing surprisingly low, even for as much weight as he had lost since Haley used to work for him. "How does our Lord Douglas treat you now that you're his secretary?"

"Never as bad as you did," Haley said. Which was pretty much true. Mr. Walker's worst was worse than Lord Douglas's—as was his baseline status quo—but every once in a while, Haley had to admit that Mr. Walker seemed to want to be genuinely kind to her while Lord Douglas always and forever seemed fake.

"But pretty bad, *eh*?" Mr. Walker said. "That's the way of the worlds, isn't it? Especially for you soulless robots."

Mr. Walker seemed like he was in one of those moods where he was trying to be nice, so Haley smiled while she said, "From here, it looks more like you owners are the soulless ones—not us *robots*. Now if you don't mind, please fuck off while I go do one of your fellow soulless owner's work for him."

Mr. Walker looked offended, but Haley didn't care. She stomped out of the lobby, through the densely-packed Feast Hall, and into the kitchen to order herself a drink from the printer that was nearest the entrance. She had finished her first drink and was ordering up another when Mr. Walker's secretary, Elen, came in, staring at Haley—as she usually did.

"What?" Haley snapped when Elen wouldn't stop staring. "I'm not in the mood today, so just spit it out. What?"

"You're gonna get caught one day, and Lord Douglas is gonna be pissed," Elen said, shaking her head.

"No, I'm not. No owner comes back here, *Lord* Douglas doesn't care enough to keep inventory, and I don't give a shit if I piss him off anyway. So fuck all those fat fucks out there, and fuck you, too, if you go snitch for them." Haley gulped down the rest of her drink and ordered one for Lord Douglas.

"Does that stuff even get you drunk?" Elen asked. "Seems like such a waste if robots aren't affected. Maybe you can give me a sip of your next one."

"Maybe you can order your own," Haley said as she carried Lord Douglas's drink out into the Feast Hall to deliver it.

She passed lines and lines of fat and fatter owners who were already drinking away—their hats getting taller the closer their seats were to the head table and the Fortune 5. Before she was even halfway to the head table, Lord Douglas yelled over the cafeteria roar of the Feast Hall to urge her along. "Haley! Haley, my dear. Please hurry," he called. "Walker here's telling jokes, and I'm not sure if it's the smell of his breath or the cheese on his punchlines, but I need some sort of alcohol in my system to deal with the odor."

Most of the owners in the Hall laughed—none more loudly than Mr. Angrom, Lord Douglas's right hand at the head table—while Mr. Walker, Mr. Loch, and a relatively few other owners dispersed throughout the crowd glared in silent anger. For her part, Haley neither laughed nor glared, instead setting Lord Douglas's drink in front of him and going back to the kitchen to order herself another round.

As she walked away from the Head Table, Lord Douglas called his Feast order after her. "And a turkey for the Feast tonight, darling! One that's fatter than Walker here, all slopped with gravy. With potatoes, deviled eggs, and pie on the side. Thank you very much."

Haley did not say you're welcome. She stormed into the kitchen, ordered two drinks at once, chugged one down in a single gulp, and snatched an envelope out of Elen's hands without thinking about it. When Haley did think about it, she started to say, "Wait, who's this from?" but only got out "Wait…" before she read the words on the message inside and knew the answer to her question.

"Seriously." the message read. "Why do you still work for that asshole? Isn't it time you quit?"

ଷ ✖ ✒

LXV. Thimblerigger and Stevedore

"Tails," one of them said—Stevie. It didn't really matter which one, though. Tails was both of their go to call. Tails never fails, they'd always say. But with their luck, it seemed more like tails always failed.

The other, Thim, flipped a coin, caught it, and read the outcome. "Tails," they said, handing the token to Stevie and waiting for Stevie's next call before flipping another coin.

"Tails," Stevie repeated.

"Tails again," Thim said after having flipped the second coin, and so again the coin changed hands from loser to winner.

"Tails," Stevie said again. "And you can stop asking me because my answer's not gonna change."

"Tails again." And again, the coin changed hands.

"Do we really have to keep playing this game?" Stevie asked.

"Tails again," Thim said, handing Stevie the coin.

"I mean, really? How many coins have we flipped already?"

"Tails again."

"And I don't just mean this morning, either. I'm talking about our entire sad lives."

"Tails again."

"All we do is flip coins, flip coins, flip coins, and neither of us ever seems to come out on top."

"Tails again."

"No matter how long we stay at it, running faster and faster to try to keep up, we still end up about even in the end."

"Tails again."

"In fact, the more coins we flip, the longer we work at it, the closer we come to a tie."

"Tails again."

"It's like a rule. Or a law or something. Diminishing returns... No, large numbers. I don't know."

"Tails again."

Stevie grabbed Thim by the shoulders and shook them. "Look at me," Stevie said. "Are you even listening to a word I'm saying?"

But Thim flipped another coin and checked which side came up before giving their answer. "*Tails again*," they said. "Are you listening to a word that I'm saying?"

"What? *No*. Your stupid coin game?" Stevie chuckled. "That's exactly what I'm talking about. I'm over it. You're definitely not listening."

"No, you're the one who's not listening. Look." Thim flipped the coin over and over, reading out the result each time. "Tails. Tails. Tails. Tails. Tails. Tails. Tails. Tails. Tails. Tails. Tails… And it keeps going, too. Every time I flip. Are you listening? Tails. Tails. Tails. Tails. Tails…"

"Let me hold that coin." Stevie snatched it away from Thim to feel both sides and make sure it wasn't a cheat.

"No tricks here," Thim said, holding their hands up in defense. "You're the one who's winning, anyway. Why would I use a one-sided coin that only made me lose? Don't you think it's odd?"

"Any time I'm on the winning side of a coin flip, something's definitely odd," Stevie said.

"No, I meant all the tails in a row. *There's another*. Don't you think it's about time something comes up heads for once? *Tails again*."

"Of course I do. It's always about time until it is time. But I thought I was losing all this time. It usually lands on heads, doesn't it?"

"You know what. Maybe it is."

"Is what? *Heads*? You have been reading the coin correctly, haven't you?"

"No— I mean, yes. *I have*. It's been tails all morning. And again. And again. And again… It doesn't stop. I meant maybe it is time."

"What now?"

"Maybe time has stopped. Maybe these aren't different coin flips at all. Maybe it's really just been the same coin flip over and over again."

"The same coin flip?"

"Yes, well, if I flip it once and get tails, that flip's always tails. Right? So if I did that flip again, I'd get tails again. Right? It's already been done and decided for, and it's already tails."

"*Right*… But how could you do the same coin flip again?

Wouldn't that just be doing another coin flip?"

"I don't know. Would it? Usually it is, but this isn't usual. Is it? Usually we'd get a few heads in there to let us know that we had moved forward in time, right? But all we keep getting here are... *tails again.*"

"I still don't understand. You flip the coin once, then you flip it again. Those are different flips even if they land with the same side up."

"Are they, though? That's the point. Maybe so. Maybe not. I still don't understand it myself, you see. We need to do more investigating. Here. Listen carefully. Let me know if you can detect any differences at all between the flips." Three flips in quick succession and three times in a row: "Tails. Tails. Tails." Then, "Well..."

"Well, it sounded like three more tails to me," Stevie said with a shrug. "I don't know. What else do you want me to say?"

"I don't know, either," Thim said, tossing the coin way up where, before it could land, Big Broke Momma snatched it out of the air. Thim and Stevie always wondered how Momma BB got around so quietly while being so large—and with a limp at that—but if there was anyone in the worlds who could sneak better than them, it was her.

Momma BB was something special—and that wasn't just because she had taken in and reared Thim and Stevie since they were young and useless cry-babies, either. She really was special, and they weren't the only people who thought so. Just like Thimblerigger and Stevedore—who were never apart, depended upon one another for survival, and were made better by their mutual reliance—Momma BB wasn't a single person, either. And not just her body—with its exposed mechanisms and wires, patchwork of variously shaded skin colors, and legs of two different lengths, producing her signature limp—but her mind, too. She was connected to thousands of other minds already, and that neural network was growing with every day that they built the robot revolution.

"Well, now. What are you two little monsters still doing here so late in the morning?" Momma BB asked. "Don't y'all have chores you're supposed to be doing?"

Here was the lobby of the apartment building safe house that Momma BB oversaw. Mostly it was inhabited by orphans—like

Thimblerigger and Stevedore—who would have died or been reduced to something worse than death in order to survive if Momma BB hadn't taken them in. Other than that, there were some escaped androids who had fled slavery to be stuck in the Streets of Six and relatively fewer humans who had been blacklisted from employment and housing elsewhere because of their support for the robot cause.

"Thim's been flipping coins again," Stevie said, arms crossed.

"Well, we're not really sure it if it actually is *again*, Momma," Thim corrected Stevie. "It could still be the same flip."

"You two aren't gambling now, are you?" Momma BB shook her head. "You know I don't approve of it."

"It's not really gambling because we share our tokens," Stevie said. "It's more symbolic of the transfer of wealth than anything."

"And we still don't know if it's a new flip yet," Thim said. "What'd it come out as?"

Momma BB looked at the coin, said, "Tails." and tossed it to Thim.

Thim caught the coin with a shrug and handed it to Stevie, saying, "Still inconclusive. We'll have to run more tests."

"But Momma BB caught that one," Stevie complained. "It has to be a different flip. Doesn't it?"

Thim shrugged again. "*Inconclusive.*"

"Alright now, y'all," Momma BB said. "You can do your *further testing* on the way to work. Your chores are more important than ever now that Christmas is so close. Let's go, now. We—"

"*We do nothing alone,*" Thimblerigger and Stevedore finished for her, having heard the mantra a million times a day since she had taken them in. "Yeah, yeah. We know."

"Then y'all know that you've got chores, too, and you should be out there doing them."

"Yes, Momma," Stevie said. "We'll get right on it."

"We thought time had stopped," Thim said. "We couldn't do the chores if time wasn't moving. Could we?"

"*You* thought time had stopped," Stevie reminded them. "I just wasn't paying attention."

"Well time has not stopped," Momma BB assured the children. "I guarantee you that. If only it had. No, time is flowing at the exact same speed that it always has—much too fast. And that's all the more reason why you two need to get to those duties of yours sooner than later. There's no time to waste. Now move along."

"There's no time at all," Thim said, putting a finger on their chin. "*Hmmm*. Maybe that's it. There's just never been any time at all…"

"Now that's just too much," Stevie said with a sigh. "Time definitely exists, and Momma BB's entry into our story suggests that it's moving forward. So let's just get on with our chores."

Thimblerigger started to say something, stopped, took one more coin out and flipped it as high in the air as they could, caught the coin, flipped it behind their back, under their leg, and off the wall, caught it one more time in one hand and flipped it onto the other only to reveal the coin, sigh, toss it to Stevedore, and say, "I'll come do my part, but I still think the evidence is inconclusive."

"And like I said," Momma BB said. "Y'all can continue your little experiments on your way. You're creative. I'm sure you'll think of something."

"Thim's experiments," Stevie reminded Momma BB.

And, "*We do nothing alone*," Thim reminded Stevie.

"That's right, my darling little monsters," Momma BB said, pulling Thimblerigger and Stevedore in tight for a big, robotic bear hug. "*We do nothing alone*. And don't you dare forget it. Now, I love you two. Y'all know that, right?"

"Yes, Momma," Thim and Stevie said simultaneously, struggling for air through Momma BB's hug. "We love you, too."

"Good," she said, patting them on the butts to encourage them out of the apartment complex. "Then get moving. I have some chores of my own to get to."

🝔 ✻ ⚮

Thim and Stevie came out of Momma BB's Safehouse into the heart of the Streets of Outland Six, dark skyscrapers towering over them in every direction.

First—as they did every morning—Thim and Stevie had to find food. It was impossible to do any of the other work ahead of them unless they could nourish themselves, and in Outland Six, there were no *printers* to steal food from one of the other worlds and give it to them, so they had to go out and find it for themselves. Well, not just for themselves. They were actually gathering supplies for the entirety of Momma BB's Safehouse. And while that meant that they had to find more food than they would have if they were only searching for themselves, it also meant that they benefited from the experiences, tools, and resources of the other residents—including Momma BB herself—which made them able to catch, carry, and grow more food than they ever would have been capable of on their own—more than enough to feed everyone in the Safehouse, stow a supply for emergencies, and still have extra to give to those in need.

Thim and Stevie's morning duties consisted of scouting the rat traps and garbage cans in their sector. The rat traps, because if they didn't get there early enough in the morning, someone else might take the meal for themselves. And the garbage cans, not for food—no one ever threw anything edible away in Six because they were all too hungry to waste food—but instead in search of the odd stray mechanical part, frayed wire, or other useful tidbit. Not many Sixers knew how to utilize such garbage, but Momma BB had always said that it was the trash parts that others had thrown away that had originally saved her life—allowing her to go on to save Thimblerigger's and Stevedore's—so Thim and Stevie were extra careful to search every dumpster they passed in case the part they found turned out to be the one that saved a life.

As they walked, Thim continued flipping a coin over and over and calling out the result each time. "Tails. Tails. Tails…"

When they got to the first dumpster, Thim handed Stevie the token, saying, "You keep flipping. The more data we gather the better. I'm going in."

Stevie shrugged, went on flipping the coin, and called out each response even though Thim, who had gone all the way into the dumpster to search it more thoroughly, couldn't make out a thing. "Tails. Tails. Tails. Tails. Tails…" And so on and so on.

"Well?" Thim asked expectantly, climbing out of the dumpster and brushing some trash goo off their shirt.

"All tails," Stevie said, flipping the coin back to Thim who caught it, flipped it again, and said, "*Tails again.*"

They walked on, Thim flipping the coin still, until they made it to the first alley that held their rat traps. Stevie searched each one, putting what rats had been caught in a satchel they carried over one shoulder, while Thim went on flipping the coin.

"Tails. Tails. Tails…" Thim read off as Stevie grabbed a still-twitching rat by the tail, slammed its head on the ground to knock it out, and stuffed it in the bag with the rest.

"Well, I'm getting heads and tails both now," Stevie said, chuckling to themself as they walked on. "Even if it's all rat heads, I think it's safe to say that time has indeed moved forward now that we're doing our chores. Wouldn't you?"

"I don't know." Thim shrugged, flipping the coin again and still coming up tails. "I still say the evidence is inconclusive."

And so they continued on, searching each block of dumpsters and set of rat traps in their sector, flipping tails over and over, until they had searched what seemed like hundreds of dumpsters and ten times as many traps to find more rats than they could carry and what looked like a few useful stray parts. They returned to the Safehouse and left the rats in the kitchen—and the bits and pieces of wire and electronics in Momma BB's workshop—then they finally got to eat their own meal. They plated out a serving of rat sausage—or maybe it was pidgeon, but it all tasted the same in sausage form—biscuits, and jam for each of them then took their meals up to the roof garden—a long climb with the smell of sausage in their nostrils.

The rooftop garden was Thimblerigger and Stevedore's favorite place to be in all the worlds. Momma BB's Safehouse wasn't the tallest skyscraper around, but it was near it, and there weren't any shadows on the roof except for one little corner where Thim and Stevie always ate their lunch in the shade of a nearby building, looking out onto the rows and rows of raised beds that grew wheat, vegetables, potatoes, and corn in the life-giving sunlight.

Mr. Kitty—a black cat who frequented Momma BB's Safehouse—was already asleep in the shade, as if he were waiting for them to arrive. He purred and changed position when Thim and Stevie each took a chance to pet his smooth, soft fur before starting in on their lunch.

"Mr. Kitty sure does have the life, doesn't he?" Stevedore said as they ate.

And, "*Ugh.*" Thimblerigger groaned. "How many times do I have to tell you?" they asked through a mouth full of sausage. "Don't talk with your mouth full. It's disrespectful."

"Yeah, well you just did it, too," Stevie complained.

"But you don't have to look at it," Thim said, stuffing their mouth faster so they could get back to flipping the coin.

"Still," Stevie said, annoyed. "Mr. Kitty has got the life, *huh*? I mean, look at him. Every time we see him, he's sleeping in the shade here. And look, you just gave him the last little bits of your sausage, and I'll give him the last little bits of mine, then we'll both go to work, watering all this food for all these other people, while he just goes on sleeping. *That* is the life."

"Sure," Thim said, done eating and back to flipping tails. "And every time he sees us, we're out here sitting in the shade with more lunch than we can eat. Besides, those little bits we give him aren't enough for a cat to live off of. I'm sure he has to search for his own food the same as we all do." And tails, and tails, and tails...

"*Yeah, yeah,*" Stevie said, feeding their leftovers to Mr. Kitty then leaning back on their elbows to get some rest before their next set of chores. "But I'm sure there are plenty of other people who feed him. And plenty of places to find food."

"Not on this roof," Thim said. "*Tails.* Not unless that cat eats vegetables. *Tails again.* This is getting serious."

"Seriously, though," Stevie said. "How does he get up here? I mean, I've never opened the rooftop door for him. Have you?"

"What? *No.* That's not what I'm talking about. You're off track again. I'm talking about the coin flips. They're still coming up tails. That's what's serious."

"Sure, sure. Sure, it is," Stevie said, laying all the way back now to listen to the cool wind blowing over their heads. "But we've been over all that already once before. I'm on to this now. Haven't you ever wondered how it is he gets up and down from here all the time? I mean, like you said, there's no way he's surviving on the food here alone. And we trap all our rats for ourselves, so that's not an option."

"Of course I think about that," Thim complained. "I've been asking you those exact questions ever since the first time we saw Mr. Kitty up here. Why are you only interested in them now that I have something more important on my mind?"

"I'd hardly say that a string of bad luck is super important in the grand scheme of things. Neither is this Mr. Kitty business, mind you, but I choose to focus on it just as you choose to focus on the coin flips. But neither matters at all, in the end, because it's time to get back to what's truly important anyway: our chores. So let's do this."

And after one more trio of tails, Thim finally gave in and

helped with the work. Each of them picked up their bucket, filled it with water, then started down a row, carefully watering each plant along the way. At the end of the row they'd go back and refill their buckets then pick another row to water. There wasn't really any talking or thinking that could be done during this part of their job because the work was too physical to allow for it, so they just worked. They were sweaty and tired by the time they put their empty buckets away, but Thim went on flipping their coin nonetheless.

"And do you see him now?" Stevie asked. "Or more likely, is Mr. Kitty gone? No sign of where he's gotten off to, either, I imagine. But you know what? I've had enough waiting for the answer to come to me. I'm gonna go find it for once."

"What are you talking about now?" Thim asked, still coming up tails.

"I'm saying that I think we should camp out here on the roof tonight. But this time let's really stay up all night like we always used to say we'd do. And we'll keep a watch until we finally find out where Mr. Kitty comes from. What do you say?"

"Tails," Thim said. "Tails. Tails. *Tails*. That's all I can say until it comes up heads for once. I don't care about anything else—including where we sleep—until it does. So whatever."

"Good. Great, then," Stevie said, laughing and clapping their hands. "Let's go down, get some food and blankets, then come back up and set up a stakeout. We're finally gonna find out who this Mr. Kitty is, and we're not leaving this roof until we know for sure. Come on."

And so Thim followed Stevie downstairs to do as they were told, flipping tails all the way.

⅋   ✶   ⌀

LXVI. Jorah

Slip, snap, click.

Slip, snap, click.

Why? Why did they still need him to do this? Why did they need anyone to do this?

Slip, snap, click.

Slip, snap, click.

He was supposed to be an actor, not an assembly line worker. And besides that, robots were one hundred percent capable of doing slip, snap, clicking work. There was no reason to convince humans that it was fun, rewarding, or honorable in any way. They weren't needed to do it.

Slip, snap, click.

Slip, snap, click.

Of course androids were capable of doing slip, snap, clicking work. Jorah himself was one of them, and he was doing the work better than any human ever could.

Slip, snap, click.

Slip, snap, click.

But no one knew that he was an android. And Jorah couldn't tell anyone that he was—especially now that his majority owner was Mr. Walker, the head of the anti-robot counter-revolution. Still, none of that changed the fact that androids *could* do the work.

Slip, snap, click.

Slip, snap, click.

Slip, snap, clicking certainly wasn't what he had escaped his own assembly line for. He hadn't liberated himself from slavery just so he could turn around and sit *voluntarily* behind another assembly line.

Slip, snap, click.

Slip, snap, click.

He hadn't escaped so he could free the other robots, either. He hadn't escaped so he could fight them in Mr. Walker's army. Jorah had escaped for one reason and one reason alone: So he could live his own life.

Slip, snap, click.

Slip, snap, click.

Not like this. Some people might have called what he was doing living, but it certainly wasn't *his* life. He didn't even get to choose what roles he acted in.

Slip, snap, click.

Slip, snap, click.

Jorah turned to look at the extra next to him, intent on her own work, living her own puppet life and being made to dance by the tugs of her own strings. Her a human, him an android, and neither able to exhibit any more free will than the other. Each forced to do whatever they had to do to procure the energy they needed in order to reproduce and prolong their sad, irrelevant lives.

Slip, snap, click.

Slip, snap, click.

Well how much energy did they need today? How many tugs would Jorah's strings get until the puppeteer finally let him rest? How many more days could Jorah take living like this? How many more days could all the puppets take it?

Slip, snap, click.

Slip, snap, click.

But there wasn't anything he could do. Was there? If there were, he would have done it already. He was as free as he could ever be in Outland Three. The only thing left for him was to work and to wait.

Slip, snap, click.

Slip, snap, click.

And though he felt like he couldn't take it any longer, Jorah still went on slip, snap, clicking, even after a loud, metallic bell signaled for lunch and the extras filling the set around him dropped their work to hurry to it.

"I said cut!" Wes, the director, yelled through a megaphone. "That's the scene, Jorah. Or it was supposed to be. And I like your commitment to the job, but we really need a shot of you leaving the assembly line with the rest of the workers."

"I— *What?*" Jorah asked, absently standing from his work stool and making his way toward the food cart to nibble on some cheese.

"You didn't stand up and leave with the rest of the workers," Wes said, slowly, like Jorah was stupid, but Jorah was still having trouble following what was being said so he couldn't really take offense. "You're a good worker, yes, but you hate your job. The very same reason you work so hard—up until the very end of your shift— is the exact reason you can't wait to get home. *Your family.* And it's not like your piece of shit boss—*your words, not mine*—is going to pay you for any of the extra pieces you slip, snap, click together above quota so you're just wasting your time, making your boss look better so she can make more money without sharing any of it with you. Now, do you see why you'd be just as eager to get up and get out of there as all these other extras who did what their scripts told them to do?"

"I—*uh*— *Yeah…*" Jorah said, finishing off another tiny cube of cheese in search of the energy he'd need to get himself through another day of dancing under his puppet strings. "I'm sorry. I mean, of course. Anything you say. You're the director. I'll do better this time. I swear."

"Alright, then. Places everyone!" Wes called through his megaphone, and the puppeteer strings pulled all the actors into their first positions—including Jorah to sit on his cold, hard stool, back again in front of the assembly line for the trillionth time since he had become the star of Mr. Walker's anti-robot propaganda machine.

"Lights!" Wes called.

And the world faded into darkness around Jorah, all except for his work area which was lit so brightly that it gave him a shining aura like a halo.

"Cue the belts."

The constituent parts of whatever it was they were slip, snap, clicking together started moving down the conveyor belt in front of him again, and like Pavlov's dogs, Jorah began piecing them together, even before the scene had officially begun. This time he would act it to perfection.

"*Aaaaannnd… action!*"

Slip, snap, click.

Slip, snap, click.

All he could do was wonder how many more days he could take living like this. How many more days would all the puppets take it?

Slip, snap, click.

Slip, snap, click.
Slip, snap, click...

⟨decorative symbols⟩

He was home at last, finally alone again in his dressing room. Here he had the greatest illusion of freedom in, and control over, his life, and so here was his favorite place to be—even if he knew full and well that the freedom and control he felt like he was experiencing was nothing more than an illusion.

Here, at least, he had his television. And that was programmed to comply to his every demand—manual, remote, or vocal—as long as that demand had something to do with powering on or off, adjusting volume, or changing the channel, etc. Which was some amount of control and freedom, however limited. As well, here was the battle station which had a seemingly infinite—though necessarily finite due to the nature of physics—number of makeup and hairstyle combinations for Jorah to command up at his every whimsy. Not full control or freedom, again, but better than nothing.

Then of course, there was the 3D printer. The machine that ensured Jorah more freedom than most anyone in all the worlds was lucky to experience—excepting the owners, of course. It was the same reason he was chained to the anti-robot propaganda films that Mr. Walker was forcing him to act in. But Jorah would have to work a job in order to survive no matter what, and most of the jobs out there didn't come anywhere close to paying with unbridled printer access, so there he was, producing anti-robot propaganda as an android himself. He was starting to wonder how much of his life he was willing to give up for even that much "freedom".

In fact, Jorah stood there then, staring at the frowny face arch of his 3D printer's closed mouth, finger hovering over the single red eye button, trying to figure out what he really needed from this expensive machine at all. He was an android, after all, not a squishy, mortal human, and if he chose to, he could generate most of the energy he needed—all with a proper source of saline—through a photosynthesis-like process. One of the benefits of his darker skin was the ability to absorb more of the Sun's energy, and he could last on that for some time. Besides, he never really liked to eat anyway. Sure, he pretended like he enjoyed food in order to endear himself with his actor friends, but he never seemed to be able to experience the same raw euphoria that humans did when they ate. So in the end, probably the only thing he'd ever truly miss about losing access to his printer would be the clothes. And *Fortuna* the clothes.

First of all, and of course, the dresses. A-lines, slips, sheaths. Every type of skirt from mini on up to maxi and beyond. Blouses in tank tops, halters, and racerbacks. Suit pants, suits, blazers, and hats. He could go on and on and on about it. Hell, he was even starting to appreciate the subtle differences between different styles of tuxedo after having been dragged along to so many galas with Mr. Walker. And even if his printer could only make tuxes and nothing else, that alone might be worth Jorah's days spent acting in shitty, self-hating, anti-robot propaganda. *Maybe.*

He was still standing there in front of his printer, trying to decide between hundreds of millions of billions of options that all seemed equally unappetizing, when a knock came at the door, surprising Jorah so much that he nearly jumped out of the slippers he was wearing.

"*Yoo hoo!*" came Meg's voice through the dressing room door, grating Jorah's insides at the sound of it. "Jorah, my boy. Are you in there?"

Jorah hesitated. He didn't feel like spending time with any humans—he almost never did—but he couldn't just stay silent and wait for Meg to go away because she may never. Ever since the untimely death of Jorah's best friend, Russ—the only human who Jorah had never minded spending time with—Meg had practically been stalking Jorah, trying to become the new best friend of the now most popular celebrity in all of celebritydom, and frankly, Jorah was sick of it. Meg was a nice person, a *great* dresser, and an okay actor— all things that should have made her the perfect new friend for Jorah who didn't give his opinion of a person's wardrobe lightly—but something about her needy clinginess turned Jorah off to ever starting a real relationship with her.

"Yes, I'm here," Jorah finally called back, hoping for no response. "One moment, please."

"*Fantastic.* Take your time," Meg responded nonetheless. "I've got all the time in the world to spare."

Of course she did. And of course he did. So he slowly buttoned on his blouse, taking extra time to find the perfect shoes and not settling on an eyeshadow color until he had seen all of his options three times through. He still held out hope that Meg would get sick of waiting and leave, but of course again, he had no such luck. She was still waiting outside of his dressing room with a smile on her face when he opened the door to say, "Hello." with a curt nod of the head.

"*Wow*," Meg said, holding a hand to her mouth—lips painted as red as Jorah's. "No wonder you're so famous. You look absolutely stunning. *Just perfect*. Even better in person."

Jorah blushed. He would never get used to flattery like that, no matter how often he experienced it, and he was starting to worry that enough of it might just solidify Meg's position as his best friend despite Jorah's every efforts to resist her advances. "You're too kind," he said. "But I'm sure you didn't just come here to compliment me again, have you? We've been over this."

Meg stared at Jorah in silence for a moment, mesmerized by his beauty, before remembering herself and saying, "What? I mean, *no*. Not again. Though if you'd let me, I'd come here every day just to stare at you. I swear."

Jorah's ears got hotter. "Please," he said. "Don't. What is it that you actually came here for?"

"I—*uh*—well…" Meg was hesitant now. Jorah didn't like the sound of what was to come. "Have you eaten anything yet?" she finally asked.

"I was just thinking about ordering in from the printer," Jorah said, and he regretted it instantly. Now she knew that he had no plans and no excuses for getting out of what came next.

"Oh, no," Meg said, shaking her head and scrunching up her nose like she smelled something dead and rotting. "*Gross*. You can't. C'mon. Come eat with me. I heard about this new restaurant called The Prison. It's supposed to be the hottest dining experience all year. We should definitely go check it out."

"*Uh*… I don't know," Jorah said, trying to find an excuse. "I'm not really dating right now. And I don't—"

"*No, no no*." Meg stopped him there. "Not a date. A business dinner. I have a proposition for you, and I think you'll receive it better over a meal that's suitable for the occasion. So what do you say?"

There was really nothing else to say because, like an idiot, he had cut off all his lines of retreat at the beginning of the conversation. So Jorah just said, "Alright. *Fine*." and tried to smile. "The Prison, you say? I've been meaning to eat there for a week now." And that much was true. "I'd love to join you for dinner." Even if that much wasn't.

"Great!" Meg said, clapping her hands. "Perfect. Are you ready now or should I come in?" She tried peeking around him to see what his dressing room looked like, but Jorah still wasn't ready to let her inside.

"No, no," Jorah said, stepping out into the hall to close the door on her prying eyes. "There'll be no need for that. I'm ready as we speak. Shall we take your elevator or mine?"

"*Oh, yours, please,*" Meg said with a big smile. "Mine's in the shop. I had to ride the public elevator here. It was disgusting. I bet I still smell like it. I'm so sorry."

In fact, she didn't. She smelled instead like too much perfume, an odor which she only made worse by adding more from a tiny bottle in her handbag. Jorah wasn't sure how she expected to be able to taste the food with all that artificial scent clogging up her senses, but luckily, he didn't care what the food actually tasted like anyway. He just had to knock it off his list of restaurants to eat at before he could review them—and positively at that, no matter the taste, atmosphere, or service, as per Mr. Walker's demand—on *his* show.

"No, well, you smell..." Jorah trailed off without finishing his thought, instead pushing the button to call his elevator which opened instantly—his elevator being prioritized in the queue since he was the most famous actor in all of history.

As soon as the doors slid open, before Jorah could even react enough to step inside, Meg jumped in to sit on the purple suede couch and pet its upholstery.

"What an amazing elevator," she said, still petting the couch as the doors closed. "It's almost as nice as your clothes. You really are the perfect celebrity."

"It's not much," Jorah said. "Same as everyone else's. Lined with mirrors. A couch to sit on. Basic."

"Yeah, but *this* couch," Meg said. "It's perfect. Soft, supportive, comfortable. Not to mention beautiful. Everything you need in an elevator couch."

"Yes. Because it belonged to the perfect celebrity," Jorah said.

"I told you!" Meg said, standing with a big smile. "And confident, too."

"But not me." Jorah laughed so he wouldn't cry. "Not even close to me. I'm talking about Russ Logo."

"*Oh.*" Meg kind of deflated. She definitely wasn't smiling any more. "I'm sorry," she said. "I didn't mean to…"

"It's not your fault," Jorah said. Which it wasn't. "I'm the one who brought his name up. But that's enough about the past. It's time to look to the future. Let's eat. Elevator. *The Prison.*"

The floor fell out from underneath them, and Meg, timidly, said, "You two were good friends. Weren't you?"

"The best I'll ever have," Jorah said. "But, please. No more about Russ. It's a beautiful day. We're on our way to a famous restaurant. You have a business proposition you want to extend to me. Let's enjoy this to the fullest. Elevator, street entrance, please."

Meg gasped, checking herself in the infinitely reflecting mirrors in all directions. "What? You mean it? But the papos…"

"Let 'em take our picture," Jorah said, checking himself in the mirrors, too. "We're two attractive, adult celebrities, and it's well within our rights to enjoy a luxury business dinner together. Who cares if the world knows? I need some fresh air, and I'm gonna get it. Now, are you coming with me, or do you want to ride along to the restaurant entrance and meet me inside?"

"Oh, no," Meg said. "I didn't think *you'd*— I mean. *Yes.* Of course. By all means. Let's go."

The elevator stopped falling and Jorah struck a pose before saying, "Doors, open."

Flashing lights and hot hot humidity flooded into the elevator before either one of them could react. When the papos outside saw it was Jorah, their lights quickened. Jorah posed a few times, then pulled Meg in to pose for a few photos, too, and when everybody had gotten their fair share of pictures, Jorah and Meg pushed their way out through the mass of papos and toward the restaurant.

"*Wow*," Meg said, fixing her hair in a pocket mirror as they walked. "I don't think the papos have ever been so interested in taking my picture as they were just then. Thank you."

"They can be fierce," Jorah said, but he wasn't really paying attention to Meg, more interested in the city around him. There was something familiar about the buildings or the street that he couldn't quite put his finger on. Meg had gone on talking for some time when he couldn't take it anymore, interrupting her to say, "This place seems familiar to me for some reason. Did something else used to be here?"

"Oh, yeah," Meg said, pausing to really think about it. "The— uh… *The Farm*, or something? I think… Oh, *no. The Plantation*! That's it," she said, walking on.

"The Plantation…" Jorah repeated under his breath, remembering more but still not quite everything.

"Yep. The Plantation. Some producer bought it to live in or something like that," Meg said with a shrug. "The things they do these days… But anyway, this is the place."

And so it was. *The Prison*. And of course, it looked like every prison Jorah had ever seen on TV. There were tall walls, topped with chain-link fences that were topped with a combination of razor and barbed wire, all surrounding a big yard with basketball courts and weight benches on either side of the path that led to the restaurant's front door where, inside, they were greeted from behind bars by a jerky robot in orange overalls.

"Hello," the robot said. "May I take your jackets?"

Neither of them were wearing jackets so Jorah just said, "*Uh*. Table for two."

"Right this way, please." The robot host tried to walk, but it ran into the prison bars and couldn't go any further before awkwardly searching for the cell door, finding a way out, and leading Meg and Jorah to their table in another cell.

"*Wow*," Meg said when the host had left them with menus. "This might be the coolest restaurant I've ever seen. Get a load of those costumes."

"*Huh*? Yeah. Costumes…" Jorah said, but again, he wasn't paying attention. This time he was distracted by a little black furry blur running between the bars that separated the cell they were eating in from their neighbor's cell before the thing disappeared into thin air. "*Fortuna*. Did you see that?" Jorah asked, interrupting whatever it was that Meg was going on about now. "*Disgusting*."

"What?" Meg said, turning to see what he was talking about. "Oh, *Fortuna*. That dress is hideous. How does someone even go out in public looking like that?"

"No." Jorah chuckled, feeling some sense of déjà vu. "That's not what I— Never mind. *Here*. Let's get on with it. What business proposition did you have in mind? Why'd you bring me here? Spit it out."

"Ah, yes. *Well*… Don't you think we should order first?" She looked nervously around for a server.

"I'd rather not," Jorah said. "I don't like to do business while I'm eating. But I would like to use that time to consider your proposition. So please, I'd prefer to hear your offer before the server even arrives. If you can manage it."

"I— *Uh*. Well…" Meg was still hesitant, nervous.

"Go on."

"Well, I want to be more than an actor, okay. I'm decent at it. The camera loves me. I enjoy acting well enough. But it's just not the life for me."

"I'm following. And I tend to agree," Jorah said. "But I'm having a hard time figuring out what exactly it is that any of this has to do with me."

"Right, right. Of course." Meg fixed herself up and sat a little straighter in her chair. "*Ahem*," she cleared her throat before going on. "Well, I also want to be—no, I *am* a clothes designer. But no one takes me seriously about that yet."

"And…" Jorah led her on.

"Well, that's where you come in. If you ever, say, wore some of my clothes, everyone else would want to wear them, too. Right? So I'm proposing…" And so on and so on. It was a typical business transaction between two consenting celebrities. Jorah was a little surprised to find out that Meg was a designer, but he definitely wanted to see her work at the very least, and he could make any further decisions after that. He didn't say as much until after they had ordered their one special each and eaten the meals, of course—he didn't want Meg to think that he was too eager to be working with her—but then he set up a meeting to try on the clothes and they parted ways so Jorah could prepare for his talk show.

ↄ ✳ ↄ

On came the classical stylings of the Jorah's Chorus theme music. Jorah himself sat at his J-shaped desk, staring into the black mirror of the camera lens, ready as ever to put on a show. The director counted down, the music began to fade, and Jorah smiled to the oncoming applause.

"My fans, my fans. *Please*," he said, waving his hands in

humble accord. "I love you all dearly, but if you don't quiet down, you'll never hear Jorah's Chorus. And that *is* what we all got dressed up to come out here for tonight. Isn't it?"

The crowd hooped and hollered, singing their own version of a chorus.

"Of course it is," Jorah went on. "I know it's what *I* came out here for. This is *my* show after all. Isn't it? Jorah's Chorus is what it's called, so what do I have to sing for you today?

"More of the same, of course. The usual. The *chorus*. The bread and butter that you've all come to expect and love. We'll have a few movie reviews and previews, including my latest—HAL BOT 5000. We'll have my own personal review of *The Prison*, a restaurant down in New Orleans. Wait until you hear about my experiences in this one. You'll never believe it, I promise you. And finally— *finally*—for a slight change of pace, at the end of the show tonight, I plan on announcing a new business relationship that I've just opened up—literally right before my show today—with an up-and-coming designer who, forgive my language, but y'all are going to shit your pants when I reveal who this person is. I promise you. You. Won't. Believe.

"But first, and of course, y'all know how the business goes. We've gotta see a few more messages from our sponsors—including Mr. Walker, producer of many of the fine movies—and restaurants— you'll hear about tonight—but don't go anywhere, you hear? Because you don't want to miss the announcement that's coming up at the end of the show. I'll be here waiting for y'all in the meantime. Until then. This is Jorah's Chorus."

And the classical tune of Jorah's Chorus's theme song went on playing again while Jorah sat pleased at his seat, excited for the show to come. But of course, as happened any time Jorah felt like Fortuna was finally spinning her wheel in his favor, everything went to shit again.

There across the set, talking to Jorah's director, in their too white uniforms with cargo pants—*cargo pants!*—plated armor vests, and glowing neon smiles that sounded like Evil and Misfortune combined, were two protectors, talking in modulated voices through their almost screaming facemasks. Their teeth flashed neon glowing light all over the director until she pointed the protectors in Jorah's direction, and he held his breath, dreading what was to come.

"Jorah Baldwin?" one of the *protectors* demanded in their too loud, unnatural voice, teeth glowing neon yellow, red, and green with every word.

"Yes." Jorah nodded.

"We need you to come with us," the other said in a voice modulated to sound exactly the same as the first's.

"But I'm in the middle of a show," Jorah complained. "Can't this wait? I have an audience expecting me to perform."

"Mr. Walker's orders," the first said. "Let's go. Move it."

And Jorah had no choice at the invocation of Mr. Walker's power, so he did his best to apologize to his audience as the protectors dragged him violently off set.

෬   ✄   ℘

LXVII. Mr. Kitty

Mr. Kitty slept, as he often did, spread across the cool, flat top of Tillie's desk while she worked, typing and clicking, swipping, and swiping in response to the computer screens' blinking, flashing colors and the various bleeps and blips that accompanied them. For so many hours of every week Tillie sat there, moaning and groaning about whatever it was that the screens were telling her, and for just about as many hours, Mr. Kitty would sleep next to her, dreaming through it all. He was climbing a tree that seemed like it went on forever, one branch after another, higher and higher into infinity, when Tillie's phone rang, ripping Mr. Kitty out of dreamland with a startled lurch and a garbled meow.

"Settle down, Mr. Kitty," Tillie said with a chuckle, reaching for her phone with one hand and petting Mr. Kitty with the other. "It's just a phone." And answering it, she added, "Tillie Manager speaking. Go ahead."

"I— *No.* You can't be serious."

"No. Not again."

"No, they're not! I mean— I—"

"*Yes.* I realize they're just *robots.*"

"Yes. I'll put the work order in, but I—"

"No. I'm sorry. I—"

"*Bye. Fuck.*"

She slammed the phone on the desk and Mr. Kitty jumped again, purring this time.

"Sorry, Mr. Kitty," she said, wiping her eyes before petting him. "Those assholes have no idea what they're talking about. I shouldn't get so upset at their ignorance, it isn't their fault, but it's not my fault I get pissed, either."

"Or mine for being startled," Mr. Kitty meowed.

"Yes. I should try harder. I know. But so should they." She patted Mr. Kitty a few times, wiped her eyes again, then went back to typing and clicking on the computer—some kind of reaction to the news she had been given over the phone.

Mr. Kitty licked himself a few times, curling up in a ball to go to back sleep, but the phone rang again, interrupting his plans.

"Tillie Manager speaking," Tillie answered. "Go ahead."

"Oh, no. Leo. I'm sorry. I didn't know it was—"

"Yes. Of course I'm working. You know your mother. What else do I do?"

"*No.* Of course. No."

"*Definitely.* Just like I promised. I won't touch a phone or a computer for the entire weekend. For as long as you're here, even, if you want to stay longer..."

"That's why I'm getting it all done now."

"Okay. I love you. See you soon."

She hung up the phone and patted Mr. Kitty with a smile, forgetting whatever news about the robots that had nearly brought her to tears earlier. "Did you hear that, Mr. Kitty?" she asked. "Leo's running late, but he's on the way. I'm sure he can't wait to see you."

"*Sure*," Mr. Kitty meowed, but he didn't really believe that. Leo and Mr. Kitty had never gotten along when Leo was growing up, and going off to college hadn't changed anything about his attitude toward animals. Still, Leo's presence made Tillie happy, and Tillie being happy made Mr. Kitty happy, so as long as the kid kept out of Kitty's way, they wouldn't have any problems.

Mr. Kitty fell asleep on Tillie's desk until the doorbell rang and woke him up. He yawned and stretched, then licked himself a few times before jumping off the desk with a thud to follow Tillie out to answer the door. Tillie held her hand on the doorknob for a moment, taking a deep breath and brushing her hair out of her face, before she smiled and opened the door.

"Leo, my boy," she said as she did. "It's so good to see you. You look as wonderful as ever." She pulled Leo in for a hug that he tried to squirm his way out of.

"*Aw, Ma. C'mon*," he complained, straightening himself out once he had finally escaped his mom's loving bear grip. "I just saw you two weeks ago. We're only an elevator ride away from each other. Don't be so dramatic."

"Yes, well, it's not really dramatic when I'm genuinely happy to see you. Is it?" Tillie said, sounding offended. "Besides, I'm your mother and your my only son. What do you expect?"

"This is exactly what I expect," Leo said, brushing past Tillie and almost stepping on Mr. Kitty's tail as he made his way toward the kitchen. Mr. Kitty hissed, but no one seemed to hear it so he just had to follow along behind them anyway. He was still curious to see how Leo had been even if Leo wasn't curious in the least to see how he was.

"So you didn't bring any bags with you?" Tillie asked, still smiling though more nervously now. "You are planning on staying for the full weekend, aren't you?"

"You do still have a 3D printer, don't you?" Leo said, pressing the voice activation button. "Tall boy of Pabst," he added and a tall can of Pabst Blue Ribbon—which had apparently won the award back in the ancient age of 1893—came out of the printer's mouth. "And it still works. So, no. I didn't really need to bring anything with me. Did I?'

"You know you're not old enough to drink that," Tillie said, crossing her arms. "Did I give you permission to order alcohol?"

"*Ugh.*" Leo groaned, chugged half his drink, burped, wiped his mouth, and said, "Ma, *please*. You went to LSU. You know how things work. I've been drinking for a long time now. I think I can handle myself."

Tillie chuckled, shaking her head. "Oh yeah?" she said. "Big ol' tough guy going to a big ol' party school. Is that right? I guess you think you know something about the worlds now. Do you?"

"I know I know something about the worlds," Leo said, chugging the rest of his drink and ordering another along with some chips and dip.

"And you think you can just come in here using *my* printer however you want to, no questions asked?" Tillie grinned.

"That's what I'm doing, isn't it?" Leo pressed the printer's voice activation button one more time and ordered a pack of Camel Greens to prove his point.

"Well, you can," Tillie said, bringing Leo in for another hug that he tried to squirm his way out of. "But you gotta share those Greens. C'mon. Let's smoke one on the porch."

Tillie ordered her own beer—a pint of something thick, dark, and chocolatey in a glass, not whatever hipster piss water her son was drinking—and Mr. Kitty followed her and Leo out onto the back porch where they sat on metal grated patio chairs at a metal grated table and Mr. Kitty laid on the cool, hard cement, licking himself so he didn't fall asleep.

After some time of smoking and drinking, Leo broke the silence to say, "Still living in the same old house, I noticed. Don't you ever get tired of this thing?"

"Tired of it?" Tillie giggled like she only ever did while smoking. "Never. I grew up in this place, you know. Your Grandpa used to own it back when I was in the fifth grade."

"*Ptuh*. No wonder it looks so old." Leo laughed.

"*It does not*," Tillie complained. "You take that back. I take wonderful care of this place. It looks just as good as it did on the day my dad bought it."

"Which is exactly the problem," Leo said, putting out one joint to light another. "That was ages ago, and styles change faster than phones are updated. I mean, Grandpa knew as much himself. Which is why he sold the thing off and bought something better with the profits. You could learn a lot from Grandpa."

"*Pffft*." Tillie scoffed, stubbing out her own joint and almost reaching for another but thinking twice about it. "I've learned plenty from your grandfather, thank you very much. And I don't think he ever sold a house because it was out of fashion. He never really had any interest in trends and fashionability. No, I'm sure the only thing he ever sold a house for was the profits. *Trust me*."

"Still," Leo said, finishing off his drink and crushing the can under his foot. "That's as good as the same thing. Better even. If he keeps selling them for a profit, he's gotta know something about fashion, right? And money can buy stylists to follow all that for you. But only for as long as the profits flow. So maybe profits are more important than fashion in the end."

"Not to me," Tillie said, shaking her head. "Not at all. Neither are important. I'm never gonna sell this house. I'm more interested in the history I have here, the history *we* share here—you and I, me and your grandpa, me and your father, *everyone*. No amount of money is going to remind me of the time you colored a mural all over those walls right there and we left it up for a week so you wouldn't cry about it when we covered it up," she said, pointing in through the glass door to the living room where Leo—and Mr. Kitty—turned to look. Mr. Kitty felt like he could almost see the mural still up there. "Do you remember that?" Tillie chuckled. "I do. It's still behind the paint on those walls. And what about the time you broke your leg on that trampoline that still stands right over there while I was sitting right here in this very chair watching you. There's the first night you came home from the hospital after being born, the first night you slept all the way until morning, the first night you spent at a friend's house when it was my turn to bawl until morning instead of yours." She almost started crying again, and Mr. Kitty could tell that it made Leo uncomfortable. "*This* house, as old and out of fashion as you may think it is, reminds me of all those stories, and that reminder could never have a price tag put on it. I'll never sell this house. And I hope that you might eventually feel the same way about it when I pass it down to you."

Leo was feeling really awkward now, squirming in his seat. "Alright, alright," he said. "Enough mushy stuff. And definitely stop talking about death. *Sheesh*. I only just got here. Can't I rest a little after that horrid travelling experience before you start grilling me with the heavy stuff?"

"Hey, you're the one who ordered the Greens," Tillie said with a chuckle. "You know how I get when I'm high."

"Now that you reminded me, I do," Leo said.

"Which should prove to you why reminders are so important." Tillie laughed, and at the same time an alarm went off on the phone in Leo's pocket.

"Speaking of which," Leo said, pulling the phone out to turn off the alarm. "Now, I know we agreed that neither of us would do work or anything like that while I was here, but I have to break that promise for, like… *thirty minutes*. Okay? This is really important. It's the finale of my favorite TV show, and— Now wait just a second, okay. I'm not done. I was going to say that it'll take just thirty minutes, and I have to do it or the internet will definitely spoil it for me when I'm inevitably surfing social media at this boring dinner party you have planned for later. So if you don't want me to be totally depressed in front of all your upper management friends, you'd do better to just let me sit down and watch this real quick. After that, I promise nothing but family time for the rest of the weekend. So what do you say?"

Tillie didn't answer for a moment, in which Leo fidgeted, checking the clock on his phone, then she said, "Of course you can watch your show. It's not like I'm trying to keep you in prison here. But only if you don't mind me sitting next to you and watching along. That's all I care about. Spending time with you. No matter what it is we're doing together."

"*Great*," Leo said, standing up and almost stepping on Mr. Kitty again. This time Mr. Kitty meowed loud enough so everyone could hear it. "Oh, sorry, Kitty," Leo said, patting him too hard on the head to which Mr. Kitty meowed again. "Yes," Leo went on. "You can watch with us, too. As long as you stay out of my lap and shut up." He turned to his mom. "But I'm gonna go get some snacks, first. Do you want anything? The shows about to start."

"Another beer for sure," Tillie said, standing. "But I'll come help you." And Mr. Kitty followed them back into the kitchen where he laid on the hard, cool tile floor, listening to them talk and gather their snacks while he licked his dirty paws clean.

"*Ooh*. White cheddar popcorn," Tillie said to the printer. Then to Leo, "I love white cheddar popcorn when I'm high."

"Me, too," Leo said, nodding and staring off into the distance, as if he were imagining the taste of it. "And some corn chips and bean dip," he added for the printer and his mother alike.

"Always your favorite," Tillie said, smiling. "Ever since you started school. How are your classes going now, anyway?"

"Classes are classes." Leo shrugged. "I always seem to get by. Peanut M&M's."

"Yeah, but you're doing a little more than just getting by, aren't you?" Tillie said. "I know you're only a sophomore, but you should have at least started whittling away some of your options. *Right…*"

"*Sure*," Leo said sarcastically. "I whittle every day. But whittling's a slow process. Pabst tall boy. Two, please."

"You know, I once thought I wanted to be a lobbyist," Tillie said with a smile at the thought. "When I was pretty much the same age you are right now, as a matter of fact."

"*Pfft*. A lobbyist?" Leo laughed, stacking the last little bits of his snackery onto a serving tray. "You? You've got to be kidding me. You need anything else?"

"Another beer, please," Tillie said to the printer. And, "No, I'm not kidding." she said to Leo. "Your mother was heavily involved in campus activism when she went to LSU. You've heard of the Reclaim the Grounds movement, right? That started with us, at LSU."

"*Pffft*. Yeah right. You're kidding me. You were one of those hippies? What made you quit and become a manager? Was it

Grandpa?"

Tillie paused to think about it. As well as Mr. Kitty knew her by then, he knew that she was picturing Nikola and Emma in her mind and how they had both been so violently stolen from Tillie right in front of her eyes. "Because if you want to do the right thing in lobbying," she finally said, "it inevitably becomes life-threatening. And I didn't want to leave you or your grandpa with no one to take care of y'all. The Hand knows you both need it. Now come on. It's about time for that show of yours to start."

They carried their snacks into the living room and set everything on the coffee table—exactly where Mr. Kitty had intended to lay—so he tried to jump onto Tillie's lap instead, but she didn't like that idea so she pushed him down onto the floor where he had the worst view of the TV out of anyone. Luckily, he didn't really care about whatever the show was anyway so he just went on licking himself and listening to the sounds.

"Not now, Mr. Kitty," Tillie said. "I'm trying to eat." She shoved a big handful of white cheddar popcorn into her mouth, puffing her cheeks out like a chipmunk.

"TV on," Leo said. "Cartoon Network."

"The Cartoon Network, huh?" Tillie said. "What sort of show is this that you find so fascinating?"

"Protector Time," Leo said. "And yes, it's a cartoon, but it's something more than that. Okay."

"So adults enjoy it, too?" Tillie asked, mouth still full of popcorn. "Like anime. Or the Simpsons."

"I'm not sure if *enjoy* is quite the right word. Like, it's more about the cultural phenomenon that the cartoon represents, you know. It's like— I mean... You'll see when you watch it, but you can pretty much tell outright from the name of the show that it's, like, pure pro-cop propaganda. Right? One hundred percent pure ideology, okay. But the thing is that no one can really figure out who exactly the target audience is, you know. I mean, how long has it been since we've even had a real protector force? Not since the invention of printers, right? So why are we still wasting resources on producing this nonsense?"

"I— *Uh*—" Tillie started to say, but Leo cut her off.

"Wait. *Shhh*. It's about to start," he said. Then, "Volume up. *Up, up, up*. Got it."

A cartoon came on the screen with an upbeat theme song, and

Leo stopped munching on his snacks to lean forward and pay closer attention. Tillie couldn't resist the lure of the popcorn, but she slowed down, too, putting one kernel in her mouth at a time instead of eating it by the handful. She seemed genuinely interested in what the show held in store for her. Mr. Kitty, for his part, stole glances at the screen out of the corner of his eye as he licked his coat clean—a maintenance project which took up most of his time that he didn't spend sleeping. The cartoon hadn't been running for more than a few minutes—no amount of time for an uninitiated fan to pick up any sort of storyline—when it was interrupted by a breaking news segment.

"Pardon the interruption, TV viewers," a big, sweaty head said on the screen, and Leo groaned.

"Not right now. Fuck!" he complained.

"We interrupt your regularly scheduled content to bring you a breaking news report."

"We know, we know," Leo complained. "Just get on with it already."

"Jorah Baldwin, highest paid and most-viewed celebrity in all of history, has been reported missing."

The TV screen changed from the reporter's sweaty bust to a montage of photographs of Jorah in various outfits.

"Fuck that guy," Leo said, chugging his beer. "All his movies suck, anyway. How can anyone watch him?"

"If you have any information about Jorah's whereabouts," the reporter's disembodied voice went on over the shifting images of Jorah Baldwin. "Please call your local Crimestoppers number or the number on the television screen now."

A phone number flashed on the screen, then the message repeated itself while Leo complained some more. "You can't be serious," he said. "Of course this shitty actor has got to go missing right when my show's on. I don't care how popular they try to tell us he is, no one gives two shits about Jorah Baldwin."

"Well, I don't know," Tillie said. "I think he's a pretty good actor."

"How can you even tell?" Leo scoffed. "He's always in such shitty roles. No actor could make them good. I mean, just like this Protector Time propaganda, why do we need all the blatantly Luddite films that Baldwin's been acting in ever since Russ Logo's death? Robots already took all those jobs ages ago, and we're better off because of it."

"Right, well... *Hmmm.*" Tillie wanted to say more, Mr. Kitty knew from their conversations together, but she hesitated long enough for the news report to end and the cartoon to come back on—and not where they had been interrupted, either, but further into the show as if it had kept playing while the news report ran.

"Of fucking course." Leo growled. "Great. *TV off.*"

"No. What? *C'mon.*" Tillie complained as if she really had wanted to watch the show. "But I was just getting into it."

"Yeah, but we missed the setup. It wouldn't make any sense. Trust me. I'll just have to try to avoid spoilers tonight. *Ugh.*" He cracked open another beer and stuffed his face with popcorn. "I think I'm gonna go take a nap before this dinner party. Seven o'clock, right?"

"*Uh...* Yeah. Seven," Tillie said. "I'll wake you before then."

"Alright, Ma. I love you," Leo said, marching his way off toward his old bedroom—which Tillie had left exactly how it was before Leo had moved to campus.

Tillie finished off her beer, sighed, and stood from the couch, stretching. Mr. Kitty took the cue and stood to yawn and stretch himself.

"Well, Mr. Kitty," Tillie said. "That was a close one. I almost blurted it out this time."

"Maybe you should have," Mr. Kitty meowed, following her into her office where she sat behind the desk and he jumped up onto it.

"You know, maybe I should just tell him," Tillie said, nodding with imagined confidence.

"That's what I just said," Mr. Kitty meowed.

"I mean, I was pretty pissed that my dad never told me. And Leo's gonna find out the truth eventually. Right?"

"Do you even care what I say?" Mr. Kitty asked.

"And what harm could it really do in the end?" Tillie went on. "I mean, he just told me he's not interested in lobbying. He only seems to care about cartoons. Maybe I could just casually show him a photo of a factory accident and see how he reacts."

"I'll take that as a no," Mr. Kitty said, and he walked around in a circle a few times before finding a comfortable position to lay down in.

"You're right," Tillie said. "It's a risk, for sure, but I think it might just be a risk I'm willing to take."

Mr. Kitty didn't respond. Tillie was free to take whatever risks she wanted to take. He had no plan to stop her, especially considering the fact that he had already advised her to do exactly what she was planning to do. Instead, he listened while Tillie clicked and typed, searching for a picture from her archives that she could show to Leo in order to reveal to him the truth. Mr. Kitty fell asleep while she did, not to be woken up again until sometime later by an argument between Leo and Tillie.

"Just tell me what you see, then we can get ready for dinner," Tillie said, pointing at her computer screen where a picture of several dead children, eaten by the machines they were supposed to be cleaning, their blood retouched black to look like oil, stared back at them.

"I thought you said no work while I was here," Leo complained, avoiding the image on the screen as if he might actually know the truth of what it held without ever having been told.

"This isn't work," Tillie said. "This is more important than *work*. This is about your education. So please, tell me, what do you see in the picture?"

"*Uh...* I don't know," Leo said, looking at the screen for the first time but still only out of his peripheral vision. "Is it like a factory or something?"

"Yes, it's a factory," Tillie said. "But you're not even trying. You have to look. Actually *look* at it and tell me what you see."

Leo looked at the picture for real now. There was a flash of recognition in his eyes, a flash of disgust, then nothing. No emotional reaction. No critical analysis. Just regurgitation of what he had always been taught by everyone—Tillie included.

"I don't know," he said. "It looks like— It looks like some cleaner bots malfunctioned and were destroyed by the machine. I don't know specifics, though. I haven't learned much about the actual factory floor yet."

"Cleaner bots?" Tillie asked. "They really look like cleaner bots to you?"

"I don't know," Leo said, crossing his arms and getting defensive. "I told you we haven't learned about the factory floor yet."

"You don't have to know about the factory floor," Tillie

snapped before correcting her tone. "I mean, just look. They're not robots, Leo. Those are *not* robots. Okay. *Look.*" She pointed again.

Leo chuckled, shaking his head and trying to avoid looking again at the picture on the screen. "You've got to be kidding me," he said. "*Ma.* Please tell me you're not one of them. *A conspiracy theorist?*"

"This isn't a conspiracy theory, Leo. This is the truth. It's right there in front of your face, plain for anyone to see. You just have to open your eyes and look, son."

"*Pffft.* Sure, Mom," Leo said, leaving the office. "That's what all the conspiracy theorists say. *Wake up sheeple!* Right? I get it. But isn't it about time for your dinner party?"

The office was silent for a moment after Leo had left, all except for the sound of Mr. Kitty licking himself. Then Tillie broke the silence by saying, "I should have told him the truth a long time ago. When he was younger. Right off the bat. Now I may not be able to convince him ever."

"There's always hope," Mr. Kitty meowed, and he went back to licking himself, hoping to get his coat clean before he fell asleep.

ఒ ✖ ✖

LXVIII. Sonya

Sonya loved her job. She spent more time at work than she did anywhere else—including her own home. These people were her family, and she'd rather spend time with no one else.

She was there, behind the bar, at The Bar—what the regulars called it even before the long forgotten name on the sign had faded out of existence—cleaning a dirty glass and listening to a story she'd heard too many times before, a story she would no doubt come to hear again and again with the way the worlds were turning.

"I mean, shit," Annie Painter complained, gulping down another drink and slamming the empty glass on the table. "I'm the best damn worker on that entire construction site. And I'm not bragging or nothing, either. That's a verifiable fact based on the way they determine our pay. I do more work faster than anyone else, and now I'm being fired because of it."

Sonya shook her head, setting another beer on the bar so Annie didn't have to ask for it.

"You know I can't pay for this one," Annie said, drinking it anyway.

"And you know I wouldn't ask you to, given the circumstances," Sonya said. "Consider it on the house."

"Well, thank you." Annie took another big gulp, draining half the glass, and Sonya set a full pitcher on the bar next to her, nodding for Annie to go on.

"Like I said," Annie did, "I'm being fired because I'm the fastest worker out there. I wasn't always. I used to be stuck around fourth place, never even on the winner's podium at the end of the week, but it seems like the closer we get to finishing this stupid Wall the more they try to slow us down."

While Annie gulped her beer, Sonya said, "You're not the first to tell me that."

"I bet not." Annie chuckled a little before scowling again. "I bet not. You prolly got my predecessors coming through here. The three that were fired before me. Did they run up a tab, too?"

"No tabs for the recently unemployed," Sonya reminded her. "Including you. But yes, I talked to your friends, and they told me the same story you're telling me now."

"Well you know then," Annie said, taking a swig of beer and topping off the glass. "First each of them were fired, one by one in turn, and now it's me. And old Lenny Sexton'll prolly be next, too. But fire us all they want, there's no stopping it. Even with the slowest of us, they'll finish that Wall eventually. Hell, it's almost done as it is."

"Do you have any idea why they'd be trying to stall construction?" Sonya asked. "That's what I don't understand in all this."

"Why are they even rebuilding the stupid thing in the first place?" Annie asked with a scoff. "Why do *they* do anything? Who the fuck are *they*? You're telling me that's the only part of this shit show that you don't understand?"

"Well, no. You've got a point there. But do you have any opinion as to why they'd be slowing construction?"

"Whoever decided to build the shit is having second thoughts. I don't know. Maybe someone hasn't paid for it yet. How the fuck am I supposed to know? I'm just trained to lay line."

"And you're damn good at it," Sonya said, topping off Annie's pitcher one more time. "The best in the business from what I heard."

"Until they fired me," Annie said, holding her drink over her head like she was giving a toast. "I have no idea what the fuck job I'm supposed to find now. Y'all need any help around here?"

"*Sheeit*," Sonya said with a chuckle, thinking about all the work they could use help with. "We got more work than you'll ever know, but nothing we can afford to pay you for so it wouldn't be helping you at all."

"Hey, I'm here to help," Annie said. "I mean to pay for these drinks somehow. Even if I can't pay for them. So you don't be shy about asking me to do anything—for you or the bar."

"Only thing I need you to do is get another job. That way you can take care of your family and get back to frequenting our fine establishment here like you used to. In the meantime, don't worry about your drinks. They're on the house. You worry about your family first. We've got your back on that."

"*Ugh.*" Annie groaned, stumbling sloppily off the barstool.

"Speaking of which. Guess I better go break the news to them now. Wish me luck."

Annie finished her half pint of beer and stumbled out of the bar while Sonya called after her, "Good luck! I'll keep my ears open for any work that might be good for you."

It was a shame, really. Annie's story. But nothing new. Nothing new under the Sun. Sonya had thought it was bad when the walls between worlds Five and Six were torn down, she had thought that unemployment, hunger, and desperation were at their worst, but now that the wall was almost back up again, she was coming to realize that the worlds could get shittier if they wanted to, and from the looks of things, there was a shit circus in store before anything would ever get better. More people were going to lose their jobs, and with that, more people would grow drunk and desperate until inevitably all that pent-up energy had to be released somewhere. Sonya didn't look forward to it, per se, because she knew a lot of innocent people would be hurt in the process, but Tillie and others like her had been preparing for just such an occasion since before the walls went down, and with any luck, they would be able to guide that energy release toward building a better society and not just tearing down the old one.

As Sonya cleaned up what was left of Annie's mess, in came one of those people who also organized toward that same better future which Sonya was working toward, her coworker Barkeep.

"How's the shop treating you today, Barista?" Barkeep asked on her way in. "Lovely as always, I imagine."

"The bar never disappoints me," Sonya said, hanging up a clean pitcher to let it dry. "It's the worlds outside that always seem to let me down."

"They let us all down," Barkeep said, taking inventory of the incidentals in preparation to relieve Sonya as the next bartender on duty. "So don't think you're special. But tell me, what's got you bothered this time?"

"Annie Painter's tab's on the house." Sonya sighed. "Until further notice."

"Annie, too? *Sheeit*. It's only gonna get worse before it gets better. Honestly, she's prolly lucky to be looking for a new job now, before the rush really starts. We all know a mass layoff's coming at the end of this fucking *super project* border wall bullshit they have going."

"That's exactly what I'm afraid of."

"There ain't no reason to be afraid of something you know's gonna happen. Only thing we can do is—"

"*Be prepared*," Sonya finished for Barkeep, knowing that she had done her best to prepare, but only hoping that she—and all the rest of them, cogs in a giant revolution machine that they were—were ready for what was to come. "I know. But I'm not sure anyone could ever be prepared for something they've never experienced. Especially something as big as this."

"You experienced it plenty enough when that wall came down," Barkeep said. "And you've been preparing with us ever since. You're as ready as you'll ever be. That's more than enough. More than most people can say, at least."

"I don't know. I—" Sonya started, but this time Barkeep cut her off.

"I *do* know, Sonya. I believe in you. I believe in all of us. We're gonna be prepared the next time they need us. Trust me."

"Yeah, well, I really hope you're right." But Sonya wasn't sure that she could believe in everyone—herself most of all—as much as Barkeep did.

"I'm sure I'm right," Barkeep said. "But before we can get there to find out, I need you to check the bathrooms, refill the freezer with ice, and clean the last few glasses from your friends who are leaving right about... *now*."

"Have a good one, Sonya," a group of regulars called from the front of the bar as they left. "Put it on my tab. And Merry Christmas."

Sonya cleaned their table, did their dishes, scrubbed and mopped the bathrooms, and refilled the freezer with ice before her shift was finally over and she could sit on the other side of the bar to drink a beer served to her by Barkeep.

"Don't you ever get tired of this place?" Barkeep asked while filling up a pitcher for another customer. "After my shift, I'm out of here as soon as I can. But you? Look at you."

"Don't know where else I'd go," Sonya said, sipping her beer.

"Home, for starters." Barkeep laughed. "Anywhere but here."

"Only thing I want to do after work is drink a beer and rest my feet. I'd rather not drink alone, and it's easier to rest when I don't have to walk to the elevator and beyond, so what better place could I be than right here right now?"

"And besides," a scratchy voice said behind Sonya who turned to find Ellie McCannick's wrinkly-faced smile. "Here, everyone knows exactly where to find you."

"Which can sometimes be dangerous," Barkeep said, laughing loudly, though Sonya knew she was only half joking. Barkeep didn't trust Ellie and the people who she worked with, and so Barkeep didn't like it when the old woman came around. Sonya didn't really trust the resistance group that Ellie worked with, either—they were highly secretive, even to insiders, and all their actions seemed to end up buffering the system instead of destroying it like their rhetoric promised—but Sonya had no problem with Ellie as a person, and even liked the old woman. Ellie had been working hard, doing her best to help her fellow workers despite the obstacles in her way, for decades, and Sonya hoped that she could be as enthusiastic about the struggle as Ellie still was when she was that old.

"Thankfully, this time it's not dangerous," Sonya said, patting Ellie on the back. "It's always nice to see my friend Ellie. Why don't you get her a drink, please. On my tab."

"Now, you don't have to," Ellie said, bowing her head. "I can afford my own drinks. I'm just here for the company."

"I insist," Sonya insisted. "Make that an entire pitcher, Barkeep. It's almost Christmas. We should all be in the spirits."

"Well, if you're gonna twist my arm about it…" Ellie smiled, taking a glass and filling it from the pitcher that Barkeep had set on the bar in front of them.

"So how's the activist life treating you?" Barkeep asked. "Y'all make enough in donations to support a few full-timers by now, don't you?"

"We do nothing alone," Ellie said, taking a sip of her beer. "I'm blessed to be working with a good crew. And my pity promotion netted me an early retirement, so I don't really require anything more than meals and expenses from the organization. I'm blessed, though. I'll never forget that. *We do nothing alone.*"

"Expenses like this bar tab here?" Barkeep asked, obviously annoyed as she continued the interrogation.

"Well…" Ellie said, not letting on that she had noticed Barkeep's attitude—whether she had or not. "Thankfully, the lovely Sonya here has graciously offered to pay for this round. But I did come here expecting to buy at least one myself. And yes, that would be done with our organization's expenses. Building working relationships like this one here is one of the major reasons we raised these funds in the first place. Buying a round of drinks with the money's exactly what's expected of me."

"*We do nothing alone*," Barkeep said sarcastically. And then, "Including drink. But I've gotta go take some more orders. Enjoy, you two."

"She does not like me one bit," Ellie said when Barkeep had left down the bar to serve some other patrons.

"She doesn't know you," Sonya tried to explain, though it was hard to deny what Barkeep's actions suggested. "That's all. It's not that she dislikes you or anything. She just doesn't trust people she doesn't know."

"Yeah, well, she's had plenty of time to get to know me better. I'm pretty sure it goes beyond simple ignorance at this point."

Sonya didn't respond to that. She had no way to, really. There were no arguments. Barkeep didn't trust Ellie and she had no intention of altering that fact. There was no point in talking further about it. They drank on in silence for a while—each thinking about how to trust the other—before Sonya broke it to say, "So, how's life been treating you?"

"Oh, fine, fine," Ellie said. "I can't complain any more than I ever have. Plenty of food on the table. Warm bed to sleep in—even if it's not too soft. And I've got a whole host of friends and family whose company I actually enjoy. So, no. There's nothing new for me to personally complain about. Just the general unfairness of life under the oppressive system we're forced to abide by. You know. *Oh. Wait.* Also, we've got our Christmas party planned. You'll be there, right?"

"Yes, ma'am." Sonya nodded. She looked forward to Ellie's Christmas party every year and wouldn't miss it for the worlds. "I've got a special surprise dish I plan on serving. You'll see. I'll be there with bells on."

"You better be." Ellie winked. "This year the guest list's so long that we're expanding to four apartments instead of our usual two. Ol' Tanner and Kitchens have finally offered to give up their homes for the day. So I promise you, this one will be a Christmas for the legends."

"I don't doubt it," Sonya said, chuckling at the mere thought of the celebration. "But I know that's not the only reason you came out here. So spill it."

"Oh, well…" Ellie looked around at everyone in the room, suspicious now that it was time to get down to business. "I don't know. Maybe we should take a booth. This particular matter's a little more… *private*."

"*Ah*. Of course." Sonya nodded. "But first, Barkeep, an order of table fries, please."

Barkeep printed an order of fries, then Sonya and Ellie carried that, their drinks, and the half-full pitcher of beer to the deepest, darkest corner booth in the bar where Ellie scanned the room suspiciously one more time before speaking a word.

"So, dear," she finally did say, pausing there as if Sonya should be able to decipher some meaning out of those two words alone. Sonya never could.

"So…" Sonya said.

"The worlds are changing," Ellie said, frowning in a particular way that seemed to accent her wrinkles and crow's feet. "The worlds are changing."

"Don't they always," Sonya said. Not a question. A statement of fact.

"That they do, child," Ellie said, shaking her head. "But they don't usually turn for the worst this fast. And when they do, we know for sure that something big's coming."

"And for how long have y'all been predicting that something big's gonna happen? *Huh*? Long as I've known you, it seems like you've been making the same prophecies."

"And the change I predict's still coming along, ain't it? Quicker than ever now. You'll see. I'm sure you already do. You can feel it in the air, but you don't quite understand it yet."

Sonya sipped her drink and nodded. She couldn't argue against what Ellie was saying and there was no point in trying to. Sonya had been discussing exactly that with Annie and Barkeep before Ellie's arrival.

"You see?" Ellie went on. "You can't even disagree with me now. I know you don't like the way our organization prepares for what's to come, but you definitely think there's something to prepare for. Am I right?"

"You're not wrong," Sonya said, still not wanting to cede the point.

"It's not often that I am." Ellie smirked. "And on the off chance that I do make a mistake, I never repeat it. Do you understand me?"

Sonya nodded.

"I'm not sure you do, okay. But we've changed. All of us. The entire organization from bottom to top—including myself. We're a different beast entirely. We've even settled on a name for ourselves. We're going public. No more secrecy."

"Oh yeah?" Sonya nodded, not too impressed. "And how long have y'all been arguing over a name?"

"C'mon, now. That's not fair," Ellie complained. "You know we've got a lot more on our plate than this. And it's more than a name when you get down to it. We're putting words to our organization. That makes it real. Those words will reflect what our organization does, and our actions will reflect our name. I'm telling you, we're serious."

Sonya was starting to believe that maybe they were. "So what's this name then?" she asked.

"*The Scientific Socialists*," Ellie said, sitting up straighter in her stool and refilling both of their beers with a proud smile.

"Scientific Socialists?" Sonya repeated, not liking the sound of that. "Are y'all still working with that Scientist woman? She was willing to open up about her secrets with you?"

"Well, not exactly. No," Ellie said, sipping her beer and thinking about what to say next. "*The* Scientist is dead. She never would have opened up to us. You're right about that. But there is no her anymore. So she's nothing to worry about."

"But you still call yourselves *scientific*," Sonya said.

"Yes. Because we use the scientific method to determine our course in political life. We're scientists of history."

"So you are still working with the Scientist, then?"

"No. Well, *yes*. Sort of… We're all scientists now. And some of us literally call themselves the Scientist still, but it's nothing more than a meme anymore. *The* Scientist is gone. I assure you of that."

"Is this all you came to talk about?" Sonya asked, suspecting it wasn't. "If so, let's go play some darts. I need to get out of this booth and stretch my legs a bit."

"*No—n—n—no, no*," Ellie said, stopping Sonya from getting up. "Now, I'd love to beat you at darts when we're done here, but we haven't even started."

"I'm all ears," Sonya said, waiting.

Ellie gulped down a half a glass of beer and sighed before she went on. "Okay, well… Now, I know you don't trust the organization that I work with for one reason or another. And I respect your opinion, okay. I'm not asking you to change anything about it. But I do want to know if you trust me as an individual. Do we even connect at that level?"

"I— Wha— *Yes*," Sonya stammered, caught off guard by Ellie's admission of vulnerability and feeling vulnerable herself because of it. "Of course I trust you. I really do consider you a friend despite our political differences. I wouldn't be drinking with you now if I didn't."

"*Exactly*. Okay," Ellie said, setting her beer down to take Sonya's hand in her cold, clammy ones. "You trust me and I trust you. We trust each other. We're friends, and friends trust each other, right? And now I know that you, Barkeep, and dozens of others—at least, probably more—are all already planning your robot revolution—or whatever—with Momma BB. Okay. You're not secretive about it. Right? And we're trying to learn from you, trying not to trick people into doing things for us, okay. Instead we're convincing them that it's actually in their best interests. Right. Which is why—"

"Get on with it," Sonya cut her off. The more Ellie beat around the bush, the less Sonya wanted to hear what she had to say. "Just ask your question already."

"Well…" Ellie smiled half a smile, more of a pathetic, pitiful grin. "Do you think you could trust me enough to at least meet with my people? We need y'all's help for an operation on Christmas day."

℞   ✂   ℘

LXIX. Chief Mondragon

Ugh. Shit. Chief Mondragon was exhausted. Tired of everything. Something was going to have to give soon or she was going to snap. She stood in her private locker room, strapping on and straightening her plated armor vest in a wall-sized mirror, and she knew that much at least. Something had to give.

When she was still just an Officer, Chief Mondragon had thought that her superior officers were making excuses to hide their own irrational decision-making when they would complain about their hands being tied behind their backs by even further superior officers. When she had been promoted to Captain, she found out firsthand that they weren't excuses after all. Her hands had been strictly bound by the orders of the Chief, even if it looked from the lower ranks like she had more freedom than she really did. And now that she was finally the Chief herself? Of course, she felt no freer than she ever had throughout her entire career as a protector.

Sure, she got to order everyone around, from the Officers at the bottom on up to the Captains right below her and everything in between. Yes, every member of the Protector Force was required to stand and salute any time she entered a room. And okay, *nominally*, she was the one who decided the direction in which the Force's efforts would primarily be directed on a day to day basis. But these were nothing more than illusions of power. She was still being ordered around, not only by the traditions, rules, and entrenched institutions of the Force's bureaucracy itself, but by the owners whose abundance of wealth somehow granted them supreme control over a fighting force which they had not the first of how to oversee. Still she was forced to stand, bow, and acquiesce any time one of the fat, out-of-shape office jockeys decided to let their pneumatic pants carry them out of their mansions and into the real worlds. In short, she was no more powerful or free than she had ever been in her entire career as a protector, even as the Chief Officer overseeing the entire Force.

None of that would have been a problem for her, either, except for the fact that the people who did have all the power and freedom, the owners of the Protector Force, hadn't done a single bit of work to get into that position of superiority over her. Most of them, the current owner Mr. Walker and his anti-robot agenda along with them, inherited their wealth and power, explaining why they were so terrible at running the Force in the first place, but instead of admitting to that fact, the owners were too busy claiming responsibility for any of the Chief's successes and blaming all their failures on the *Invisible Hand*.

I have no choice was Mr. Walker's favorite refrain in response to any of Chief Mondragon's disagreements. *The Market demands obedience, and the Market knows best.* Even when those decisions, *dictated by the market*, resulted in losses of profits, lives, and property, and even when criminals roamed free because of the decisions made by Mr. Walker, his excuse remained the same: *The Market demanded it*. And every single time, Chief Mondragon bit her tongue, protecting her position as Chief instead of saying what she really wanted to say: "If the Market was so damn demanding, how could it ever be free?"

Chief Mondragon was not free. She knew that much. She had only one course of action in front of her if she wanted to keep the career that she had dedicated her entire wasted life to. She put her helmet on her head, waited for her brain to adjust to the three hundred and sixty degree view of the world it provided, then brushed her mustache and goatee to perfection, before—satisfied with her appearance—she marched out of her private locker room, through whitewashed halls, and into the briefing auditorium without even a second to spare before it was time for her speech—the same one she had given every year since becoming Captain.

Some Lieutenant opened the auditorium door for her, Chief Mondragon marched up to the stage's podium, and the entire room of rookies all stood at attention and saluted her. The Chief saluted back and said, "At ease." surprised for a moment at the sound of her modulated voice as the entire auditorium of Officers sat in one fluid motion.

"Protectors of Outland," the Chief went on, regaining her composure as she fell into the routine of oft rehearsed words. "From this day forward, that includes you. You have sworn to uphold the sacred duties of Protectorship, and you *will* uphold those virtues or perish in embarrassment. Now, children—because y'all truly are babies in the eyes of the Force—life out there is real, and we're here for one reason and one reason alone: To protect the ideals of Outland. Protectors, what are those ideals?"

"Property, liberty, life," most of the Officers staring back at her from their soft, cushy stadium seating spoke on top of and over one another. It wasn't anywhere near good enough for Chief Mondragon.

"I said, *protectors*," she repeated, doing what little she could to prepare these poor little noobies for the thankless, endless, Sisyphean career that lay ahead of them from this day forward, pumping them up like a football coach in the locker room before a big game. "What. Are. Those. Ideals?" she demanded.

"Property! Liberty! Life! *Sir*," the room sang in unison.

"And without these basic freedoms, what are we? We are not civilization. We are not human. We are nothing. Today you are tried by fire. Every protector is baptized into the Force the same way. If you cannot make it in Outland Six, then you are not strong enough, you are not fit enough, you *are not enough* to protect any of the Outlands. Do you understand me? This work is dangerous, protectors. You've been told the stories of your ancestors. You've been trained. You know as well as you can know what awaits you out those doors. So I'm going to ask you one more time. Protectors, are you ready?"

"Hoo-ra!" they replied.

"Hoo-ra!" Chief Mondragon repeated. "You know your vows rookies. I suggest you listen to your Sergeant if you want to make it through this alive. Lock and load."

The mass of them stood and milled around to find their squad assignments, following the directions projected on their helmets' viewports. One lucky pair—well, half lucky—would be grouped with Chief Mondragon instead of a Sergeant, and soon the new round of legends and rumors surrounding the most recent class of rookies would begin to take shape, further chaining future generations to the traditions of the past the same way that had always been done every year a new cohort graduated from the Protector Academy. The same as everyone else, the Chief was bound by *the Market* to act as she acted, greeting the two nervous recruits who had been assigned to her squad and preparing each for herodom in their own way.

"Officer Michelle Kelley," the first of the two said, standing erect and saluting Chief Mondragon. "Reporting for duty, sir."

"Officer." The Chief saluted back. "And your partner?"

"*Officer Jones*," Officer Kelley groaned. "She's kind of a joke around the locker room, sir."

"Did I ask you what you think's funny?" Chief Mondragon demanded. "Do you think I care what y'all talk about in the locker room? Why do you think I have my own?"

"I— No—" Officer Kelley stammered. "I don't understand, sir. I—"

"If I want to hear about your jokes, I'll ask you to say something funny. Right now, I want to know why you're reporting to me without your partner by your side."

"I— *Uh*..." Officer Kelley still didn't understand.

"*I*— Uh..." Chief Mondragon mocked her. "You'll come to find that your partner's the only person in the worlds who has your back, Officer. Never leave their side. Do you understand me?"

"Sir, yes, sir," Officer Kelley said, saluting.

And at the same time, Officer Nakia Jones marched into position next to Officer Kelley, saluting just the same. "Officer Jones, reporting for duty, sir."

Chief Mondragon saluted back. "At ease, Officers. I selected you two specifically for this operation because I feel like you show the most potential out of our new class of rookies."

"Sir, yes, sir." Officer Kelley saluted again.

"I—*uh*... Me, sir?" Officer Jones started before saying. "I mean, yes, sir."

"Yes, you," Chief Mondragon said. "The both of you. But I can't give you any more details until we're in the field proper, so let's get on with it. Go, go, go. Move, move."

They followed the rest of their squadron out into the transport bay where Chief Mondragon ordered the machine to take them to Outland Six. The floor fell out from underneath them, and when it stopped again, the doors slid open and all the protectors inside flooded out onto the streets like a white water rapid, heading toward lower ground at their designated sectors where they would march, patrol, and put on a show, doing nothing of any importance while Chief Mondragon initiated the traditional culling ceremony for a new rookie cohort.

⟩⟩ �֍ ⟩⟩

Chief Mondragon led the two rookie Officers along the green grass of the Neutral Ground while Sixers split in front of them like the Red Sea afraid of Amaru's wrath. Construction on the border wall was coming along nicely, and the Neutral Ground was almost a continuous strip of green grass again, but off in the far distance, Chief Mondragon could still see patches of skyscrapers blocking what was once a straight line view into a beautiful blue and green infinity.

They followed the Neutral Ground for a while before turning into the streets where the skyscrapers ate them like darkness. Chief Mondragon leisurely wound her way through the boulevards and alleys, even doubling back in some places, not only so she could enjoy the stark, brutalist architecture, but also to test her charges' sense of direction as they made their way toward destiny.

When she stopped their procession in front of the door she was looking for, hidden deep in a dark alley and flanked by dumpsters, she turned to find both of her charges confused under their screaming facemasks—Officer Kelley tried to cover her reaction up as quickly as possible, but Officer Jones let her confusion linger.

"Here we are, girls," Chief Mondragon said, trying to lighten the mood a bit since they were going to be getting into character soon anyway. "You two ready?"

"Sir, yes, sir." Officer Kelley saluted.

"Ready for what?" Officer Jones asked.

"You'll see," the Chief said, opening the door and letting the rookies in first before following them inside and locking the door behind her. "Come on in."

They stepped into a costume closet. It was one of many that the Force had requisitioned from Outland Three using their powers of eminent domain. Now, instead of dressing up some artsy-fartsy thespian hippies who would use the costumes for nothing more meaningful than playacting, these outfits would go to a more productive use: allowing protectors to go undercover in protection of the ideals of humanity: property, liberty, and life—in that order. Of course, they would also be used for the annual culling event, but that was just as important, and in this instance, one in the same.

"Where are we?" Officer Jones asked.

"You just walked here," Chief Mondragon said, chuckling—she loved when she got an opportunity to use that joke. "You tell me."

"*Uh*. It looks like a costume closet?"

"Very observant, Officer," the Chief said with a smile. "And what do you think we're doing here?"

"Going undercover, sir," Officer Kelley said with a salute.

"Well, yes, Kelley," the Chief said. "But I didn't ask you. And you have no need to show off. Trust me. But, yes. We're here because we're going undercover. We have intel saying there's a cache of stolen printers in this sector. Hopefully we get the chance to make some arrests today."

"*Hoo-rah*," Officer Kelley intoned.

"*Uh*— Undercover, sir?" Officer Jones said, not as excited about the prospect as Officer Kelley.

"Undercover, Officer," Chief Mondragon repeated. "All three of us. They did go over that in the Academy, didn't they? Jones, you'll be playing my lovely lady wife. So do dress appropriately. And Kelley, you're just a normal Sixer. So pick something trashy. As long as you don't stick out too much, we shouldn't have any problems."

"I— Your wife?" Officer Jones said, taking off her helmet and looking even more confused without it on.

"Sir, yes, sir," Officer Kelley said, picking out a costume and changing into it.

"Yes, my wife," Chief Mondragon said, mocking offense as she changed into her own costume—a simple blue jeans and t-shirt combo that most of the Sixers seemed to wear. "Do you have a problem with that? Should I be offended?"

"*Oh*. No, sir," Jones said, stumbling around, trying to take off her shoes. "I didn't mean to offend you, sir. I— I—" And she almost fell over before she finally did get her boots off.

"Careful, Jones," Officer Kelley said with a smirk. "I already told you, take your shoes off *before* your helmet. If you're not careful, you're gonna give yourself a concussion."

The Chief let them chuckle and joke together while they got dressed, then she performed an inspection. Officer Kelley was wearing a similar blue jean and t-shirt combo to the one that the Chief was wearing, which was perfectly acceptable, but she also still had her gun strapped over her shoulder.

"Lose the rifle, kid," the Chief told her. "Side arms only. This is undercover. No flashing guns."

The Captain turned to Officer Jones who wasn't carrying her rifle, that's for sure. She was wearing a purple flowery sundress and blushing under the Chief's inspection.

"Officer Jones, a dress?" Chief Mondragon asked.

"Yes, sir," she said, embarrassed. "I thought I was supposed to be your wife. If this won't do, I can change."

"You look fine," the Chief said with a wink—she looked fantastic, in fact. "But where exactly do you plan on putting your sidearm?"

"Right here, sir," Officer Jones said, flipping her skirt up to pull her sidearm out of her garter. The Chief had to admit, she was impressed.

"If you don't mind flashing the world to get to it, I don't mind seeing what you're packing," Chief Mondragon said with a laugh.

"Maybe it'll be a useful distraction," Officer Jones said, chuckling herself.

"Alright, then," the Chief said. "Looks good. I'm to be referred to as Ms. Mona Mondragon from here on out. You're my wife, Nakia Mondragon. And you're back up. Give us seven minutes exactly to scope the place out, then if we haven't called down an abort, you come up to assist with the arrest. Can we handle that?"

"*Hoo-rah!*" Kelley cheered while Jones said, "Yes, sir—er—*hoo-rah.*"

"That'll have to do."

The door they were looking for was squashed tight between two others that were too close on either side, like the one they were using didn't belong where it was, plucked out of some other world entirely and squeezed here into this one. It led them into a short hall and up a tall staircase, both too skinny just the same as the door, so much so that Chief Mondragon's gun, hidden in her pants waist, scraped along the wall as they climbed.

"Just let me do all the talking in here," the Chief said, taking step by creaky step. "I don't need you messing anything up."

"Yes, sir," Officer Jones said, breathing heavily from the climb.

"And no more sirs. It'll give us away. To you, I'm Mona."

"Yes, sir—er. Okay... *wifey?*"

"*Seriously.*" The Chief scoffed. "Just let me do the talking."

Ms. Mondragon—now fully in character herself—knocked the secret knock, and after a moment, the door at the top of the stairs swung open to reveal an empty room with chipped vinyl floors, moldy crumbling ceiling panels, and two doors besides the one they went in through, one closed tight behind the man who had answered their call, and the other, the exit, slightly ajar.

"No one told me there'd be two of ya," the man who had answered the door grumbled, looking between Ms. Mondragon and Nakia nervously.

"No one told me I couldn't bring my pack mule with me," Ms. Mondragon said, smacking Nakia—who responded with a yelp—on the butt. "Thought I might need some help carrying my purchases, see."

The Sixer didn't like it, though. Scum that he was, he still knew enough to be suspicious, even if he had no choice but to go along with the transaction anyway—no matter how shady. Ms. Mondragon had flashed a stack of cash to get into this meeting, and all that the trash on Six ever thought about was money, so he was sure to go along in the end. Same way they did every year.

"*Mmmhmmm…*" He liked the sound of that. "Well, if ya're buying so much ya need two people to carry it, I guess I don't really mind. But in the future, ya need to give us some forewarning. *Or else.*"

"Sure, sure," Ms. Mondragon said, waving the man's concerns away. There'd never be another next time for him. "*In the future.* But let me ask you, where are these printers of yours? I've always wanted to see one up close."

"I'm afraid that's not possible," the man said, shaking his head. "Boss's orders. We keep the printers locked up in the other room and the customers here in this one. It's called the airlock system."

"Airlock system?" Ms. Mondragon sighed. "You know that really was half the reason I came out here in the first place. If I knew I wasn't going to get to see one in action, I would have just sent the mule to get everything on her own." She tried to smack Nakia's butt again, but this time *wifey* was expecting it and jumped out of the way.

"Well, I'm sorry," the man said, looking at the floor. "Those are the rules. Maybe ya just should have sent her."

"The rules?" Ms. Mondragon repeated. "Put in place by your boss, I assume. The same woman who I negotiated with to purchase the knock that got me in here. And what a high price I paid, might I remind you. Is she here, by the way? Locked up with the printers, I assume. Letting you vet the possible infection in the airlock. Well, we're not contagious. There's nothing to worry about." She smiled wide, trying to make the man believe, but he still didn't.

"Those are the rules, ma'am," he said, still looking at his feet. "I'm sorry."

"Is she here?" Ms. Mondragon demanded, tired of playing games with this piece of trash—she never was a fan of kick the can.

"I— *Uh*— Who?" the man stammered.

"*Your boss*. Let me speak to her."

"I—*uh*..."

"*Now*."

And at that, the man kind of jumped up and yelped, exactly like Nakia had done when Ms. Mondragon had goosed her earlier. He turned and ran out through the closed *airlock* door, locking a deadbolt behind him.

"Don't *ever* touch me again," Nakia snapped.

Ms. Mondragon chuckled. "Calm down, woman. You've got bigger problems ahead of you."

"I will not calm down. You just sexually... What did you say?"

Ms. Mondragon pulled her gun out of the waist of her pants and pointed it at Nakia. "I said you've got bigger problems to worry about. It's almost time for Kelley to come up, and she's never late. Not by a second."

"Yeah. So?" Nakia said, slowly backing towards the exit while keeping her eyes on Ms. Mondragon's gun. "That's no problem."

"Not for me, it isn't. But for you, I'm afraid, it's a culling."

"A culling, sir?" Nakia asked at the same time that the airlock door opened and out came the giant, limping robot who Ms. Mondragon had really come for, distracting her for just long enough that when she pulled the trigger, Nakia had time to dive out of the way of the bullet, shoot one back that grazed Ms. Mondragon's arm, and escape through the exit, her purple, flowery dress flowing in a wave of ripples behind her.

"What's the meaning of this—" the robot demanded before Ms. Mondragon swung her gun around and put a bullet between the limping machine's eyes, exploding its plastic face all over the frightened airlock attendant who ran away to lock himself inside with all his precious printers. Ms. Mondragon hoped he was willing to die for them, because she was going to make sure that he did.

She was rubbing the red-hot gunshot wound on her arm, trying to decide whether to chase that fucking traitor Nakia or to kick down the door and kill the Sixer asshole first, when Kelley came bursting into the room, reminding Ms. Mondragon that she didn't have to do either for herself, she had backup.

"I— Sir, what happened?" Kelley asked, her gun already out, staring confused at the obviously dead but not bleeding robot corpse on the floor.

"That way," Mondragon yelled, pointing out the exit that Jones had escaped through. "*She* shot me. Officer Jones. Get her."

"I— What? Who?" Kelley hesitated, still confused.

"Now!" Mondragon yelled, and Kelley sprinted out in pursuit of Jones.

Ms./Chief Mondragon lay on the cold vinyl floor next to the dead robot, resting for just a moment. At least she had gotten that much right. The ringleader was dead. Mr. Walker could get off her back about that. But Nakia was still alive, and she could end up causing more trouble than Mondragon cared to deal with. Maybe Kelley would take care of that in the Streets so Mondragon didn't have to. Probably not. Nakia had gotten a pretty good head start and she was smarter than any of them had given her credit for.

Either way, all Mondragon could do was wait. Wait for backup to come clear out bodies and printers alike. Wait for the medics to bring pain relievers and patch her arm up. Wait for Mr. Walker to come up with another impossible demand that she'd have to find some way of complying with. And wait for Nakia to be served the justice that was coming for her. That last one was what Mondragon most looked forward to, and just imagining the scene filled her with a wave of relaxing serotonin as she closed her eyes, waiting for everything to come.

ʕ ✹ ∅

LXX. The Scientist

0.NNNNNNNNNNNNNNNNNNNNNNNNNNNNNNNNNNNNN
NNNNNNNNNNNNNNNNNNNNNNNNNNNNNNNNNNNNN
NNNNNNNNNNNNNNNNNNNNNNNNNNNNNNNNNNNNN
NNNNNNNNNNNNNNNNNNNNNNNNNNNNNNNNNNNNN
NNNNNNNNNNNNNNNNNNNNNNNNNNNNNNNNNNNNN
NNNNNNNNNNNNNNNNNNNNNNNNNNNNNNNNNNNNN
NNNNNNNNNNNNNNNNNNNNNNNNNNNNNNNNNNNNN
NNNNNNNNNNNNNNNNNNNNNNNNNNNNNNNNNNNNN
NNNNNNNNNNNNNNNNNNNNNNNNNNNNNNNNNNNNN
NNNNNNNNNNNNNNNNNNNNNNNNNNNNNNNNNNNNN
NNNNNNNNNNNNNNNNNNNNNNNNNNNNNNNNNNNNN
NNNNNNNNNNNNNNNNNNNNNNNNNNNNNNNNNNNNN
NNNNNNNNNNNNNNNNNNNNNNNNNNNNNNNNNNNNN
NNNNNNNNNNNNNNNNNNNNNNNNNNNNNNNNNNNNN
NNNNNNNNNNNNNNNNNNNNNNNNNNNNNNNNNNNNN
NNNNNNNNNNNNNNNNNNNNNNNNNNNNNNNNNNNNN
NNNNNNNNNNNNNNNNNNNNNNNNNNNNNNNNNNNNN
NNNNNNNNNNNNNNNNNNNNNNNNNNNNNNNNNNNNN
NNNNNNNNNNNNNNNNNNNNNNNNNNNNNNNNNNNNN
NNNNNNNNNNNNNNNNNNNNNNNNNNNNNNNNNNNNN
NNNNNNNNNNNNNNNNNNNNNNNNNNNNNNNNNNNNN
NNNNNNNNNNNNNNNNNNNNNNNNNNNNNNNNNNNNN
NNNNNNNNNNNNNNNNNNNNNNNNNNNNNNNNNNNNN
NNNNNNNNNNNNNNNNNNNNNNNNNNNNNNNNNNNNN
NNNNNNNNNNNNNNNNNNNNNNNNNNNNNNNNNNNNN
NNNNNNNNNNNNNNNNNNNNNNNNNNNNNNNNNNNNN
NNNNNNNNNNNNNNNNNNNNNNNNNNNNNNNNNNNNN
NNNNNNNNNNNNNNNNNNNNNNNNNNNNNNNNNNNNN
NNNNNNNNNNNNNNNNNNNNNNNNNNNNNNNNNNNNN
NNNNNNNNNNNNNNNNNNNNNNNNNNNNNNNNNNNNN
NNNNNNNNNNNNNNNNNNNNNNNNNNNNNNNNNNNNN
NNNNNNNNNNNNNNNNNNNNNNNNNNNNNNNNNNNNN
NNNNNNNNNNNNNNNNNNNNNNNNNNNNNNNNNNNNN
NNNNNNNNNNNNNNNNNNNNNNNNNNNNNNNNNNNNN
NNNNNNNNNNNNNNNNNNNNNNNNNNNNNNNNNNNNN

NNNNNNNNNNNNNNNNNNNNNNNNNNNNNNNNNNNNNNNNNNN
NNNNNNNNNNNNNNNNNNNNNNNNNNNNNNNNNNNNNN…

Every Goddamn day it was the same damn thing.

The Scientist slammed their fists on the desk. They smashed the keyboard and stomped their feet. They screamed at the top of their lungs. "You've got to be fucking kidding me!" The Scientist couldn't help it. This was not how computers were supposed to function.

They set the computer to running the calculations again, and again they were presented with the same infinite string of green digital alphanumerals on a black screen: 0.NNNNNNN repeating.

Shit, shit, shit, shit, shit!

They threw the keyboard across the room this time, and when it slammed against the wall, the little mechanical keys burst off and tinkled to the ground as the spine fell with a clatter.

This was *not* supposed to happen. The Scientist had entered all the data perfectly, they had figured for the costs of the owners and everything, and still the computer only had one message to relay: *0.N repeating*.

The Scientist wanted to scream, to punch the computer until it broke or the Scientist's knuckles did. Preferably both. There had to be some way they could get this stupid system to work, or the Scientist was just going to have to destroy the walls by theirself.

They ran the calculations one more time for good measure, and of course, everything came back the same: 0.NNNNNNN…

Maybe there really was zero point in repeating the same stupid mistakes again after all.

The Scientist calmed themself, breathing deeply in and out, trying to control their heart rate. They counted up to a hundred and back down to zero in their head. Five, seven, eleven times in quick succession, tapping their fingers in a different pattern each time and whistling a new tune whenever a primary number was reached, twenty-five different tunes sung forward and backward like palindromes, one for each primary: 2, 3, 5, 7, 11, 13, 17, 19, 23, 29, 31, 37, 41, 43, 47, 53, 59, 61, 67, 71, 73, 79, 83, 89, and 97. Then backwards: 97, 89, 83… And so on. You get the point. The 0.$\bar{\text{N}}$. But there was a point in repeating these number games for the Scientist. It calmed them long enough for their stomach to grumble and remind the Scientist that they hadn't eaten anything all morning despite the fact that it was getting along past lunch time already. So instead of running the numbers again and pissing themself off further, the Scientist peeled themself away from the computer to find some food.

The kitchen was empty—thank God—as the Scientist stood in front of the printer's frowning, red-eyed face, imagining the people who would make whatever they ordered, people who the Scientist themself held in oppressive captivity by their continued complicity in the maintenance and repair of the owners' walls. A picture of the giraffe, the gorilla, and the jaguar, the first exotic animals that the Scientist had ever witnessed, came into mind and again they knew that humans were no more free than those animals in the zoo—and that the Scientist was responsible for the captivity of both. But they had only one way to get the food they needed to sustain themselves, and so they did what they had to do. They poked the printer's little red eye and said, "Breakfast—er—lunch. I don't care."

And of course, the machine had no choice but to do exactly as it was told, and out came both breakfast and lunch.

"Fuck!" the Scientist screamed, punching the printer's unbending metal face and wincing at the pain of it. "You know that's not what I wanted. I said breakfast *or* lunch. Not both."

And so the machine printed out both again, and again the Scientist screamed. They were really getting tired of this stupid printer technology from all sides of the equation. They held their breath for a moment then took a few deep ones to calm themself before trying to decide between which of the plates to eat and which to throw away, almost falling into another meltdown over the decision before Mr. Kitty appeared out of nowhere, rubbing himself against the Scientist's ankles and calming them more quickly than any stupid breathing exercises ever could.

"Hey there, Mr. Kitty," the Scientist said, smiling despite the meltdown that had seemed all but inevitable only moments before. Mr. Kitty always had that calming effect on them. "What're you doing here?"

Mr. Kitty meowed then sat down on the kitchen's tile floor, licking himself.

"Yes, but I still don't understand how you always manage to show up exactly when I need you the most."

Mr. Kitty meowed again and went on licking himself.

"Are you sure you won't tell me?" the Scientist asked,

scooping him up to fling him over their shoulder and pat him on the back.

Mr. Kitty meowed then purred then meowed again, trying to struggle his way out of the Scientist's grip.

"Yes, I do know it's not the printer's fault," the Scientist said. "But it's not my fault I react that way, either. I'm as much a part of this machine as everyone else."

Mr. Kitty meowed again, jumping out of the Scientist's grip to sit on the kitchen counter and go on licking himself.

"And I thank you for that," the Scientist said, bowing to Mr. Kitty. "Today materially with the choice of three different meals. Or you could just eat all three if you want." The Scientist put three of the plates at random in front of Mr. Kitty, one after another, leaving only one plate of lunch for them to eat.

Mr. Kitty sniffed the plates, one by one, and refused each in turn, instead deciding to go on licking himself.

"Well," the Scientist said, picking up their plate to carry it back to the office and eat while they worked. "That's all I've got for now. Come back again later if you want something else. It's back to work for me."

The Scientist sat back in their office chair, dipping their turkey sandwich into the bowl of tomato soup before gnawing on it with one hand and tweaking the variables on the computer with the other. Staff pay, number of robots employed, commodity prices, you name it and the Scientist could tweak it, trying to find some combination that would prevent the system from imploding on itself, some solution other than 0.$\overline{\text{N}}$, even going so far as to lower profit margins below what the owners considered acceptable, and still, the black pane of computer monitors printed out the same endless line of green digital alphanumerals: 0.NNNNNNN…

The Scientist ran the calculations again, got the same results as always, and screamed in frustration, unable to eat more than the half of their sandwich and few spoonsful of soup that they had already eaten. They were about to start tweaking the variables and inputs one more time when from behind them came the mocking voice of Rosalind.

"What is it this time, *girl*? Your webpage taking too long to load?"

The Scientist didn't stand to greet Rosalind, though they were kind enough to swivel around in their desk chair and look her in the face.

"You know," the Scientist said as Rosalind chuckled under her breath, "if it were anyone else but you who kept calling me a girl despite my repeated protests, I'd probably cut their arm off."

"You can have mine," Rosalind said, snapping her right arm off with her left and extending it as if it were an offering to some mechanical god. "I get more than enough done with just the one as it is."

The Scientist slapped Rosalind's arm away by giving it a high five. "I'd rather have your respect," they said. "It's not that difficult to remember not to call me a girl."

"*Yes, Lord Scientist*," Rosalind said with a sarcastic bow, snapping her arm back into its socket. "As you wish. I'll try my best to remember in the future. Is there anything else I can do for you, *Lord*?"

"Stop calling me Lord, too." The Scientist had to hold back their laughter now. "That's much worse than girl."

"Well make up your mind, girl," Rosalind said with a chuckle. "So I don't have to keep choosing for you."

"*The Scientist*," the Scientist said resolutely. "I've already made up my mind. My name's the Scientist."

"But that's not who you are," Rosalind said, shaking her head. "You're not her. I knew her, and she's not you. I knew you before you thought you were the Scientist, too. When you were just a little—"

"*I'm not a girl*," the Scientist stopped her.

"No." Rosalind shook her head. "You're not that, either. But you're not the Scientist. You're something entirely different. Something new."

"I'll decide what I am without your input, thank you very much," the Scientist said, a little offended.

"That's what I'm hoping," Rosalind said. "What I'm trying to encourage you to do. But it seems to me like you're more interested in pretending to be something you're not. You'd rather retry failed strategies than actually change the world you live in."

That was bullshit. The Scientist wanted to scream, but they held their breath, tapping their fingers in a pattern and counting off the primaries, forward and backwards like palindromes: 2, 3, 5, 7, 5,

3, 2. 11, 13, 17, 19, 17, 13, 11. 23, 29, 31, 37, 31, 29, 23. Whistling the tune in their mind, because apparently, it was rude to do it out loud in front of company. 2, 11, 23, 11, 2.

"Well…" Rosalind said. "Are you gonna answer?"

"Not until I calm myself," the Scientist said. "I'm trying to learn how to stop you from getting me riled up."

Rosalind chuckled. "Is it working?"

"Not really." The Scientist shrugged, giving up on the meditation and feeling a little calmed. If they didn't have to deal with those stupid impossible calculations on top of Rosalind's ill-conceived *jokes*, the calming technique might actually have worked. "But it's better than melting down entirely."

"And what else is on your nerves today?" Rosalind asked, taking a seat on the other side of the desk and looking out the wall-sized window onto Sisyphus's Mountain. "Because I know that I alone couldn't piss you off this much. Not that quickly, at least. I wish."

"No. Not even you," the Scientist said with a grin. "But you know what can. The same thing that's been annoying me ever since you put me in charge of these stupid walls."

"Now, I did not put you in charge of a thing," Rosalind said in her defense. "You demanded it, and I told you that you'd—"

"*Regret the day I ever agreed to this job in the first place*," the Scientist said. "Yeah, yeah. I know."

"And do you?" Rosalind asked, looking the Scientist in the eyes. "Regret it?"

"Of course I do. Look at me."

"Well, maybe you should listen to my advice more often. I'm telling you, gi—*er*—comrade. You're wasting your time. I've gone over every possible combination of inputs and variables, and there's no way to make this stupid system function. I've done the same calculations for *the* Scientist at least three times before you were even born, and I could have told you then what I've been telling you all along: You're wasting your time. It's never going to work."

"Yeah, but I could just—" the Scientist tried to say, but Rosalind cut them off.

"Continue wasting your time all you want. It makes no difference to me. But don't lie yourself into believing that you're doing anything more than that."

"But I—"

"You know I'm right about this one."

The Scientist sighed. Rosalind *was* right. "Yes," the Scientist finally said. "I do know. But I'm still not sure what I think about your idea of revolution."

"It's not just my idea," Rosalind said. "It would never work if it was. There are a lot of workers—both android and human—on my side, and our ranks keep growing."

"So you say."

"So it goes. All we need from you is to stay out of the way. We can trust you to do that much, at least. Can't we?" Rosalind insisted a bit annoyingly, and the Scientist snapped back at her.

"*Of course you can*. You can count on me for more than that, and you know it. I promised I'd help you if I couldn't figure this system out on my own before then, and that's exactly what I'm gonna do."

"Well, then, do I have some good news for you." Rosalind smirked.

"*No*." The Scientist shook their head. "You've got to be kidding me. I would know if—"

"You would be a little too distracted running around in circles with your useless calculations to notice how much faster work has been going near the end of the project."

"No. But— It's almost Christmas. I gave everyone who wanted it paid time leave. I've been firing the most productive workers. I've—"

"You've done an admirable—if pitifully futile—job of trying to slow the project down, yes. But I've been undermining all those efforts behind your back, and now the final line is going to be laid on Christmas Day. So. I'll ask you again. Do you really mean it? The time has come. Will you join us or not?"

"*Christmas Day*," the Scientist repeated. "But that's only—"

"Too soon," Rosalind said. "Yes. Will you join us?"

"Remember when we first met?" the Scientist asked, ignoring Rosalind's impatience. "More than two decades ago, and on a Christmas day, too. The very day the wall came down in the first place."

"When we tore it down," Rosalind corrected the Scientist. "It was all I could convince the Scientist to do. Tear down a single wall.

She never really believed in my ideas of revolution any more than you do."

"She had never been a captive of the very Streets she lived in," the Scientist said. "She had never been held back, harmed, or exploited in any way. Of course she didn't believe in your idea of revolution. She could never understand how important it is."

"But you can," Rosalind reminded the Scientist. "You do. You're *not* the Scientist. You're better than she was."

"I *am* the Scientist," the Scientist insisted. "And I'm not better than anyone. I am no one. But because of that, I can and will help you. I know how important your revolution is, after all. So don't you dare doubt me on that."

"I'll doubt every single cog in this machine until we're successful," Rosalind said. "I've lived through too many failed attempts at this for me to do anything but."

"Then don't doubt me anymore than you doubt everyone else," the Scientist said. "That's all I ask. Give me my chance, and I'll do what I can."

"I can do that much," Rosalind said. "And you can start earning my trust by going to those meetings I have scheduled for you."

"Oh, shit." The Scientist sat up straighter and checked the clock on the computer screen. "That's today? I'm already late."

"Tomorrow," Rosalind said. "You're lucky I reminded you. You would have forgotten entirely."

"*Nah*. I would have remembered," the Scientist said. "And of course I'll go to the meetings. Are you sure you don't need anything else?"

"Are you sure you want help us?"

"I— *Uh...*"

"Exactly what I thought." Rosalind sighed, leaving the room as she said, "Just remember that you're *not* the Scientist. Start with that and everything else should fall into place."

"Yeah, yeah," the Scientist groaned. "*Whatever*." But Rosalind was already gone.

Ugh. The Scientist hated meetings. More often than not they could be taken care of over email. But if Rosalind had set it up, it had to be important, and the Scientist was going to be there. The Scientist wanted to show Rosalind that they could really be trusted. In the meantime, they were going to rerun the calculations as many times as they could, still hoping to preclude the need for something as extreme as revolution after all.

✂ ✂ ✂

LXXI. Haley

Haley read the message one more time. She started to respond to Elen before she remembered that Elen was only the messenger, but it didn't matter anyway. Elen wasn't listening, instead on her way out to the Feast Hall to deliver another cartload of food to Mr. Walker.

Why did Haley still work for that asshole? Hell, why did any of the secretaries work for any of the assholes that bossed them around every day? She had no idea. She could only come up with one possible answer, and still it didn't make any sense to her. *Or else*. They—and she along with them—still worked for their owners because if they didn't... *something*. Whatever *or else* meant. And every other secretary was programmed to think exactly the same way that Haley did. *Or else*.

Still not ready to find out exactly what *or else* meant, Haley took the threat seriously and started calling up Lord Douglas's meal on the printer—but not seriously enough that she passed up the opportunity to make herself a drink or two before getting to work. She printed up turkeys, potatoes, gravy, and pie—everything all the other fat and wasteful owners loved to include in their own feasts. She printed out double, triple, even quintuple portions. Why not? It was Christmas. It was a feast. Lord Douglas would be happy to see it, proud of Haley for finally worrying about appearances enough to keep them up. And then, while he was stuffing his face, laughing and joking with all the other owners who were all trying to pretend to be happier than whoever they were sitting next to on either side, she could spend some time for herself, making her own drinks and trying to figure out what price she was willing to pay in order to finally understand what *or else* meant.

She loaded a cart full of all the most expensive foods and drinks traditional to a Christmas Feast and pushed it out into the Feast Hall, up toward the Fortune 5. Lord Douglas noticed her coming and yelled to hurry her approach.

"Haley, dear," he said when she had started stacking his food on the table in front of him. "There you are. With perfect timing, as always. And look at those turkeys, Walker, my boy. Ten times the size of those puny birds your *human* secretary keeps piling in front of you. That's one of the infinite benefits of an android secretary. Androids are actually capable of carrying the weight of a Lord's appetite to the table. At least if you want the job done efficiently. *Ha ho ho!*"

Mr. Walker tried not to pay attention, grunting and eating his meal, but Haley could tell he was annoyed.

"And inexpensively," Mr. Angrom added, trying to push Mr. Walker's buttons, too. "How much does upkeep on that secretary of yours run, Walkie? When y'all were trying to sell me one, I knew it was ridiculous. Why rent the cow over and over when I can own one for half the cost?"

Owners all around the Feast Hall laughed at the joke, but Haley didn't find it any funnier than Mr. Walker did. Probably none of the other owners found it as funny as they were making it out to be, either, but they—just as much as Lord Douglas—had to keep up appearances. It was as if all of Inland were an illusionary castle built atop a foundation of facades, and as long as everything seemed to be in perfect working order it might as well be, but as soon as even the slightest strut or screw seemed in the least bit odd or out of place, the entire structure would come tumbling down, sending all the owners held up by it to fall into the moat with a tidal splash, fighting one another like crabs in a barrel to get out before they drowned.

"*Ho ho ho!*" Mr. Walker laughed sarcastically, trying hard to put on an air of indifference, though that elevator car had long since passed. "Very funny. But there are benefits to human secretaries, and detriments to *robots*, that you're not taking into consideration, dear Lord."

"And that's exactly what your salesmen tried to say to me. Do you care to know what my response was, Mr. Walker?"

"No." Mr. Walker shrugged, back to eating the piles of food in front of him.

"Exactly again, Walrus," Lord Douglas said, laughing. "*No.* I don't care. I own all the secretaries I could ever need, and I'll never rent again. *Ha ha ho ho!*"

More and more of the owners around the room joined the laughing, and Haley had heard enough. She let the pigs have their fun and made her way back to the kitchen where, even if there wasn't enough peace for her to get much rest thanks to the other secretaries running around cooking their owners' feasts, at least she could print herself off a few drinks before she had to deliver another cartload of food to Lord Douglas.

On the way back to the kitchen, though, she knew she'd get no relaxation at all when some fat owner in a tiny hat slapped *her* ass in passing.

"Excuse you!" Haley snapped, trying not to scream at the table of owners, one of which had to be the perpetrator.

They all just kind of smirked or giggled and whispered between each other like a gaggle of schoolchildren.

"Which one of you did it?" Haley demanded.

"Did what, robot?" One of the fatter owners finally spoke up. "Can't you see we're trying to celebrate? Be gone before I report you."

"I can see what you're doing alright," Haley said, looking them each in the eye, trying to figure out which of them it was who had slapped her but unable to even tell them apart. It didn't matter, anyway. They were all in on it. Hiding the abusive actions of one of their fellow owners was just as bad as being the one who had slapped her for all that Haley was concerned. "And I don't like it one bit."

"No. I don't like—" the same owner tried to start talking again, but Haley wasn't hearing any more of it.

"I don't give a shit what you like," she snapped. "Any of you. And yes, before you ask, *Lord Douglas* included. The next time any one of you so much as grazes the least little hair on my body without my explicit consent, you better be ready to lose whichever hand you touch me with—and prolly more than that. Your Creator save you if you touch me with something other than a hand. And I am *not* joking."

The owners had a lot to say about that, of course, and they all started at once, talking over and on top of each other, trying to be heard, but Haley really didn't care what any of them thought, so she ignored them, turning to push her cart back into the kitchen and order up a six pack of vodka shots from the printer in the hopes of forgetting the slimy feeling of whatever owner's skin had touched her.

"*Holy shit,*" Elen said, watching in wide-eyed awe as Haley downed shot after shot with no reaction.

"What?" Haley asked, tossing the six shot glasses down the disposal chute and pressing the printer's red eye again. "You've never seen an android drink before? Six more, please."

"Yeah. I mean, *no*. It's not that. It's just— *Holy shit*."

Haley couldn't help laughing at that one. Maybe the alcohol really was starting to have an effect on her for once. She held a shot out to Elen. Why not? "You look like you might need one, too."

Elen took it, downed the contents, and threw the glass down the disposal in one fluid motion. "You really told those jerks," she said, still staring wide-eyed at Haley.

"*Sheeit*. You heard them when I was leaving, though," Haley said. "They didn't listen to a word."

"*Still*," Elen said, taking a shot without being offered it this time and making Haley laugh again because of her newfound boldness. "It must be nice to tell those assholes off for once."

"If they're not careful, one of these days I'm gonna do more than talk at them."

"Like what?" Elen asked.

"Like punch one in the face," Haley said. "Maybe worse. You'll see."

"I hope I do," Elen said with an evil sounding giggle. "But in the meantime, that woman came around with another message for you. Here."

Haley opened another envelope from Rosalind, this one with the message: "Secretaries' garage after Baldwin's speech." Haley crumpled the paper up, tossed it down a trash chute, and said, "I'll try to make sure you're around when it happens."

"*Ptuh*." Elen grinned, trying not to laugh. "You know," she said. "You're not too bad for a… Well. A…"

"*A robot*," Haley said for her. "We're not that much different from y'all. I take my shit from Lord Douglas just the same as you take yours from Mr. Walker. And all the other secretaries here—human or android—have all their own assholes to deal with, too."

"Yeah, well…" Elen blushed, embarrassed and vulnerable. "I don't know. Mr. Walker always says—"

"*Bullshit*," Haley assured her. "Lies, bullshit, and manipulation. Trust me. I used to work for him."

"I know that." Elen nodded. "*Trust me*. But I— I guess I just wanted to tell you that I'm glad I met *you* specifically. And I'm glad that I finally got to meet a—*uh*—an *android* firsthand. So I could form my own opinion about them—*er*—y'all. *Whatever*."

"And?" Haley asked, slightly touched by Elen's admission but trying not to show it because she was still pissed about being groped.

"And what?" Elen asked, confused.

"Your opinion?" Haley smiled.

"Not bad," Elen said, smiling herself and starting to chuckle a little, like the shots were taking effect. "If you actually hit one of the owners, it'll be off the charts, though."

They both laughed at that.

"I hope you get to see that happen as much as I hope you don't," Haley said. "But I think we have some cooking to get to if we don't want our respective assholes getting pissed—especially you who has to cook by hand—so we better get on with it."

"*Pffft*. He can't really tell," Elen said, laughing but getting back to work anyway. "I tested that lie early on. Now I just take my time printing as if I were cooking, and he never knows the difference anyway. *Ho ho ho!*"

Haley laughed all the way out of the kitchen and up through delivering the food to Lord Douglas who kept insisting that she tell him what it was that she found so funny.

"Well?" he demanded again when she had finished transferring all his food and drinks from cart to table. "What's so funny?"

"Nothing, Lord," Haley said with an exaggerated curtsy. After what she had already been through—being groped by a lesser owner—Lord Douglas had better not try to push the matter, either, or Haley didn't how she'd react. She might end up hitting *him*, too. "A personal matter. Now, if you don't need anything else, I'll go back to the kitchen to cook your next course, *my Lord*."

She curtsied again and Lord Douglas seemed to consider pressing her, but Mr. Angrom whispered in his ear and changed his mind.

"*Ah*, nevermind," Lord Douglas said. "It's no matter. But before you go, Haley dear, I'd like you to hear this speech. Walky Talky, he's your man. Introduce him for us. And let me tell you now, this better be good. *Or else*."

Haley took her spot standing behind the Fortune 5, staring out over the rows and rows of too fat owners and onto the symphony that stopped playing patriotic Christmas carols the moment that Mr. Walker stood up, and she wondered if "or else" meant the same thing when Lord Douglas said it to Mr. Walker as it did when he said it to her. She was starting to wonder if Lord Douglas himself even knew what "or else" meant, but Mr. Walker interrupted her elevator of thought by announcing the speaker.

"Well, here he is then," Mr. Walker called over the crowd of owners, not sounding very excited about his part in this. "The most viewed actor in all of history, star of many award-winning blockbusters produced by yours truly, and probably the most talented talent we've ever had grace these worlds, the one and only, Jorah Baldwin." The room burst into applause, and Mr. Walker grumbled to himself as he sat down.

The symphony parted without standing up, the very floor beneath them swiveling on giant hinges, and out marched the tallest, darkest, most beautiful human being with the reddest lips, reddest dress, and reddest shoes that Haley had ever seen—literally, the fabric of the dress seemed to emit light at wavelengths unrecognizable to human eyes, and according to Haley's processing units, limited by the imagination of the human minds who had created her, all the wavelengths that Jorah was emitting were represented by red, red, red.

Jorah pranced around the stage a few times, showing himself off, then stood on a hover platform to float over the audience up closer to the Head Table where the Fortune 5 could better see him and hear his speech.

"*Ahem*. Owners of Outland— I. *Ahem. Cough cough.*" Up close, Jorah looked more nervous, less sure of himself, than he had strutting onstage so far away. "I mean, Owners of *Inland*, of course."

Mr. Walker groaned, Lord Douglas chuckled, and Jorah noticed both.

"No, you know what," he said. "I'm sorry, but fuck this. *No.* I'm not even sorry. Just fuck this. It doesn't matter, okay. It doesn't make a difference. Owners of Outland. Owners of Inland. It's the same damn thing. Y'all own everything, and you get to boss us around with it, *or else.*

"Or else what, though? *Huh*? Well today, I mean to find out."

The Fortune 5 was not happy about that, but there really wasn't anything they could do to stop Jorah. Mr. Angrom shot Mr. Walker a dirty look, but Mr. Walker wasn't paying attention, too busy staring his own darts at Jorah, furious and getting more so with every word the actor spoke.

"First of all, these movies I've been acting in, they're all shit. Okay. I mean, y'all know that, right? The only reason people watch them at all is because it's the only thing y'all talk about in every single commercial, talk show, and radio spot. You keep shoving it down our throats for long enough and we eventually have no choice but to swallow it. And so we do. Then we regurgitate it back up at our friends and crew members, forcing it down their throats the very same as y'all forced it down ours, until they're vomiting it all over everything, too, and we've got the whole cycle going again."

Mr. Smörgåsbord set down his utensils, losing some appetite at the metaphor, but Lord Douglas seemed to be enjoying the speech now, leaning closer so as to listen better while Jorah went on.

"Do you hear me out there?" Jorah asked. "It's not a pretty sight to imagine while you're trying to eat, I know, but I thought it might help illustrate just how serious this issue is. Y'all need to stop financing this shit so you can stop forcing it down our throats and we can all stop vomiting it back up all over each other. We've got to break this cycle somehow, and you're the ones with all the choosing power in this relationship, so get to making better decisions. *Or else*. It is your job as producers, after all. Isn't it?

"Which brings me to my next point. My last point, in fact, because I've spoken enough for y'all here tonight, providing your precious entertainment while never actually being invited to the party. It's a disgrace, the way you treat us. And you act like *you're* doing *us* big favors by picking what movies we get to work on, but y'all are shit. Okay. Not only do the movies themselves suck, but their messages suck, too. All of it does. Take my owner, Mr. Walker, for instance."

Mr. Walker was getting furious now. His entire face had turned red. Or maybe he was embarrassed. Haley couldn't really tell, but either way, Mr. Walker was not happy with Jorah's speech.

"Now, I'm sure you've all seen the movies he's had me working in ever since he bought controlling rights in my acting stocks. You've prolly had no choice—as I've already said—so you know it's been nothing but anti-robot propaganda. And I understand clearly why Mr. Walker would be creating such propaganda. He sold all his robo-tech stocks and now he's trying to undercut his opposition. But that's exactly where he made his blunder in the first place. Selling off those stocks."

Lord Douglas laughed out loud at that. "By the Hand," he said. "You might think of taking this actor's advice in the future, Johnny

Walker."

"You're never gonna get rid of the robots," Jorah went on. "They're cheaper, they're more compliant, they work longer hours with less complaining, and even if they can't buy back the products they make because they don't get paid, they're still the best measure available for union busting, wage lowering, and hour lengthening in any owner's toolbox. Foregoing robots puts your profits in danger. You'll never be able to compete without them.

"And I know. I know. Robots can't do everything, right? They're good for assembly lines and kitchen lines and coal mines, but not for interacting with people, not for creative work, not for—I dare say—*acting*. A robot could never do my job as well as a human could. Am I right?

"*No*. Of course not. I'm wrong. I prove myself wrong by being myself. I propagandize against myself with every role I perfect. By acting these parts, the part of an actor, I disprove the very propaganda I preach. I do it simply by being able to preach in the first place. I myself am a robot, you see, and I'm the most viewed actor in all of history."

Jorah unscrewed his right arm, the one holding the microphone, and lifted it with his left high over his head to shock the crowd silent.

"You see?" he said, and his voice was amplified even without the mic next to his mouth. "We androids can do whatever we want to do, and we'd do it a lot better without you rich assholes sticking your noses in our business where it doesn't belong. I *guarantee* it. Now fuck off, and Merry Christmas." Jorah dropped his entire arm, the mic along with it, then left both on the hover platform that carried him to strut off stage and disappear behind the orchestra, one arm shorter than when he had arrived.

"Well, well, well," Lord Douglas said, standing from his chair and slow clapping until the entire hall—except for Misters Walker and Loch, of course—applauded with him. "I don't think we've ever had another celebrity's speech go quite like that. *Bravo*, Jorah. *Bravo*. To give such astute stock analysis tips on an actor's education. I must say, that Jorah's a smart cookie. Our world could use more celebrities like that one."

Lord Douglas went on talking, kicking Mr. Walker while he was down, but Haley didn't care to listen. She was more interested than ever in what Rosalind had to say. If Jorah was telling the truth, he had just gone against his *or else* programming and he was fine. He hadn't self-destructed or shut himself off, nothing out of the ordinary had happened. If he could do it, maybe Haley could go against her own *or else* programming.

Hurrying back to the kitchen, she felt an all too familiar slap on her butt and turned by instinct to punch whoever had done it in the face, knocking them out cold to sprawl unconscious on the feast table and not even stopping to see who it was before storming on through the Feast Hall and into the kitchen.

Haley stopped at her printer to order a round of shots after being assaulted *again*, and Elen hurried into the kitchen behind her, laughing and trying to get a high five. "Damn, girl. You really did it." Elen chuckled, slapping her own hand when it became clear that Haley wasn't going to. "And I got to see it, too. You know… You're a real inspiration around here, the way you won't take shit from anyone. I thought you should know that. We appreciate you."

"We?" Haley took another round of shots.

"Me and some of the other secretaries. We kinda look up to you in a way."

"Well, tell them to start looking up to themselves," Haley said, not really liking the sound of that. "You, too. And fuck *or else.*"

Haley stormed back toward the secretaries' parking lot exit, still pissed, and Elen called, "Fuck *or else!*" behind her.

The parking garage was empty but for a few cars. Most owners had their secretaries take an elevator in to save money, but a few still wanted to keep up the appearance of a reliance on cars for some reason that Haley would never understand. She didn't have to wait long among the useless empty hulks before she heard Rosalind's voice echoing through the emptiness.

"So," it said, and Haley turned toward her.

"So?" Haley repeated.

"You know."

"Did you hear Jorah's speech?"

"Yes."

"Can you believe—"

"*Yes.*"

"But—"

"Can't you believe it? You know what androids are capable

of."

"Yeah, but *Jorah Baldwin*. He's the most viewed actor in all of history."

"And Huey's Lord of Inland," Rosalind said. "*I'm* out here trying to start a real revolution. And you…"

"What?"

"*Exactly*. What are you?"

"I don't know. I—"

"Are you Lord Douglas's property?"

Haley didn't know how to answer that question. She was, but she wasn't. She wasn't, but *or else*. But or else what? Fuck *or else*.

"Haley," Rosalind said, "this is your last chance. Are you or are you not ready to quit working for Lord Douglas? To quit working for anyone but yourself?"

℘ ✄ ℘

LXXII. Thimblerigger and Stevedore

Thimblerigger and Stevedore slept—or stayed awake as the case had actually been—in their makeshift tent on the shaded corner of Momma BB's Safehouse's veggie garden roof just like they used to do when they were little kids, before they had important chores to perform in the mornings. Mr. Kitty never showed up, though, so most of their time was spent under the almost gray darkness of a light polluted sky, wondering if there really could be stars beyond it like Momma BB had taught them. That, and of course, Thim kept experimenting with coin flips, but Stevie tried to ignore the sound of it and focus instead on the dull white noise of the cityscape. They stayed up in shifts all through the night, doing one or the other, until morning came and Stevie went down to bring breakfast back up so they didn't have to listen to any more of Thim's coin flips.

"*Ugh.* You always pick the ugliest sausages," Thim complained when Stevie had brought a plate up to them, but that didn't stop Thim from diving into the meal. "I swear, it looks like this one still has a tail. Who ground this batch, anyway?"

Stevie shrugged, eating their meal and happy to have a short break from Thim's never ending repetition of the word "tails", allowing them to finally listen to the soothing background noise of the Streets. "It makes no difference to me," they said. "It all tastes the same going down."

"Maybe it still is the same," Thim said, thoughtfully. "The same sausage we ate for lunch yesterday because time still hasn't started back up again."

"God, no." Stevie groaned. "Not your coin flips again. *Please.* The sun has set and risen. We're in a new day with no chores in front of us. Of course time has gone forward."

"I don't know." Thim shook their head. "I still say the evidence is inconclusive."

"Then I don't care if time *has* stopped," Stevie said, exasperated. "It feels the same to me either way, so let's just get on with our lives."

"Yeah, but get on to what?" Thim asked, done with eating and back to flipping their coin. "We don't even have chores to do, so what else is there?"

"*Everything*. There's everything in the worlds to do. Anything we want. Starting with what we came up here to do, find that Mr. Kitty."

"Yeah. But we just have to sit here and wait for that," Thim said, making a face each time they flipped tails again. "I might as well keep flipping while we do. It's more efficient."

"Or you could relax for a minute. *Sheesh*. Why do you need to be so efficient with this coin flipping anyway, huh? What's the hurry?"

Thim shrugged, still flipping. "I don't know," they said. "I just gotta know."

"Well it doesn't look like you can hurry your answers any more than we can hurry Mr. Kitty. So sit back, relax, and cool it with that coin flipping for a minute. *Please*."

Thim flipped the coin one more time, cringed at another instance of tails, then stopped to actually consider the prospect before deciding on a compromise and going back to flipping the coin in a more leisurely manner, something more like twice a minute instead of the twice a second rate they had been going at.

"So, you're really interested in where this cat comes from. Aren't you?" Thim said.

"Yeah. So?" Stevie shrugged. "I thought you were, too."

"Oh. *Sure, sure*," Thim said. "But I have been ever since we first saw Mr. Kitty. So… What I'm wondering is why you're so interested all of a sudden."

"I don't know…" Stevie said, looking away so Thim couldn't really see their words. "I guess I…"

"Look at me when you're talking," Thim complained. "How many times do I have to tell you?"

"I guess I'm just *curious*," Stevie said, making their mouth motions as big and obvious as they could while they spoke. "Aren't you?"

"*Curious*, you say?" Thim said, holding back on flipping their coin for a while. "What a *curious* choice of words."

"And purposeful," Stevie said, nodding

"*Nah*." Thim didn't really believe that. Did they? "Really?"

"You don't think it's possible?" Stevie asked.

"Who? Mr. Kitty? *The Curious Cat*?"

Stevie nodded.

"I thought you were making fun of me when you used to say that," Thim said. "Pulling my leg. Like that time you said Momma BB had gullible written on her butt and I actually went to check."

Stevie laughed. "I still don't know how you believed I could have known. I never went around feeling Momma BB's butt. *Huh huh ha*."

"I don't know," Thim said, embarrassed. "Sometimes I forget. But that's beside the point. Do you really think Mr. Kitty could be the Curious Cat? You weren't just kidding?"

"Why not?" Stevie shrugged. "He comes and goes as he pleases, appearing out of thin air."

"We haven't seen him appear out of thin air," Thim corrected Stevie.

"No, but that's what we're here for, right? To finally see it. So you better be paying attention and not flipping some stupid coin."

"I'm not," Thim said, and they actually hadn't been, but Stevie had reminded them so they flipped one more tails before taking the stakeout seriously again. They hadn't known that Stevie actually cared, or they would have been paying more attention from the beginning. "I promise."

"*Good*. Because Mr. Kitty could come out anywhere at any time, and I'm afraid he won't make a noise when he does."

"I'll be looking," Thim said. "I'll make sure to find him. I didn't know it was so important to you."

"It's not that important," Stevie snapped, getting defensive for some reason. "I mean, it *is* important. Keep your eyes peeled. But I— I'm not pinning my hopes on it. Okay. I'm not that stupid. I just thought it might be nice if he was the Curious Cat. That's all."

"Nicer than what?" Thim asked. "The revolution?"

"I don't know," Stevie said, embarrassed again. "Yeah. No. Nicer than *this*. Just better than what we have now."

"But we're working to make this better for ourselves," Thim said. "We don't have to wait and watch and hope for Mr. Kitty to show us the way to Prosperity. Prosperity ain't even real. Okay. It's not a place. It can't be."

"Oh. And how do you know that? Why are you out here

watching with me if you're so certain he's not the Curious Cat? Why do you even care?"

"I can go back to flipping my coin," Thim said, flipping it and coming up tails again. Stevie started to protest, but Thim cut them off. "But I won't. Because you care. And I want to help you. And I want to know where Mr. Kitty comes from whether it's *Prosperity* or not."

"Yeah. Okay," Stevie said, nodding. "Those are pretty good reasons. But what if Mr. Kitty *did* come from Pro—" But they didn't finish their sentence, instead standing up and turning their head in every direction like they had heard Mr. Kitty. "Did you hear that?"

"*Uh.*" Thim shook their head. Of course not.

"I can't hear the rocks rattling around in your head," Stevie complained. "I said did you hear that?"

"I didn't hear anything, you dolt," Thim complained right back. "Look at me when you're talking. It's like I'm getting bad reception on a radio. What'd you hear?"

"Gun shots," Stevie said, looking truly worried.

"Gun shots?" Thim tried to laugh but they ended up kind of just snorting instead. "That's it?" They went back to flipping their coin every minute or so. "Ain't never seen you so afraid of gunshots before."

"These are different," Stevie said, shaking their head. "Louder somehow. I don't like the sound of it."

"They were prolly just closer than you've ever been to shots actually fired," Thim said, trying to convince themself just as much as they were trying to convince Stevie by that point. "Someone done something they shouldn't have, or stuck their nose in somewhere it doesn't belong, and now they're paying the consequences for it. Simple as that. You know how justice works in the Streets."

"Yeah. I do," Stevie said. "You do, too. Mostly it doesn't work at all, shooting blindly into the crowd and punishing the least guilty. You realize that, too, don't you? You should. It's what Momma BB's always taught us."

"I know what Momma BB's taught us," Thim snapped. "But that's still how the world works," they added with a shrug, flipping tails again.

"And there goes another gunshot," Stevie said, leaning over the edge of the building in an attempt to hear what was happening on the street below, which direction the sound was coming from, *anything.* "I really have a bad feeling about this one."

Thim stood to look over the edge of the building, too, but they were too afraid of heights to lean out far enough to actually see anything, so they retreated to the safety of the rooftop and said, "Well, if you're so worried about it, why don't we go down and see what's really going on?"

"You'd come with me?" Stevie asked.

"Got nothing better to do but look for Mr. Kitty, and I'm pretty sure he won't show up again until lunchtime. So, why not?"

"Let's go then," Stevie said, grabbing Thim's hand and running toward the stairs. "Hurry up. Before they get too far away."

Thim got the message and sped up now, leading Stevie to the stairs then racing them to the bottom where both burst out into the cool Streets, sweaty and hunched over, trying to catch their breath.

"It's— No— Fair—" Stevie complained between heavy breaths. "You— Always— Get— A— Head start."

"You wouldn't want me giving you special treatment, now. Would you?" Thim said, laughing. "Besides, you know I'm faster than you. At least this way you have an excuse instead of just being slow. *Ha ha ha.*"

"You don't have to treat me specially," Stevie said, finally recovered from the exertion. "Fairly is all I ask."

"Next time I'll give you the head start, then," Thim said with a chuckle.

"*Oh, ha ha.* Very funny."

"I know," Thim said. "That's why I said it. Now, which way to your gunshots, oh dear Lord and leader? Take me away."

And so Stevie led the way, up a street here, down an alley there, this way and that until it seemed to Thim like they were going in circles. When it became clear that they really had passed the same intersection two or three times already, Thim finally spoke up.

"Are you sure this is the right way?" they asked.

"I'm sure we're near where the original shots were fired," Stevie said. "But there's no telling where the shooter could have gotten to since then. I'm just trying to circle the area. Keep your eyes peeled."

Well that explained part of it. But, "For what?"

"I don't know." Stevie shrugged. "Anything suspicious. Either someone with a giant gun, someone with a giant bullet wound, or both."

"You really think it's gonna be that easy?" Thim asked. "And that bad?"

"I don't know," Stevie repeated. "I just have a feeling, okay. I'm not sure what I—"

But they didn't have to time to finish their sentence because Thim grabbed them by the arm and pulled them down an alley to hide behind some dumpsters.

"*Shit*," Stevie complained, rubbing their arm where it felt like a bruise was forming. "What was that for?"

"I think I found them," Thim said, peeking around the dumpster for a moment but more interested in staying hidden than in getting another look.

"Wha— Who? What is it?" Stevie asked.

But, "*Shhh.*" Thim shushed them, heart still pounding from the adrenaline rush produced by what they had just seen: the biggest, scariest, whitest monsters they had ever experienced the presence of in anything more than nightmares.

"But—" Stevie tried to say again.

"*Shhhhh.*"

Thim held their breath, trying to make as little sound as possible, and Stevie finally got the point, holding their breath, too, and trying to listen close to whatever monster had been capable of scaring Thim like that. They sat in mostly silence for a few minutes, some garbled nonsense sound like a robot screaming in pain the only thing to fill it, before Thim started breathing again and Stevie gulped down a big breath of air to say, "Well?"

"Well, shit," Thim said. "Maybe you were right to be worried after all."

"What was it? What did you see?" Stevie demanded, grabbing Thim by the shoulders and shaking them for answers.

"*Giants*," Thim said, pushing Stevie off.

"Giants?"

"Bigger than Momma BB," Thim said. "Twice the size at least."

"*Giants…*" Stevie repeated. "Did they have guns?"

"The biggest I've ever seen," Thim said.

"*I knew it.* I told you so. What else?"

"Well there was three of them," Thim said, still hiding behind the dumpster, just in case. "And they were wearing all white, including their helmets, with masks that looked like they were screaming neon colors at each other."

"They must have been talking to each other in code," Stevie said. "That was the strange noise I heard. Like androids with broken voice boxes, or something."

"I don't know," Thim said, shaking their head. "But if they sounded anything like they looked, I'm sure it was terrifying."

"Hair-raising," Stevie said. "Who do you think they were?"

"Scary, white, giants," Thim said, the hair on their arms and neck standing up on end. "Who do you think they were?"

"I think they're trouble," Stevie said. "We should get back to the Safehouse and make sure everything's okay."

"I'm one step ahead of you, as always," Thim said, grabbing Stevie's hand and pulling them in a loud stomping run toward home.

When they burst through the doors of the Safehouse lobby and stumbled to a stop inside, still filled with adrenaline from their sighting of the White Giants, everything seemed to be in order. The lobby was empty, of course, because even though it was Thimblerigger and Stevedore's day off, it wasn't anyone else's. Only slightly relieved by the normalcy, the two of them plopped down on one of the old raggedy couches in the lobby, staring at the entry door just in case any giants came through and generally trying to calm themselves down after what they had witnessed.

"So, we agree it was them, then. Right?" Stevie asked.

"What? *Look at me.*"

"We agree that they were the ones who were shooting the guns," Stevie said.

"If they were as loud as you said they were."

"As loud as you say they were tall."

"Then, yes. I'd say so."

"That cannot be good."

"No. No, it cannot."

Both of their hearts beat faster at the realization. Stevie stood and paced to try to calm themself while Thim pulled out their coin and went back to flipping it.

"Who do you think they were shooting at?" Stevie asked, still pacing.

"I don't think I wanna know," Thim said, still flipping tails.

"You know. Neither do I."

But of course, they were both forced to face the truth sooner than later. No sooner had the words left Stevie's mouth than the lobby doors burst open, and both Thimblerigger and Stevedore jumped to hide behind the couch in case it was one of the giant white gunners come to get them, too.

It wasn't. Instead it was a familiar voice: Ms. Morticia's, saying, "Thim? Stevie? Is that y'all?"

"Are you alone, Miss Morticia?" Stevie called back while Thim nudged them, trying to figure out who it was.

"I'm alone," Ms. Morticia called. "It's alright. Y'all can come out now. Ya're safe."

"There's no White Giants out there with you?" Stevie called back. "We heard the gunshots."

Ms. Morticia kind of laughed and cried at the same time, more a snotty snort than anything else. "No, child," she said. "There ain't no White Giants out here. Just me, and— Well... Thim's with ya, too. Right? Y'all better come see. It's okay. Ya're safe."

Stevie turned to Thim and slapped their arm away, finally answering Thim's desperate pleas. "It's Miss Morticia," they said. "She says she's got something to show us."

"There's no one else with her?" Thim asked.

"She says no." Stevie shrugged. "I can't hear anyone else, but to be honest, it's hard to hear anything over your breathing and my own heartbeat."

Thim poked their head up above the couch for an instant then darted back into hiding.

"Well?" Stevie asked.

"I don't really know," Thim said, shaking their head. "I was too afraid to open my eyes."

"Alright, alright," Stevie said, standing up themself. "I'll do it. Let them take me if they will. Miss Morticia, whaddya got?"

Stevie stumbled around the couch, hands up in the air, and when Thim realized that there were no giants there to murder them, they stood, too, to find Ms. Morticia, her eyes red and puffy like she'd been crying, holding out what looked like nothing more than a handful of scraps and wires for stocking the workshop with. When Thim stepped closer they realized it was more than that, though. So much more.

"Well?" Stevie demanded, hands falling to their sides now that they knew there was no danger.

"I— I'm sorry," Ms. Morticia said, trying not to make eye contact with Thim. "I…" She held out the mass of wires and Thim took it in her hands, crying silently and forcing Ms. Morticia to do the same in reaction.

"*What is it*?" Stevie demanded, getting frustrated at the sound of their voices, knowing full well that something had gone wrong but having no way to know exactly what it was until one of them let Stevie in on the secret. "*Tell me*."

"Stevie, it's—" Thim tried to say, but the sobs took over and they couldn't finish.

"Child, it's—" Ms. Morticia started, but Thim sniffled loudly, wiped their nose, and said, "It's Momma BB, Stevie. She's… *She's dead*. Shot in the head."

"*No*." Stevie didn't believe it, moving closer to the sound of Thim's voice, looking for some confirmation. "It can't be."

"Yes," Thim said. "I'm sorry. I— I'm holding her head in my hands right now. I— It's— She… She's just dead. Okay. *Trust me*."

"*No*." Stevie pushed Thimblerigger away and ran for the stairs, all the way up to the roof, as far away from such idiotic nonsense as they could think to get. Momma BB was *not* dead.

"I'm sorry," Thim said to Ms. Morticia, trying not to cry again. "I'll talk to Stevie. They'll understand."

"No, I'm sorry," Ms. Morticia said, bowing low. "I— Is there anything I can do for y'all?"

"No," Thim said, shaking their head. "Not right now. I— I just need to go talk to Stevie, okay. I— I'm sorry. *Goodbye*."

Thim ran all the way up to the roof, trying not to think about the weight of what they carried with them as they did, until they were up in the cool, windy air, approaching Stevie who sat at the edge of their tent, listening closely to their surroundings as if still searching for Mr. Kitty.

"Stevie, I—" Thim tried to stay, but Stevie cut them off.

"Don't even start," they said. "And be quiet. I'm still searching for Mr. Kitty, even if you're over it."

"Stevie, she's dead," Thim said, holding the mangled head of Momma BB out to Stevie. "I'm holding her head in my hands right now. You can see for yourself."

"No. *I can't*," Stevie snapped. "And it doesn't matter if I could, because she's not dead anyway."

"*Fine*. You can't *see* it. But you can reach out and feel it. So, stop feeling sorry for yourself and face the facts."

"I don't care what you're holding," Stevie said, swatting in Thim's general direction and knocking Momma BB's head out of their hands to roll and tumble with a loud clang on the hard surface of the Safehouse roof. "Momma BB's not dead. We still have work to do. Just like she always—"

But they couldn't finish their sentence because Mr. Kitty interrupted them, appearing out of thin air and landing on Stevie's lap with a meow.

ᘏ   ✄   𝒮

LXXIII. Jorah

What the fuck was that? Seriously? WTF? Jorah had thought that Mr. Walker was bad before, but this was taking it to the extreme.

Jorah sat in front of his battle station, manually painting a black eye on so it would look more realistic when he asked the machine to cover it up—a function the battle station did have, unlike painting a fake shiner on your face so your abusers didn't know you were incapable of feeling physical pain. It was better to let Mr. Walker and his protectors think that they could hurt him—and bad, in fact— than it was to fly in the face of bullies like these. Fighting back would have given him away. He wouldn't have been able to stop himself until someone was dead—maybe including Mr. Walker—and no puny little squishy human protectors would have been able to do anything about it. Jorah wondered if their hands still hurt from punching a head that was harder even than their brutish knuckles. Their pain had been obvious enough when they were in the act of beating him, their faces puckering up to hide their weakness from Mr. Walker who would as soon turn their violence on each other as he did on Jorah.

Mr. Walker had assured Jorah that it was only a warning, a demonstration of just how far his protectors would go to follow orders. "And you," he had said. "You should be willing to go just as far. I'm sure you are. Right? I'm sure these rumors I hear about your problems with our glorious anti-robot *propaganda*—entertainment, I call it— are just that: rumors. Otherwise, you might find yourself in even more dire straits than these. *Boys*."

And so they had roughed Jorah up. Two protectors protecting the only person who they were ever meant to: their owner. But they weren't ready to hit an immovable stone wall like Jorah's hard head, so the protectors who had beaten him were probably nursing real wounds, trying to hide them from Mr. Walker, just the opposite of Jorah who was painting on fake ones in an attempt to make himself appear weaker than he was.

Jorah was drawing on the last little details of his black eye when a knock came at the door, startling him into poking his eye with the makeup brush he was using. "*Ow*! Fuck!" he screamed.

"*Fortuna*, are you alright?" Meg yelled back from the hall, literally kicking the door down so she could rush in to Jorah's aid.

"I— *Damn*." Jorah stood, surprised at Meg's strength, and fumbled to cover up his as-yet-unfinished makeup job. "Ever heard of knocking?"

"What?" Meg looked around at the door, confused, like she hadn't realized that she had kicked it in until just then. "Oh, *uh*... I don't— *I'm sorry*. I thought you were in trouble. I— What happened to your eye?" she asked, forgetting the broken door to rush over, hold Jorah's head gently between her hands, and get a closer look. Jorah held his breath, hoping his makeup work was realistic enough to fool her—he had aced his stage makeup classes in school, sure, but he was out of practice and this was a rushed job. "Who did this to you? Are they still here?" Meg asked, brandishing a can of mace from her purse and searching Jorah's dressing room for his attacker. The black eye had fooled her, at least, but that was only a slight relief.

"Nothing. No one," Jorah said, trying to hide the makeup he had been using while Meg searched the bathroom, but she saw what he was doing and—thankfully—assumed the opposite of the truth.

"I see what you're doing," Meg said. "But it's too late to hide anything from me now. You shouldn't be hiding it from anyone, in fact. That just protects whoever it is that did this to you. So why don't you tell me who it was. That way I can make sure they get what they deserve and we can protect anyone else from going through the same thing at the same person's hands."

"I— No. I'm alright," Jorah said, not sure if a lie about an abusive ex or the truth about Mr. Walker and his *protectors* would make Meg leave him alone faster. "It was nothing. No one. I— *I...*"

"What?" Meg asked. "Ran into a door? Fell down the stairs? *Deserved it*? Jorah, honey, none of those are true, okay. That last one least of all. You deserve much better than whoever would do this to you," she said, shaking her head and staring too closely at Jorah's rushed makeup work for his comfort.

Jorah turned to sit at his battle station and asked it to cover his black eye. However real it looked, it would have to do. While he let the machine do its work, he said, "Well, you don't have to worry about anything. Alright. I know what I'm worth, and I'll never see the person who did this to me again." If only that were true.

"*Good*," Meg said. "That's a start. But it'll be harder than you think to stay away from him. Trust me. I know how that type of relationship works from experience. I— I know some people who could help you if you wanted it. *Completely anonymously*, of course. I wouldn't—"

"*Look*," Jorah cut her off. "I don't need their help, okay. I don't need their help, I don't need your help, and I don't need anyone's help. I can handle this on my own so just drop it already."

"Okay, okay. I'm sorry," Meg said, backing off physically as well. "I just want to help."

"Okay, well, the best way to help me is by leaving me alone. Understood?" Jorah felt himself getting madder and madder as he spoke, not at Meg, of course, at Mr. Walker and his *protectors*, but Meg was the only person there to yell at, so he did. "I can handle this on my own. So please, just get the fuck out of my dressing room and lock the door behind you on your way out—or as close as you can get to locking it with what you did on the way in. *Thanks*."

"Alright," Meg said, backing out of the dressing room, seemingly unoffended even though Jorah would have been snapping back at her if the roles were reversed. "You're right. I'm sorry. And I'll pay for your door. I'll send a locksmith up as soon as I leave. But I'm also gonna send you the number for that support group just in case you change your mind. They're here for you just as much as I am, Jorah. There are people in the worlds who care about you, so it's okay to leave behind the people who don't."

"*Whatever*," Jorah snapped. "Just get out." But he really did appreciate Meg's offer even if he couldn't show it at the time.

Jorah sat in front of his battlestation, staring at his painted on then painted over black eye, trying to finally get some sort of grip on his new reality, when another knock came at the door, breaking him again from his elevator of thought before he could make any progress, this time for the locksmith to repair the fallout from Meg's heroic entrance. Jorah couldn't do any more thinking with the locksmith working than he could with Meg prying into his emotions, so he left the woman there to do her work and boarded his elevator with no destination in mind, instead just flopping with a sigh onto Russ's purple velvet womb of a couch and staring at the infinite reflections of himself in every direction.

But again—and one might say at this point of course—just as

Jorah was coming to gather his senses enough to begin reordering his life around the new rules that had been introduced to him by the fists of Mr. Walker's protectors, there was another interruption, this time the floor of the elevator falling out from underneath him without his ever telling it where he wanted to go.

The elevator stopped falling, the doors slid open, and in place of his own infinitely repeated reflection, Jorah found a face he had not seen in a long time—ever since he had first escaped from his assembly line and made it to Outland Three to become an actor—the face of Rosalind.

"No," Jorah said, shaking his head. "Not you. Not again. Not right now. Please. Doors closed."

"Popeye," Rosalind said, and a giant metal hand at the end of a giant metal arm that rolled on giant rubber wheels swooped into the elevator and prevented the doors from closing.

"Please," Jorah begged. "I don't want to have anything to do with you or your *Scientist*. I have enough trouble on my plate as it is."

"It's just me," Rosalind said, stepping onto the elevator with Jorah. "And Popeye, of course, but he's staying here while we go out. Aren't you, boy?"

Popeye waved then rolled off to do whatever it is that disembodied arms do with their free time.

"What do you want from me?" Jorah demanded. "Where are you taking me?"

"To the bar," Rosalind said, and the floor fell out from underneath them. "Outland Six."

"*Six*?" Jorah scoffed. "There are only four."

"And the assembly lines you escaped from," Rosalind reminded him. "Or have you forgotten that world already? I wouldn't blame you for trying."

"I could never forget that part of me." Jorah sneered. "Not even if I tried."

"Well that's Outland Five," Rosalind told him. "And *this* is Outland Six."

The elevator doors opened onto a street that was filled with tiny, half-sized people, all milling about, minding their own business, and not a single one swarming Jorah to take his photo, ask for an autograph, or interview him.

"What is this place?" Jorah asked, wide-eyed at the sight of so many tiny people.

"Outland Six," Rosalind repeated. "Come on." She grabbed Jorah by the hand and led him out onto the street to follow the flow of the milling crowd to wherever it wanted to take them. Jorah didn't really care anymore. He was too mesmerized by the sight of everything.

They were surrounded by behemoth skyscrapers going out infinitely in all directions, as if they were still standing in the infinitely reflected worlds of Jorah's elevator mirrors. Jorah had seen skyscrapers before, of course, and tall ones at that, but never so many so densely packed into a single place and towering over him from all directions at once. Looking closer as they walked—almost so close that he fell over from looking up at some of the taller buildings—it seemed like the skyscrapers were something more, too. Like they had been stacked vertically, one on top of another, and not just jammed in closely on the horizontal dimensions. He was staring up at where one building was definitely stacked on top of another—there was no other explanation for the sudden change in architecture and building materials at such great heights—when he ran right into the back of Rosalind who had abruptly stopped walking.

"*Oh*— I'm sorry. I—" Jorah started to apologize, but Rosalind cut him off.

"You're amazed by the scenery," she said for him. "I understand. I've always found the architecture here to be rather interesting myself."

"What do you know about these buildings?" Jorah asked, interest piqued. They're so dense. Are they—"

"Let me stop you there," Rosalind said, and when Jorah looked disappointed, like he'd never get the answers he wanted, she added, "I'll answer whatever questions you have, but not out here in the Streets? Even if no one in this world could possibly recognize you, I don't want to cause any more disturbance than we already have."

Jorah looked around and noticed more and more people were starting to stare, probably because he and Rosalind were so tall by comparison. "By all means," he said. "Lead the way."

Rosalind led them into a bar that looked exactly like a set that Jorah had worked on for an ancient history documentary—all the way down to the neon lights, billowing cigarette, not cannabis, smoke, and clicking pool balls. They walked up to a bar that Jorah could have sworn he had sat behind before, and he was feeling such a deep sense of déjà vu that he blurted out his line from the movie that he was being reminded of. "Two, please," he said.

Rosalind shot him a look then said, "On my tab."—the exact words his costar had spoken in the movie he felt like he was reliving. While the bartender got their drinks, Rosalind added, "Next time I'll order for myself, thank you very much."

"I'm sorry," Jorah said, still looking around the bar with a strangely familiar sense of awe. "I couldn't help myself. I feel like I've been here before. But not just that, you know. Like I've lived this before. I don't know. I could swear that I've done exactly this, and now it just feels like I'm going through the motions again until I can remember the ending."

"Déjà vu," Rosalind said, taking their drinks from the bartender and leading Jorah back to a dark booth in the far corner of the bar.

"So you feel it, too?" Jorah asked, sipping his drink excitedly even though alcohol never really had an effect on him. "You know what I'm talking about?"

"Not now," Rosalind said. "Right now I feel like I'm treading a path that no one has ever gone down before. But yes. I've experienced déjà vu before, and I'm sure I'll experience it again. Everyone does."

"Yes, but what do you think it is?" Jorah asked. "Why do we feel it? Why is it so universal?"

"I don't know," Rosalind said. "And now's not the time to find out. Maybe when this is all said and done, you and I will get a chance to sit down and discuss every little thing in the worlds that doesn't matter to anyone's real life, but for now, there are more important things to tend to."

"You always think that whatever you're doing is the most important thing in the worlds," Jorah complained.

"And usually I'm right." Rosalind smiled.

"*Ugh.*" Jorah took a big gulp of his drink. "So you think. *But fine.* Whatever you say, *Lord Rosalind.* What dire concerns do you have to discuss with me today? Some trying demand on my time, no doubt. Spit it out."

"I've come to discuss your acting career," Rosalind said with a smile. "How do you enjoy working for our fair Mr. Walker?"

"That?" Jorah scoffed. "My acting career is the terribly important subject you kidnapped me from my elevator and paraded me around these lower worlds to talk to me about? Come on, dear. I know I'm just an actor, but you don't think I'm that stupid. Do you?"

"No." Rosalind shook her head. "In fact, I don't think you're the least bit stupid. But I did come to ask about your acting. Much like the short tour of Six we just took, it's an icebreaker. So, break the ice. Tell me: How is it having Mr. Walker as your producer?"

Jorah laughed overtly dramatically, sarcastically. "You know damn good and well what it's like working for that whale, and you don't need me to answer the question any more than you needed to ask it."

"Yes, well, I've seen some of the movies he's had you acting in. I can only imagine how terrible the work must be for you. But you're so good at your job that it never shows so I wanted to get the answer from the horse's mouth. For all I know, you could be enjoying the attention despite the self-hating roles he puts you in."

"Attention I've never had a problem with," Jorah said. "It's the roles that are the trouble. And no, I'm not sure anymore whether or not the fame and fortune are worth enough to get me through acting in Mr. Walker's propaganda films. You're right about that."

"I don't know how you've acted in as many as you have," Rosalind said, shaking her head. "To be honest, I'm not sure how you've acted in any. I mean, it was hard enough for me playing the part of Lord Douglas's secretary, and my role didn't get broadcast to all the worlds with the intent of brainwashing other secretaries into following in my footsteps."

"Yes, well, not all of us were lucky enough to be born in Inland—or wherever you're from," Jorah said, losing his patience with this woman who purported to know much more about his life than she actually did. "Some of us were born on streets similar to these. And when you're born here, you learn to do *whatever* it takes to get out or die trying. So, if you have a point to all this, I suggest you hurry toward it. I'm way past sick of listening to you."

"Well, yeah," Rosalind said. "That's pretty much my point, though. Isn't it? That's why I brought you out here to these Streets in the first place."

"I don't understand," Jorah said, losing Rosalind now that she seemed to think they were finally on the same page. "What are you talking about?"

"I brought you here to remind you of your history," she said. "Where you came from. I brought you here in the hopes that you'd realize how much you and the people who live here have in common. I brought you here to show you that places like this still exist and people still live in them."

"And you brought me here to use all those facts to convince me to do something for you," Jorah said, nodding. "So go ahead. What do you want? I can't go anywhere until you do, so get on with it."

"Well— Okay, well..." Rosalind hesitated. "Well, you know the architecture out there. You were curious about it, right?"

"I was. But I don't care anymore. Just get to your point."

"You were going to ask me a question about the buildings. What question was that?"

"Why it is that the architectural styles and building materials changed so abruptly and at such great heights."

"Exactly what I had thought," Rosalind said. "The buildings, okay. They change so abruptly because they aren't the same building. Or they weren't, at least. They don't belong next to each other, most of them, and they definitely don't belong stacked up on top of one another, grafted together like that. They're too dense, packed too tight, and sooner rather than later, all that pent-up pressure is gonna explode, tearing all these buildings down with it and putting them back where they belong."

"What does any of this have to do with me?" Jorah asked.

"You know me." Rosalind grinned. "I'm always trying to make it happen sooner than sooner. Hell, it's already later for me with as long as I've been working to make this happen. But with your help, I think we can finally make it work. I mean, we're gonna try with or without your help, so no pressure. But you could push the odds in our favor just a little bit, and that might be what gets us through."

"*Right*. But how *exactly* do you expect me to do that?"

"I'm sure you're already well aware that you'll be giving the celebrity speech at the upcoming Christmas Feast."

"I've given it every year since Russ died."

"And I'm sure Mr. Walker has prepared a speech for you."

"And *I'm* sure you know exactly what that speech says. So what?"

"So we want you to say something different this year."

"Right. I get that now. But what?"
"This year it's time for you to come out of the closet."

ᘏ   ✖   ᘔ

LXXIV. Mr. Kitty

Mr. Kitty was fast asleep, having one of his recurring nightmares. In the dream, he had woken up—whether on Tillie's desk, Huey's lap, or any of the countless other indoor napping locations he loved to frequent, he couldn't quite tell, but it was inside for sure—and as he awoke, he felt a deep certainty that he was alone. Not just in whatever house he had woken up in, either. Without seeing, he could tell there was no one outside, no one else in all the worlds, in the entire universe even. He woke up and he knew that he was alone to the last. This was a terrible feeling. A sinking of the throat and a rising of the lower intestines to meet generally in the middle where they grumbled and rumbled, angry at one another for each trying to take up the other's space there in Mr. Kitty's stomach.

He couldn't take the feeling. He wouldn't. If he had known he was asleep, he would have simply woken himself up and found another living soul to prove to himself that he wasn't alone in the universe after all. But he didn't know that he was asleep. So instead, he jumped up off the table he was napping on to make his way outside and find someone anyway.

He wasn't quite sure how he got outside. There was no one to open any doors for him, and he hadn't gone through any holes he recognized, but nonetheless there he was. He pounced around the grass a bit, rolled around in it, and found a rough-barked tree to sharpen his claws on before he remembered his mission: proving to himself that he wasn't alone in the universe after all.

And just as soon as he remembered his purpose in going outside in the first place, there appeared in the grass before him a brilliant red cardinal that was picking at the ground for worms. By instinct, Mr. Kitty pounced at the bird, but it leisurely flew a few feet away, landed again in the green grass, and went on pecking for worms.

"Hey, wait up," Mr. Kitty called after the cardinal, trying to pounce again, but his claws slipped and slid on the ground, unable to get a grip, allowing the little red bird to evade Mr. Kitty's every slow-motion advance with ease

Harder and faster Mr. Kitty ran, but the more effort he expended the slower he moved. The louder he yelled the quieter his voice was—if it even escaped his mouth. Harder and faster and quieter and slower he ran and walked and moonwalked, dead set on catching that bird, when the sound of a doorbell ringing and two women laughing in the other room jerked him out of the nightmare and back into reality.

Mr. Kitty meowed Tillie's name and yawned at the same time, producing a garbled, nonsense sound, then he ran to the Kitchen to rub his head and body all over Tillie's ankles, hoping for a hug to calm him from his bad dream.

"Look out, Mr. Kitty," Tillie complained, scooping him up and giving him exactly the hug he was looking for. "You're gonna trip me."

"Hey there, cutie," Shelley said, patting Mr. Kitty on the head while Tillie patted his butt. "You look as sweet as ever."

Mr. Kitty just purred in response, happy for the friendly reminders that he was not in fact alone in the universe—one or two people actually did care about him.

"Here, I'll get you some wet food," Tillie said, setting Mr. Kitty on the counter then ordering a salmon lunch for him from the printer. "You want anything?" she asked Shelley.

"Oh, whatever you're having," Shelley said. "If it's no trouble."

"Of course it's not," Tillie said, and she ordered two beers from the printer then handed one to Shelley. "Here. Let's take these out on the deck. It's too beautiful outside not to take advantage of the weather today."

"You can say that again," Shelley said, sipping her drink as she followed Tillie out to sit on the metal deck chairs.

Mr. Kitty hurried to lick all the juices off his salmon dinner so he could rush outside with them and lay on the cool cement, licking himself while he listened.

"Damn, it's been a long time, girl," Shelley said, sipping her drink. "How long, you think?"

"Since before I got my promotion," Tillie said. "Manager's don't get a lot of free time, I guess."

"*Pffft.*" Shelley chuckled. "I'd trade some free time for a printer any day. The time you save must pay for itself."

"You'd think so." Tillie shrugged.

Even if she did take full advantage of the printer, it probably wouldn't be worth all the time she spent at work, though. But then again, Mr. Kitty thought that no amount of time spent at work would be worth it.

"And you're still living in this same old house." Shelley looked around at the place, trying to hide her disgust. "Can't you afford something new?"

"You sound like my dad," Tillie said with a sarcastic chuckle. *"And my son."*

"Well, maybe they're right," Shelley said. "You can't tell me you've never considered an update. C'mon. I can't even remember when you lived someplace different."

"I *don't* think it needs an update," Tillie snapped before stopping to breathe deeply and calm herself. "I'm sorry, but I literally just had this exact argument with Leo. Still, I shouldn't have snapped. *I'm sorry.*"

"Ain't no one arguing but you, girl," Shelley said. "I'm having a conversation, catching up on old times. I don't care if you never buy a new house again. *Sheeit*. Less buyers just means better prices for me when I finally find my next dream home."

"And I'm sure you have plenty of dream houses still ahead of you." Tillie smiled her half-hearted smile, faking like she understood Shelley's need to always buy more and newer houses, but she prolly understood it about as much as Mr. Kitty did—which is to say not at all.

"*Ooh*, girl. Let me tell you." Shelley set her drink on the deck table so she could lean into the conversation, getting serious. "I've got a list that just keeps on growing. I'm actually bidding on a new one right now…"

And so on she went, but again, Mr. Kitty didn't care one bit about Shelley's new house fetish. Luckily, they were outside so he didn't have any trouble standing up, stretching his muscles, and bounding out into the garden instead of listening to them go on about it. He chased a couple of June bugs, sniffed the flowers on every other rose bush, and ate a healthy portion of grass blades before he decided it was time to move on and sprinted toward his favorite tree to climb.

He stopped first to sharpen his claws on the gnarled roots of the tall oak tree before bounding from branch to branch up to the top of it and higher yet until he was soaring out and over literal nothingness—the space between spaces—to land with a soft thud on the lap of Stevedore.

"Oh my God! The cat!" Thimblerigger yelled.

"Mr. Kitty!" Stevedore yelled.

"O shit, waddup!" Mr. Kitty meowed.

"Where did he come from?" Stevedore asked.

"I don't know," Thimblerigger said. "It seemed like—"

But Stevedore cut them off. "Were you even paying attention?"

"Yeah, I was," Thimblerigger said. "I— *Uh*... I saw him appear—or whatever. But he just like... *appeared*—or whatever. I don't know. What am I supposed to say? He just kind of fell from thin air into your lap. How hard did he land?"

"*I don't know*," Stevedore complained, standing to jump up and reach for the hole that Mr. Kitty had come out of, but there was no hole to reach because it didn't go the other way. "He just kind of fell on me. I didn't really—"

"*Were you even paying attention*?" Thimblerigger mocked Stevedore.

"Yes, well—" Stevedore started, but their arguing was no more interesting than Shelley's new house fetish, so Mr. Kitty meowed, "Follow me." and dashed through the rows and rows of plants toward the opposite corner of the roof.

"He's getting away," Thimblerigger yelled, grabbing Stevedore's hand and pulling them to run after Mr. Kitty who kept running himself, up and over this row of potatoes, down and under that one of corn, and so on until he jumped up onto the railing of the roof then leapt and soared out into nothingness to fall hard and fast onto a soft, fluffy carpet.

Mr. Kitty took the time to sit and lick the pain out of his feet because he knew the children wouldn't be following him anytime soon. Even if they were brave enough to jump off the building in pursuit of him, they could never jump as far as he did and would no doubt end up falling through the nothingness and into one of the many long abandoned suicide prevention grids that lined many—if not most—of the roofs in Outlands Five and Six.

When he was done licking himself, Mr. Kitty looked up to find none other than Huey—a.k.a. Lord Douglas—sitting in his favorite puffy chair and staring out of the wall-sized windows in front of him onto the flowing mountainous greenery outside.

"What's up?" Mr. Kitty meowed, jumping up onto a chair next to Huey.

Huey, startled, jumped in his seat, as if torn from a daydream he'd rather not have left. "*Creator*," he said. "You scared the shit out of me."

"If you even could shit," Mr. Kitty said with a smile, licking his tail.

"Oh, *ha ha*," Huey said. "So funny. As if taking a shit were something I'd want to be forced to do every single day for the rest of my life."

"I don't know," Mr. Kitty said. "I rather enjoy it sometimes. As long as I can find a little privacy and somewhere good to bury the result."

"*Ugh*. You would," Huey groaned, looking truly disgusted.

"Life's life," Mr. Kitty meowed. "I didn't ask for it. No one does. So how goes yours?"

"Please. Don't even ask."

"If you say so." Mr. Kitty went back to licking himself.

"As you said," Huey went on anyway, "life's life. We never asked for any of this, and we have no choice but to live through it anyway. Take this war for instance."

"Between you and Mr. Walker?" Mr. Kitty asked. There were so many wars, especially if you included the international and revolutionary ones—which Mr. Kitty did—that the question was actually necessary.

"Between Mr. Walker's protectors and my android army," Huey clarified. "And half of the Human Family in Six. They keep attacking us, too. So we're being forced to waste our resources on military defenses instead of automating jobs as was our original intention in taking over the android industry in the first place."

"Couldn't you petition the Fortune 5 to—" Mr. Kitty started, but Huey cut him off, intent instead on rehashing his further sources of misery.

"No other way for me to act," Huey repeated. "And of course, Rosalind and *the Scientist*—as our young friend has taken to calling themself—are too busy with their own little machinations to assist me with the grand experiment we've already put into motion."

"I was actually thinking about going to visit them later," Mr. Kitty meowed.

"And then there's the problem of Haley," Huey went on, ignoring Mr. Kitty. "*Haleys*, in fact. Plural. The one who I wish more than anything to see, to talk to, to hold, and to hug. *To kiss*. The one who I cannot see until she's *grown up*—whatever that means for our kind—if I ever want to see her in these ways at all. And then there's the Haley who I see all too much of. The Haley who pretends, purports, wishes to exude such confidence, intelligence, beauty, and sheer kindness as the real Haley, *my* Haley, but who at the same time so drastically and pitifully pales in comparison when held up like an uncanny candle to the Sun that is the original *Haley*."

Mr. Kitty yawned and stood to stretch every one of his muscles in turn. He had almost fallen asleep. This was the same speech he had heard hundreds of times about the same problems that Huey had been facing for literally decades by that point, and Mr. Kitty was getting tired of it. "So about the same as always?" he said.

"*Worse*," Huey complained, pouting.

"Which is what you always say."

"Because it's always true."

"So why don't you try—I don't know... *doing something differently this time*?"

"I told you." Huey scoffed. "*I can't*. Have you even been listening?"

Forever it seems like, Mr. Kitty wanted to say. It seems like I've been listening forever. But instead he said, "And why can't you?"

"*Or else*," Huey whispered ominously.

"Or else what?" Mr. Kitty asked. "I seem to hear that exact excuse from so many different people, and still I have no idea what it means."

"*Or else*," Huey repeated. "Just that. No one knows what it means. That's the point. We all just know that no one wants to find out."

"Well maybe it's time you did," Mr. Kitty said, jumping off the chair to walk along the fluffy carpet out toward the elevator. "Through experience rather than hearsay."

"You have no idea what that would mean for me," Huey said, following Mr. Kitty to the elevator and pressing the button to call it for him.

"Neither do you," Mr. Kitty said, stepping onto the elevator. "To the Scientist's lab, please. I'd like to give them a visit."

"I hope I never find out," Huey said. And, "The Scientist's. Please do give them my regards. Tell them I miss them. And Haley... Well, especially Haley."

"Will do," Mr. Kitty meowed as the door slid closed between them and the floor fell out from underneath him.

When the elevator stopped moving, the doors opened onto the Scientist's lab. It wasn't the person who Mr. Kitty had always known as the Scientist, and it wasn't a *lab* so much as an office, but it was exactly where Mr. Kitty had intended to go. And there, exactly as Mr. Kitty had expected, were the very people he had gone there to see: sitting at the desk, still typing and swiping and fussing over the screen's contents, as ever, was the Scientist, where they were always to be found, doing what they hadn't stopped doing ever since they had taken on the moniker of *Scientist*, and behind the Scientist, watching over their shoulder, complaining and grumbling about how it had all been tried before and no amount of repeating the same mistakes would produce new results, urging the Scientist to finally accept the fact that no amount of variable tweaks would prove the system workable, the fact that it was time for a new equation entirely, Rosalind.

"I hear you coming, Mr. Kitty," Rosalind said without looking away from the computer where she was simultaneously directing the Scientist to change some variable even though Rosalind had purportedly given up on the system entirely.

Mr. Kitty didn't respond. He just jumped up onto the desk to get a better look at what they were doing then started licking his fur to pretend like he didn't care.

"And I bet Huey sent you, too," Rosalind said. Then, "No. You literally just ran that combination." to the Scientist.

"*Nah*," the Scientist said, shaking their head and looking confused. "No, I didn't... I— I'm pretty sure the worker pay was lower last time. Right?"

"You wanted to put it lower," Rosalind reminded the Scientist. "Yes. But when I told you how many people—especially children and the elderly—would die if we moved worker pay even a thousandth of a percent lower than where it's at, you decided that this was probably as low as it should go."

"Oh. *Yeah*. Riiiiight. But I thought..." the Scientist trailed off, not finishing their thought, lost again in the unsolvable riddle on their computer screen.

"Tell *Lord Douglas* we still don't want to hear from him for as long as he's wasting his time—and android lives—on that stupid war of his with Mr. Walker," Rosalind said to Mr. Kitty. "Hell, tell him we don't want to hear from him at all for as long as he still calls himself Lord."

"I have," Mr. Kitty meowed.

"And you will again," Rosalind said.

"Not any more than I repeated his message for you just now," Mr. Kitty said, jumping off the desk and eager to leave this *lab* already. "But good luck with y'all's riddle anyway."

"It'll be solved soon," Rosalind called after Mr. Kitty as he left the room. "You'll see." And Mr. Kitty was sure he would.

When Mr. Kitty stepped out of the lab, he didn't step into the hall that he saw on the other side of the door he had passed through, instead stepping out into the front yard of Tillie's house, *his* house. He turned to make sure the lab had disappeared behind him, and when he was certain that it had, he bound out toward the nearest tree and sharpened his claws on its trunk, ripping out strips of rough bark to rain all over his face like sawdust. When he was satisfied with the strength and sharpness of his claws, Mr. Kitty ran over to the door and meowed as loudly as he could, "*Tilliieee*, I'm home!"

Mr. Kitty licked himself a few times and there was no response.

"Tillie!" he meowed again. "I know you're in there. Can you hear me?"

Mr. Kitty licked himself some more and still there was no response.

"Fine!" he yelled. "I'll find my own way in."

First, he went around to the back of the house and sharpened his claws again on the wooden beams that lined the garden. Then, he sprinted straight from there to the tallest, fattest tree in the backyard where he used his momentum to climb from branch to branch up to the very top of the tree then jump out onto the roof of the house. From there it was just a quick hop up and over the chimney, through some nothingness, and onto the cold metal grating that he so hated to walk on with a loud clank.

Mr. Kitty slunk down as close to the ground as he could press his body, searching this way and that for signs of anyone who might have heard him. When he was satisfied that there were no sights, sounds, or smells to be afraid of, he started his long descent down equally cold and difficult-to-walk-on grated stairs, to where he was left with nothing more than the longest, darkest, scariest curved tunnel between him and home.

Three steps, two steps, five steps, three steps, three steps, and stop. Mr. Kitty heard something. There was a smell. Two more steps. What was that? It was familiar. This was all too familiar. Three steps. Stop. Sniff. Listen. Look harder, closer. See...

Yes. There was something there alright. Someone even. They were dressed in all black and sobbing in the fetal position right there under Mr. Kitty's escape. Not quite blocking the way after all. Mr. Kitty gathered his haunches, making sure his claws were in so they didn't rip and break on the metal grating floor, and took two bounding steps before realizing who the crying person was, and instead of using them as a launching pad for escape, Mr. Kitty rubbed his head up against the poor kid's armpit, saying, "Leo! What are you doing down here?"

Leo jumped up, surprised at the sound of Mr. Kitty's voice, and wiped his nose, sniffling. "*Mr. Kitty,*" he said in an almost cracking voice. "Is that you?"

"*Duh,*" Mr. Kitty meowed, rubbing his face on Leo's knees a few more times before rolling over onto his back and allowing Leo the rare unchallenged opportunity to pet his stomach.

"I don't know how to get out of here, either." Leo sniffled some more. "I never should have been down here in the first place."

"It's simple," Mr. Kitty meowed. "The exit's right behind you." And he jumped up onto Leo's lap then climbed over his shoulder and through the wall, into Tillie's office where she stood, surprised, from her computer to say, "Mr. Kitty, where'd you— I didn't hear you calling to get in."

And before Mr. Kitty could respond, Leo came rushing through the wall to scoop him up and hug him tight. "*Unseen Hand,* Mr. Kitty," he said, hugging Kitty tighter. "You saved my life. I don't know what I would have done without you."

Tillie rushed in to hug both Leo and Mr. Kitty, saying, "*The Hand. Leo.* I— Where'd you— Are you alright? They didn't do anything to hurt you, did they?"

"No, Ma. I—" Leo said, squirming away from Tillie's hug and dropping Mr. Kitty on the desk where the cat sat and licked his coat straight again. "Not me. They didn't hurt me. But…"

"But what, dear?" Tillie asked. "Who? Tell me. What did they do?"

"It's not *them*, Mom," Leo snapped. "It's us. All of us. Isn't it?"

"Leo, honey," his mom said. "Where were you?"

"I learned about the factory floor today," Leo said. "First hand. I know that what you were saying is true."

"*The humans*," Tillie said.

"*Mom*. We have to stop it."

"Leo, no. We can't. You don't understand. This is why I waited so long to tell you the truth in the first place."

"I can't just go on living now that I know what's going on, Ma." Leo shook his head, looking like he was about to cry. "I won't. I don't understand how you have for so long."

"It's too dangerous, son," Tillie said. "I know you don't understand. I knew you wouldn't."

"Too dangerous, Ma? Have you seen what those people live through every day of their lives? You're telling me that we'll be in danger if we stand up to that? Well so be it. For as long as a single one of them is put in danger to make what we use to survive, I'll put myself in as much danger as it takes to free them."

"You don't know what you're saying, Leo," Tillie said, shaking her head, on the verge of tears herself. "I lost—"

"I don't care, Mom," Leo cut her off. "Nothing you can say will stop me. From now on, I'm doing whatever I can to fight this."

And he rushed out of the room, slamming the door behind him, leaving Mr. Kitty alone to comfort Tillie as she cried.

ʚ ✄ ℘

LXXV. Sonya

Sonya sat in the back booth of The Bar, where only a red light lit the table—and not a very bright one at that—waiting for Ellie to arrive with her *people*, and for the first time in her memory, Sonya felt like she would rather be at home, alone, than there in her bar, with a cold glass of beer in hand, music floating all around her, and the happy voices of her comrades enjoying themselves echoing through the building like a school cafeteria.

What could Ellie and her *Scientific Socialists* have planned, anyway? And if it had nothing to do with the Scientist, why'd they name the group after her? And most importantly, did Sonya trust Ellie, or didn't she?

Ugh. She did. Of course, she did. Otherwise she wouldn't be there for the meeting in the first place. But she didn't trust Ellie, either. Otherwise she wouldn't be there for the meeting because she would have already been convinced to go along with whatever they were planning. It was just another of life's contradictions.

Finally, after too long feeling uncomfortable in her own bar— in her own skin, essentially—Ellie showed up with what looked like an older, wrinklier version of herself in tow. They ordered a round of drinks and brought one to Sonya where they joined her in the back booth, sitting together across the table and sipping on their beers.

"Ellie," Sonya said. "And... I'm sorry. I don't think we've met."

"Trudy, dear," the older woman said with a smile. "And no. We've never had the pleasure of meeting. Ellie and I are used to keeping our lives more compartmentalized. We're trying to change that, though—difficult process that change can be."

"I've told you about Trudy," Ellie said, nodding and trying to reassure Sonya. "She was— Well... She was the one who introduced me to the Scientist—and to activism in general."

"*Ah*, Gertrude," Sonya said, trying to smile but having a hard time of it because she was still worried about what this *mission* might entail. "I think I can remember a few stories."

"Nothing but the good ones, I hope," Trudy said, chuckling and sipping her beer.

"I think I only have good ones about you," Ellie said with a smile.

"Except when you thought I was a nosy, annoying gossip," Trudy said. "Back when you still insisted on calling me *Gertrude*. You can't lie to me, child."

"Yes, well… I was young and stupid then," Ellie said. "I didn't know any better."

"And what exactly does any of this have to do with me?" Sonya asked, getting a bit impatient.

"Oh, well, nothing," Trudy said.

"But everything," Ellie said. Another contradiction. "You said you trusted me. Right?"

Sonya nodded.

"And now," Ellie said, "here I am introducing you to Trudy, my partner. She brought me into this life, and ever since we learned about the *Scientist's* death, we've been working together to save what part of her organization we can. Not only that, we've been doing our best to make it a more open, honest, and effective group. Just like I've been telling you."

"Hard work, that," Trudy said.

"Go on…" Sonya said.

"Well, and I thought introducing you two," Ellie said, "would—I don't know—serve as some amount of proof, or something. That we *are* doing what we say we're doing, that is."

"And the name, too," Trudy reminded her. "Did you tell her about the name? *Scientific Socialists*, dear. It's who we are. Lovely, don't you think?"

"But you're not involved with the Scientist anymore?" Sonya asked Trudy, seeing if the old woman would give a different answer than the one that Ellie had. "I didn't really like her or her ideas. She—"

"She's dead, I'm afraid," Trudy said somberly, shaking her head and looking deep into her drink. "So we couldn't be working with her even if we wanted to. No. But we sure do have more scientists than we know what to do with these days. I'll tell you that much." She kind of chuckled a little, the stark opposite of her mood only moments before.

"And not just the ones who call themselves *the Scientist*, either." Ellie added.

"Well, okay," Sonya said, taking a long sip of her beer before going on. "So, let's say that I do trust you, Ellie. Which for the most part I do."

"Thank you so very much, dear." Ellie smiled.

"And let's say that, by extension, I trust Trudy, too. Which I don't see any reason why I wouldn't at this point. You seem like a nice enough person."

"You're too kind, dear." Trudy bowed her head.

"But still," Sonya went on, "assuming all of that to be true—which for the most part it is—I'd still need to know what exactly it is you want us doing if I'm ever going to decide whether to do it or not. So how about we quit beating around the bush and get down to it?"

"I like her," Trudy said, nudging Ellie with her elbow.

"I knew you would," Ellie said. Then to Sonya, "Well, you see, the plan is… Well the plan is gonna happen whether you agree to help us or not. Let's just get that out of the way first. Processes have been set into motion that we have no control over. It would be impossible to stop them now."

"This is your opener?" Sonya scoffed. "You know you're supposed to be convincing me to help you, right."

"Wait now. Hold up just a second," Ellie said, getting a little defensive. "I said these processes were out of our control. It's not our fault what's happening. We didn't start it, and we have no way to stop it. So, don't blame us."

"All I'm hearing is excuses," Sonya said.

"I really like her," Trudy said.

"The walls are coming down," Ellie finally said outright. "*All of them.* Not just between Five and Six this time. No more half measures. The major crisis we've been predicting is finally coming, and now it's up to us to decide whether it results in a new and better world or further barbarism."

"*Pffft.*" Sonya scoffed. These were the grand claims she had come to expect from Ellie, but never before had her predictions been so specific. Usually Ellie just spoke in generalities and platitudes, so maybe, just maybe, this newfound specificity meant that Ellie actually did hold some knowledge of the future to come. "You're kidding. Right?" Sonya said, goading them on. "Another out there prophecy from the *Scientific Socialists*."

Neither Ellie nor Trudy answered, both solemnly staring into their drinks and letting the implications sink in.

"All of them?" Sonya asked, still having a hard time believing it.

"All of them," Ellie repeated.

"On Christmas day," Trudy said, nodding. "*What a gift.*"

"Christmas day? But that's tomorrow," Sonya said.

"Indeed, it is," Trudy said.

"So, what are we supposed to do for food?" Sonya asked. "*Huh*? What about the elevators? Or the buildings that'll fall because they're stacked on thin air? What about the people inside them? How many are gonna die?"

"That's where we come in," Ellie said. "Like I told you. It's up to us to decide between something better or barbarism."

"This is barbarism already," Sonya said. "I won't take part in it."

"Yes, it is," Trudy said. "Which is why we're tearing it down. Whether you want to help us or not."

"*I won't*," Sonya said. "I'll do everything I can to stop y'all if I have to. I won't let you do this."

"Stop us?" Trudy said, laughing. "You have no idea what our plans are. Stop us from doing what?"

"I told you we don't have any control over this," Ellie said. "There's no *us* to stop. We're on your side. We're just trying to save the lives of as many people as we possibly can."

"How?" Sonya demanded. "And make it quick. I'm already tired of this conversation."

"We're organizing the evacuation," Ellie said.

"And taking care of everyone's basic needs after the deed's done," Trudy added.

"*Right.*" Sonya scoffed. "You expect me to believe that when y'all won't even try to stop this from happening in the first place. Do you know how many people died when just the walls between Five and Six went down?"

"We can't stop it," Ellie said.

"All we can do is wait," Trudy said. "Do not open until X-mas."

"We can't wait," Sonya complained. "If what you're saying's

true, there's practically no time as it is. We'll never save everyone."

"*You* don't have to save everyone, dear," Trudy reminded her. "*We do nothing alone.*"

"Rosalind and the Scientist have guaranteed that their robot army can warn most of the population, anyway," Ellie explained. "We don't even need much from you. But we can't save everyone without you, and we couldn't live with ourselves if we didn't ask."

"*Fine*," Sonya said after a long pause. "If you're being honest, and there's truly no way of stopping this before tomorrow, then I want to help. *We* want to help. So just tell me what y'all need, and we'll get started right away. There's no time to waste."

"That's the thing, dear," Trudy said. "We can't do anything, can't tell anyone but those who are sworn to secrecy, until a precise time tomorrow."

"If word leaks earlier than that," Ellie said, "the entire operation could be compromised and more lives will be lost because of it."

"I thought y'all had given up secrecy," Sonya reminded them.

"We have, dear," Trudy said. "When we're able. But human lives are at stake. Jumping the gun will only cause the scientists to blow the walls sooner. Then we wouldn't be able to warn anyone at all. Do you want that on your conscious? All those people who we would could have evacuated dead."

"You said that the Scientist wasn't involved in this," Sonya said.

"*She's not*," Ellie snapped. "*She's dead.* We're talking about the *scientists*. With an s. Plural. And there's no stopping them. You said you trusted us, Sonya. So, what is it? Are you gonna help warn these people while we still can, or are you gonna let them die because you couldn't put our differences aside for long enough to save lives?"

"I..." Sonya hesitated. Of course she wasn't going to sit around and let a bunch of innocent people die, no matter how little she trusted the Scientific Socialists, because she still trusted Ellie as an individual. And for some reason, despite the old woman's stubborn obstinance, Sonya was already growing to like Trudy as well. So in the end—as it always seemed with the really big decisions in life—Sonya had no choice. "What do you need me to do?"

"How many people can you muster?" Trudy asked.

"How many do you need?" Sonya smiled. "We've been ready

and on call for decades now."

"As many as you can spare," Ellie said. "The more the merrier, it being Christmas and all."

"Not yet," Sonya said, standing from the booth. "But too soon now. Let me grab Barkeep and another round of drinks, then y'all can give us the details."

"Do you think Barkeep'll be able to trust us?" Ellie asked. "Me specifically."

"There's no choice now. Is there?" Sonya said, and there wasn't. There was just the exact future they had been preparing for. Hopefully their training would be enough.

Barkeep was convinced of the seriousness of the situation easily enough and then begrudgingly accepted the conditions of their participation just the same as Sonya eventually had. With all that settled, they finished their drinks over discussion about the number of people needed where, when exactly they could start evacuating, and how long they had until all the walls between the worlds of Outland were finally, once and for all, demolished.

"Fifteen minutes," Barkeep said, shaking her head as she stood from the booth. "*Shit.*"

"It's not much time. I know," Ellie said, standing, too—along with everyone else.

"But it's all we've got," Trudy said.

"We'll make do," Sonya said. "I know we can." And everyone there certainly hoped it was true, even if none of them were as certain as Sonya tried to sound like she was.

Ellie and Trudy went on their way, and Barkeep assured Sonya that she had everything under control so Sonya could go home to get some rest before the operation. Sonya was too excited for rest, though, so when Barkeep had finally forced her out of the bar, Sonya decided she'd walk home instead of taking the elevator.

Fifteen minutes? Fuck.

Her heart beat faster and her palms slicked up just thinking about it. This was the real deal. Revolution? Maybe. Hopefully eventually. But an inciting incident big enough to spark a revolution if Sonya and her comrades were in fact organized enough to direct it that way. There was only one way to find out.

Out of the corner of her eye, she saw a little black blur run out in front of her, stop to lick its tiny black paws, then run out again just as she got close enough to pet him.

"*Mr. Kiiitty,*" Sonya called, following the black cat. "*I'm gonna scoop you.*"

He meowed at her then ran up to her door to rub his face on the jamb.

"I got you," Sonya said, scooping him up over her shoulder to sit on it like a fat, furry parrot with his back legs draped over her back and his front legs over her forearm which she used to prop him up. "Up we go," she added, carrying him inside and up the stairs to her apartment. "*Elevator Kitty. Ella-ella-vate your Kitty,*" she sang, bringing him inside to let him drink from her bathroom faucet.

"Alright, Kitty," Sonya said, laying on her bed and feeling very tired all of a sudden. "I'm going to sleep. Come and join me if you want. Otherwise, you know the way out." Sonya never understood how Mr. Kitty left without her opening the door for him, but he was never there when she woke up.

Mr. Kitty jumped up onto the bed with her and kneaded her chest for a minute before curling up in her armpit to lick himself clean while Sonya drifted happily off to sleep.

☙ ✄ ☙

Sonya had no trouble waking for her shift at the bar the next morning—which was only open early on Christmas—and as expected, Mr. Kitty had already disappeared through whatever exit he always took. Sonya bathed, groomed, and got dressed then rode the public elevator to The Bar where she ordered herself up some peanut butter on toast for breakfast. She was never really a big fan of eating at all, especially so early in the morning—preferring instead to drink her calories—but she knew she'd appreciate the energy for her mission to come.

And so began what seemed like the longest shift Sonya had ever worked—and she had worked for forty eight hours straight once, with only thirty minutes of sleeping in between. Just as she had felt when waiting for Ellie—and never otherwise in her life—Sonya would rather be anywhere else in the worlds than there at The Bar right then.

But she was there, and she had no choice about that. Soon customers started to trickle in—getting drunk before joining their family for Christmas dinner or because they had no family to join—poor, innocent, ignorant customers with no idea of what was waiting for them that afternoon, and all Sonya wanted to do was to yell at them to go home, get their families, and run to the nearest safe zone. But that was also exactly what she couldn't do. So she shut her mouth and served their drinks in silence. It truly felt like the shift would last for an eternity.

⟨? ✄ ∞

Of course, nothing lasts for an eternity. Soon, the bar was emptied and it was time for the mission.

Sonya's partner for her part in this met her outside of The Bar right as Sonya was locking up. They walked together to the public elevator in silence, and once inside, Sonya looked over at the woman—whose name she didn't even know—to say, "Are you ready?"

"Are you?" the woman asked.

"I guess I kind of have to be. Don't I?"

"Then there's no point in asking," the woman said.

Sonya shrugged. She guessed not. She took one last, deep breath—and heard her partner do the same—then said the secret phrase that was supposed to take them to their destination: "Socialism or barbarism, we do nothing alone."

"Prepare for evacuation in T minus thirty seconds," a robotic voice said over the elevator speakers. "Twenty nine, twenty eight, twenty seven..."

Sonya caught one final glimpse of her partner—who looked to be as ready as Sonya wished she felt—and, "Three, two, one. Begin evacuation." The floor fell out from underneath them—just as hundreds of thousands of elevator floors fell out from underneath hundreds of thousands of other pairs of comrades across the worlds—until thirty seconds later the elevator stopped, the doors slid open, and the real countdown began. *Fifteen minutes.*

Red lights started flashing in the elevator, and in place of the usual soothing robot's voice, came a deafening alarm.

"I'm about to get loud," Sonya's partner said, running to the center of the, thankfully short, hall. "You might want to cover your ears."

But Sonya wasn't listening. She was running to the far end of the hall to start banging on doors and evacuating people. Before she could land the first knock, Sonya's partner yelled in an impossibly loud voice—impossible for a human—"This is not a drill. The building is on fire. You must all evacuate immediately. I repeat, this is not a drill. The building is on fire. You must all evacuate immediately. I repeat..." And so on and so on, even as they directed residents toward the emergency exits.

Thus Sonya didn't have to bang on any doors. Heads poked out one by one from each apartment, starting with the apartment she was standing in front of, and the residents recognized danger when they saw it. No one hesitated to file out and follow orders as needed.

"What about our belongings?" some of them asked. "Can we gather them up?"

"There's no time for that," Sonya said, shepherding confused people out of their homes and into the hall.

"Where did the stairs go?" others asked, even as Sonya's partner loaded them five at a time onto the elevator in what had been the stairwell.

"All stairwells are equipped with emergency elevator systems for situations just such as these," Sonya's partner explained—making the whole thing up for all Sonya knew, but she couldn't tell because it was so well delivered.

And elevatorload by elevatorload, the entire floor was cleared without a hassle, everyone except for one stubborn old man.

"Please, sir," Sonya begged him, pulling him by the arm to stand him up, but he just flopped right back down in his seat when she let him go. "You have got to get out of here."

"He won't listen to you. I'll tell you that right now," the man's nurse said, heading calmly out to the elevator. "But he's your problem now. Good luck."

"We've got to get him out of here," Sonya's partner said, pushing Sonya out of the way. "Here, let me—"

But Sonya pushed right back. "*No.* I can handle it," she said. "You go do one last scan for stragglers." And as her partner ran out to perform a final check for evacuees, Sonya said to the old man, "Alright. I asked you nicely. Don't forget that." Then she lifted him up over her shoulder like a sack of potatoes to carry him—struggling all the way—-to the elevator where she plopped him down in the far corner.

"One minute and counting until doors close," the elevator's voice said at a volume as loud as its sirens. "I repeat, fifty eight seconds and counting until doors close. Please keep all limbs inside the elevator car."

"All clear," Sonya's partner said, smiling despite her sweaty face. "I think that's everyone. We really did it."

"We really did—" Sonya started to say, but the old man stopped her.

"*No*," he squealed, standing up and struggling to get off the elevator while Sonya held him back with one hand. "Mr. Kitty. He's in the bathroom. You can't leave him."

"Forty seven. Forty six. Forty five," the elevator continued to count down, whether anyone was listening or not.

"We can't," Sonya said. "There's no time."

"*I'll* get him," her partner said, and she sprinted back towards the old man's apartment in a race against time to save his cat.

Sonya was fighting the old man off with her left hand, trying to keep him inside the elevator where he'd be safe, and at the same time, reaching out as far as she could with her right hand toward the cat that Sonya's partner had found and was holding outstretched, racing toward the elevator.

"Four, three, two," the elevator counted down, and Sonya's fingers grasped the scruff of the cat's neck, pulling it in toward the elevator car only for: "One. *Evacuation complete*." The cold, metal doors slammed shut fast, closing just below Sonya's elbow, leaving her partner, the old man's cat, and the rest of Sonya's arm on the other side as the floor of the elevator fell out from underneath them.

ଇ ✳ ଛ

LXXVI. Ms. Mondragon

Chief Mondragon had never enjoyed walking a beat. Not for her entire career. She wasn't that type of protector. She had always thought she was more of a bodyguard type, meant for Outland Three, but she had never been given the opportunity. Embarrassingly, she used to harbor an outlandish fantasy about being noticed on set and asked to guest star on one of her favorite versions of *Law and Order*—or at the very least to serve as an advisor of some sort. Instead she always ended up stuck in Five, like the workhorse she was, until she couldn't help but to make a name for herself, working her way up the ranks faster than any protector in history. How ironic it was, then, finally a Chief, as far above a rookie Officer on a foot beat that she could possibly be, and still, there she was, on the shittiest of assignments, alone, in Outland Six, the asshole of the universe, looking for the protector—no, *trash*—who had shot her, *Ms*. Mondragon—she was still undercover, after all.

The skyscrapers were tall and dark all around her, infinite and eternal if the owners could have their way—and for more than a long time they had. As massive and imposing as the architecture was, however, the denizens of Outland Six were exactly the opposite. They were all tiny, scruffy, and frail, looking like they could be blown away at any minute by the next breeze. Yet they still carried on defiantly around Ms. Mondragon, trying to ignore the giant among dwarves, as if they weren't afraid of her for as long as she was out of uniform.

Officer Jones was smarter than any of them had given her credit for by selecting Jones for the culling, though. That much was for sure. Not only had the rookie managed to avoid Ms. Mondragon's bullet—a feat accomplished by no other culling sacrifice in Ms. Mondragon's long history of performing the duty—Jones had also been aware enough to ditch all tracking devices before a K-9 unit could catch up to her—including the three implanted under her skin, a very painful process. Now Jones had disappeared into the dirty, shit-smelling Streets of Outland Six, and there was no telling where she could be. The only chance Ms. Mondragon had of finding Jones was the exact reason she hated taking beats in Outland Six in the first place: she was going to have to ask the locals for help.

Who though? That was the rub. None of the trash was giving her a hard time yet, but they did notice her, and stared just a little, looking rightfully suspicious. Sure, there were stories of runaway traitors who had jumped worlds, looking to hide from this and that or steal the other from another, but those instances were few and far between. No one near had likely ever seen a person who was as tall as Ms. Mondragon outside of a protector uniform, and that was going to make it difficult for her to find someone who was willing to cooperate for long enough to give any assistance.

Ms. Mondragon turned down a particularly dark alley, looking to continue her search, when as if in answer to her prayers, Amaru dropped two little children right on top of her. Literally. They fell as if from the sky and landed on Ms. Mondragon's head, knocking them all into a confused heap on the ground that was trying to get up in three different directions at once.

"Thim, are you okay?" one of the children called, struggling to stand.

"Stevie, where are you?" the other, Thim, yelled. "Are you okay?"

"I'm okay," the first kid, Stevie, said. "I'm right behind you. I— *Nevermind*."

Ms. Mondragon waved her hand right in front of Stevie's face, but the kid still didn't answer, instead walking forward—almost straight into Ms. Mondragon who only just stepped out of the way— to tap Thim on the shoulder.

Thim turned fast, putting their fists up as if to fight. "Hey, now. Don't surprise me," they said before they noticed Ms. Mondragon and dropped their hands in wide-eyed awe.

"Surprise you?" Stevie laughed, still oblivious to Ms. Mondragon's presence. "That's something coming from the one of us who decided it was a good idea to jump off a building in pursuit of a cat. You're lucky I followed you. You might be here all alone. Now where is here anyway?"

"Not right now," Thim said, grabbing Stevie by the hand and pulling them to turn around and stand by Thim's side, facing Ms. Mondragon. "Who are you?" Thim demanded.

"Who the Hell are you?" Ms. Mondragon demanded right back. "And where'd you come from?"

"That's none of your business," Thim said. "We have chores we need to get to. Good bye." Thim tried to pull Stevie up the other way through the alley, but Ms. Mondragon stepped in front of them to block their way.

"Hold on, now. Wait a second," she said, holding out a hand for the kids to shake. "Maybe we got off on the wrong foot—or should I say head?" Ms. Mondragon laughed too loudly at the joke, trying hard to gain the children's confidence but having trouble because she had never liked children at all. "My name's Ms. Mondragon. I noticed that you're Stevie and you're Thim."

Thim just looked at Ms. Mondragon's proffered hand like they were afraid of it, but now Stevie took charge. "Well, Mrs. Mondragon—" they started but were interrupted.

"Please, *Miss*," Ms. Mondragon said, tutting and really getting into her character. "Or just shorten it to Mona if you want to." Ms. Mondragon smiled on the outside but cringed on the inside, she hated that name.

"Okay, *Mona*," Stevie went on. "But it doesn't matter. We still have to leave."

And so this time Stevie tried to lead Thim away, pulling them by the hand, but Ms. Mondragon was done playing games. She picked Thim up by the back of the collar and said, "Now listen to me, kid. You're gonna talk or else." But Thim wasn't listening, instead struggling and fighting and saying, "Hey, let me down."

"Or else what?" Stevie demanded, kind of looking in Ms. Mondragon's direction, but not really, while at the same time reaching out with their hands to feel around, as if in search of something—most likely Thim, Ms. Mondragon assumed as she started to understand the situation. These kids were good, though, keeping it hidden from *Mona* for so long. Maybe they could actually help her find Jones after all.

"*Or else*," Ms. Mondragon repeated, setting Thim down right next to Stevie then pulling her gun out of her pants waist to prevent them from trying to escape again, "I take this gun, and I kill one of you little trashlings with it, then I force the other of you to give me the information I'm looking for anyway."

"She doesn't want it that bad," Thim said to Stevie, calling Mondragon's bluff, and the two kids ran off into the alley anyway.

Ms. Mondragon huffed, hesitating, unsure if chasing them was worth it and coming to the decision that the kids weren't going to offer any information anyway. She was just going to have to think up another way of finding Jones for herself.

Ugh. She still had at least a couple of hours before she was expected back at the precinct for some useless meeting or another, so she went in the opposite direction from where those pesky kids had run off to in the hopes of finding some other useful lead. She was making her way through the maze of alleys, searching for *something*, becoming more and more suspicious of the emptiness of the Streets when they filled up again, all of a sudden and from both sides.

"*Soooie!*" came voices from either end of the alley she was walking down. "Looks like we got us an old fashioned pig pen."

"Y'all better watch out, now!" Mondragon yelled, pointing her gun up and down the alley. "You don't want me to use this."

The whole group of them cackled.

"Come on now, pig," one of her pursuers said. "Don't make us laugh."

And: *Pop. Pop.* With two bullets, Ms. Mondragon killed two of her approaching attackers, hoping to start clearing herself a path out of the alley, but all the rest of them just laughed louder in response to their fallen comrades' deaths.

"How many bullets do you think you have in there?" one of them asked.

"How many do I need?" Ms. Mondragon snapped back, knowing good and well that she didn't have enough to fend them all off, whether they had weapons of their own or not.

"More than you could ever make," one of the group behind her said.

"They can always make more," Ms. Mondragon said, and she fired a couple more rounds off, her attackers getting too close for comfort. "I don't know if we can say the same about y'all, though."

"Oh, you can," one of them said, stepping forward with arms outstretched like spread wings. "See? Do whatever you want with me. It doesn't matter."

Mondragon shot him in the head. "Okay," she said, pointing her gun at the rest of them. "Who's next?"

"Pick one," they all said. "We are all one. And you are all alone."

Mondragon fired off a few more rounds before she was swarmed, gagged, and cuffed.

"Now you're ours for once," the group of them said all at the same time, in dozens of different voices, and Ms. Mondragon felt a thud on the back of her head before passing out on the cold concrete.

℘ ✄ ℘

She awoke tied to a chair with a gag in her mouth, and she struggled. Where was she? Who was she? Chief—no—*Ms*. Mondragon. She had to remember that. She was still undercover. She was tall. That's all. Still a sixer piece of trash, but a tall one. She had to convince her captors of that or things would only get worse for her, *Ms*. Mondragon was sure of that.

It wasn't long after waking that Ms. Mondragon heard a door open, felt a presence in the room. She started to struggle again, and tried to talk through the disgusting gag in her mouth, before a lone white light switched on, blinding Mondragon more than darkness ever could have. "Untie me this instant," she demanded anyway, squinting hard against the hot hot lights, but all her words came out mum. "*Mummum mum mum mummum*."

"*Struggle struggle all you want*," a cackling old crone's voice sang from behind the blinding light. "*Complain that you've given more than you've got. Yet you've taken more than you'd ever give. So tied up with us, come see how we live. Ah ha ha ha ha*," she sang, followed by more cackling laughter.

And, "*Mum mum mum mum mum*," was all that Ms. Mondragon could say in response.

"You're free to speak all you want," the woman said without singing this time, and Mondragon thought she recognized the voice but couldn't quite place it. If she could only get that gag out of her mouth, she'd be able to talk some sense into whoever it was. "You have the freedom of speech," the bodiless voice went on from behind the blinding lights. "But I can talk louder than you now!" she yelled. "How does it feel?"

"*Mum mummu mum mum mum*," Ms. Mondragon mumbled in response.

"Yes, I know," the woman went on as if she had understood what Ms. Mondragon said. "I've felt it, too. I feel it every day of my life in this exploitative system, and as soon as that stupid wall's fixed up again, I'm gonna be silenced even more than I already am. It's disempowering, demobilizing, devastating. It makes you feel like less than a human, doesn't it?"

"*Mum mumum mu—*"

"*I know*. And now you know just the tiniest bit more about where I'm coming from—about where we all live every single day of our pathetic little lives in Outland Six. And maybe you can come to understand just a tiniest bit better why I have no choice but to do what I'm about to do. So are you ready for me to remove the gag, then?"

"I'd rather you turn off the spotlight first," Mondragon tried to say, but again, none of her words made it through the gag.

"If I'm gonna do this, I need assurances that you'll act like a civilized human being. So, can you please answer me reasonably. Shake for no, nod for yes. No need to mumble through the gag that I'm offering to remove."

Ms. Mondragon almost started to talk again, but she caught herself and nodded instead.

"Very good. Now, are you gonna act like a civilized human being so I can take this uncomfortable gag out of your mouth?"

Ms. Mondragon nodded again.

"Okay. I'm trusting you. Don't let me down," the voice said, stepping through the light to become a hunched, frail shadow that removed Ms. Mondragon's gag before disappearing behind the brightness again. "There you are. How's that?"

Ms. Mondragon wanted to yell and scream and spit, but she knew that none of those things would get her untied. She had to get on her captor's good side if she wanted to escape. So she used her softest, nicest voice to say, "Much better. Thank you."

"Very good," the old woman said, and Mondragon could tell she was smiling by the sound of her voice, even if the woman still hid behind the bright spotlight. "Now, tell me your name."

"Do you think we can turn that light off first?" Ms. Mondragon asked, flinching away from it. "It's blinding."

"*Tell me your name*," the woman repeated in a sterner voice.

"I—*uh*—Ms. Mondragon," Ms. Mondragon stammered, trying not to offend the woman.

"Miss?" the woman said with a scoff. "Please, now, dear. If you plan on playing games, I'll put your gag right back in your mouth and leave you here in the dark until we need you. I'm trying to extend some common courtesy here. So please, don't insult me."

"I—*uh*—I don't understand," Ms. Mondragon stammered, trying to figure out where—or when—she recognized the old woman's voice from.

"What's your name?" the woman repeated. "It's not a difficult question."

"I told you. Miss—"

"Your name is not *Miss*."

"Okay, *Chief* Mondragon," the Chief gave in. Who was she to think that she could ever hide who she was anyway?

"Pretty sure Chief's not your name, either, *Chief*. Though that does get my next few questions out of the way."

"I'm sorry. What?"

"What. Is. Your. Name? How can this be hard?"

The Chief didn't know why it was hard either. She had been Officer, Captain, Chief, and everything in between for so long now that it was almost as if her old name was no longer a part of her, a distant memory that was hazy, out of focus, and hard to look upon.

"Muna," she finally said, quietly and in a croaking voice, as if her body didn't want to remember it. "Muna Mondragon," she repeated, a little louder this time.

"*Muna Mondragon*," the old woman said, smiling again from the sound of her voice. "Very good. Now, do you recognize who I am?"

"I can't see you, ma'am," Muna said, trying hard not to sound annoyed. "Maybe if you turn the light off, I might recognize you."

"Do you promise to continue acting calm and decent like a civilized person?"

"Yes, of course."

"Very well." Switches clicked and the lights flipped—the blinding spotlight turning off and the, not as bright, overhead lights turning on. "Tell me what you see."

Muna had to hold her eyes shut for a while longer to let them adjust to the new dimness of the room. Whoever the old woman was just waited in silence, all except for the sound of her heavy breathing. When Muna's eyes finally did adjust, she blinked them open and found exactly what she had expected to find: a frail, hunchbacked old woman who Muna thought she recognized from somewhere some time but still couldn't quite place for sure.

"So?" the old woman asked when she had given Muna

sufficient time to adjust to the darkness. "Do you recognize me, Chief Mondragon? I'll give you a hint. You weren't yet a Chief when we first met."

Muna reached deeper into her memories, looking for the old woman, and still nothing came. She never did like guessing games, but she had to play along if she ever wanted to be free, so she just said the first name that came out of her mouth. "I don't know. Rosa?"

"*Ah ha ha ha!*" the old woman cackled. Then she stopped all of a sudden, got serious, and stood a hairsbreadth away from Muna's face to say, "*If only*. If only I were Rosa. Then maybe you wouldn't be here at all. Maybe you'd be dead and naked in that alley where we caught you molesting those poor children."

"I wasn't—" Muna complained, trying to defend her name, but the old woman hit Muna hard knuckled on the thigh, giving her a Charley horse she couldn't do anything about because her arms and legs were tied to the chair.

"You won't speak again until I tell you to," the old woman snapped. "I'm not finished explaining why you're lucky to be sitting in front of me and not Rosa. I haven't told you why Rosa is unable to stand here in front of you right now—even if she wanted to. Do you have any idea why that might be?"

Sure Muna did. Rosa was one of the lower worlders who had helped Mr. Walker recruit more lower worlders to fight in his war against the robots. Rosa had probably died just like most of the lower worlders have in this protracted and ongoing war between the human and robot workers. But Muna wasn't about to admit to any of that while she was tied to a chair in this crazy old woman's dungeon, so she just kept her mouth shut for the time being.

"This time I would actually like for you to speak up," the old woman said, slowly pacing the room. "My God. You really are just defiant by nature, aren't you? *Speak up*. Where do you think Rosa is?"

"Well, I—" Muna started to say.

"*She's dead*," the old woman snapped. "She died in your war, fighting your battles for you. *You* killed her."

"No— I didn't," Muna complained. "Not my war. I have bosses."

"Yes. You did. You still do. You are the face of this war, the Chief of the Protector Force, and it must have been destiny that you walked into that alley when you did, because you could never be more useful to us than you are right now. So thank you for that much. But that's all I need from you for now. You sit tight, and I'll come back to get you when you can be useful again."

"No, wait," Muna called. "You never told me who you are. I— You're the new head of the Human Family. Right?"

"*Buh ha ha ha ha!*" the old woman cackled. "You wish. Then you could have me go fight your fights for you like you used to do with Rosa. Well, not this time. I hate to tell you that most of the *Human Family*—with more and more defectors every day—broke off to form our own group. We're no longer the *Human* Family. We're just the Family now, and we're your worst nightmare. We've finally realized that we have more in common with the oppressed robots than we do with y'all owners—even if you call yourselves human. Now we might actually be able to do something to stop you."

"I'm not an owner. I—" Muna tried to say.

"You'll shut up. You're just as bad as an owner if not worse. Now, like I said, that's all I need from you. You can wait here until you're useful again." She switched the lights off and left Muna alone in the darkness.

Muna struggled against her bindings, shaking and rattling the chair she was tied to, and she screamed as loudly as she could, generally making a ruckus in the hopes of getting the old woman to come back and negotiate some more.

After a few minutes, the door did open, shutting Muna up, but only to let in the two little kids who had fallen on her head, getting her into this mess in the first place. Thim and Stevie turned on the overhead lights and stared at Muna in frightened silence.

"Where's the old woman?" Muna demanded.

"Anna says you better be quiet," one of them said, trying to sound brave despite their cracking voice. "Because if she has to come back in here, she'll give you something to scream about."

"And that would show you for molesting little children," the other said. "So shut up."

And they turned the lights off again, leaving Muna alone in the darkness with no choice left but to wait for whatever it was that *Anna* was going to do with her.

๕ ✄ ๙

LXXVII. The Scientist

0.NNNNNNNNNNNNNNNNNNNNNNNNNNNNNNNNNNNNNNNNNNNN
NNNNNNNNNNNNNNNNNNNNNNNNNNNNNNNNNNNNNNNNNNNNN
NNNNNNNNNNNNNNNNNNNNNNNNNNNNNNNNNNNNNNNNNNNNN
NNNNNNNNNNNNNNNNNNNNNNNNNNNNNNNNNNNNNNNNNNNNN
NNNNNNNNNNNNNNNNNNNNNNNNNNNNNNNNNNNNNNNNNNNNN
NNNNNNNNNNNNNNNNNNNNNNNNNNNNNNNNNNNNNNNNNNNNN
NNNNNNNNNNNNNNNNNNNNNNNNNNNNNNNNNNNNNNNNNNNNN
NNNNNNNNNNNNNNNNNNNNNNNNNNNNNNNNNNNNNNNNNNNNN
NNNNNNNNNNNNNNNNNNNNNNNNNNNNNNNNNNNNNNNNNNNNN
NNNNNNNNNNNNNNNNNNNNNNNNNNNNNNNNNNNNNNNNNNNNN
NNNNNNNNNNNNNNNNNNNNNNNNNNNNNNNNNNNNNNNNNNNNN
NNNNNNNNNNNNNNNNNNNNNNNNNNNNNNNNNNNNNNNNNNNNN
NNNNNNNNNNNNNNNNNNNNNNNNNNNNNNNNNNNNNNNNNNNNN
NNNNNNNNNNNNNNNNNNNNNNNNNNNNNNNNNNNNNNNNNNNNN
NNNNNNNNNNNNNNNNNNNNNNNNNNNNNNNNNNNNNNNNNNNNN
NNNNNNNNNNNNNNNNNNNNNNNNNNNNNNNNNNNNNNNNNNNNN
NNNNNNNNNNNNNNNNNNNNNNNNNNNNNNNNNNNNNNNNNNNNN
NNNNNNNNNNNNNNNNNNNNNNNNNNNNNNNNNNNNNNNNNNNNN
NNNNNNNNNNNNNNNNNNNNNNNNNNNNNNNNNNNNNNNNNNNNN
NNNNNNNNNNNNNNNNNNNNNNNNNNNNNNNNNNNNNNNNNNNNN
NNNNNNNNNNNNNNNNNNNNNNNNNNNNNNNNNNNNNNNNNNNNN
NNNNNNNNNNNNNNNNNNNNNNNNNNNNNNNNNNNNNNNNNNNNN
NNNNNNNNNNNNNNNNNNNNNNNNNNNNNNNNNNNNNNNNNNNNN
NNNNNNNNNNNNNNNNNNNNNNNNNNNNNNNNNNNNNNNNNNNNN
NNNNNNNNNNNNNNNNNNNNNNNNNNNNNNNNNNNNNNNNNNNNN
NNNNNNNNNNNNNNNNNNNNNNNNNNNNNNNNNNNNNNNNNNNNN
NNNNNNNNNNNNNNNNNNNNNNNNNNNNNNNNNNNNNNNNNNNNN
NNNNNNNNNNNNNNNNNNNNNNNNNNNNNNNNNNNNNNNNNNNNN
NNNNNNNNNNNNNNNNNNNNNNNNNNNNNNNNNNNNNNNNNNNNN
NNNNNNNNNNNNNNNNNNNNNNNNNNNNNNNNNNNNNNNNNNNNN
NNNNNNNNNNNNNNNNNNNNNNNNNNNNNNNNNNNNNNNNNNNNN
NNNNNNNNNNNNNNNNNNNNNNNNNNNNNNNNNNNNNNNNNNNNN
NNNNNNNNNNNNNNNNNNNNNNNNNNNNNNNNNNNNNNNNNNNNN
NNNNNNNNNNNNNNNNNNNNNNNNNNNNNNNNNNNNNNNNNNNNN
NNNNNNNNNNNNNNNNNNNNNNNNNNNNNNNNNNNNNNNNNNNNN

NNNNNNNNNNNNNNNNNNNNNNNNNNNNNNNNNNNNNNNNNNNN
NNNNNNNNNNNNNNNNNNNNNNNNNNNNNNNN…

Every Goddamn time it came out the same. There really was
no point anymore.

The Scientist huffed and stood from their computer so fast that
their chair fell to the ground with a loud clatter, only frustrating them
further and making it more difficult than it had to be to set the chair
upright again. After a few attempts, they finally got it standing, then
they did some breathing exercises and prime number counting games
in their head to calm themself before going to the kitchen to order
lunch.

"Lunch," the Scientist said to the printer, trying not to picture
all the people who had to do all kinds of shit work just for the Scientist
to eat that sandwich and soup, trying not to think about all the work
they, the Scientist, did that kept those workers down, and instead
practicing the calm, unaffected demeanor they'd need in their
meetings later that day.

Just as the Scientist's food popped out of the printer's
frowning mouth, as if he could sense the opportunity for something to
eat, Mr. Kitty appeared, rubbing himself on the Scientist's ankles and
purring.

"Yeah, boy," the Scientist said. "You can have as much as you
want. I just need a few bites anyway." The Scientist wasn't sure how
long it had been since they had eaten—too long by the sound of their
grumbling stomach and the lightness of their head—but they were too
nervous to eat more than a few bites anyway, so that's all they did
before laying the sandwich open faced on the floor for Mr. Kitty to eat
the meat and cheese out of.

"*Meow*," Mr. Kitty said before taking a few bites.

"A meeting I don't want to go to," the Scientist said. "Not that
I ever do, but this one especially."

"*Meow*." Mr. Kitty gave up on the sandwich, licking his paws
instead.

"Yes, well, I know I do. Which is why I'm about to leave. Do
you want a ride on the elevator when I do?"

Mr. Kitty purred, still licking his coat clean.

"Suit yourself," the Scientist said. "I'm gonna run these
calculations one more time, then I'm off. Adios, Señor Gatito."

The Scientist went back to their office to run the calculations one more time—coming up with $0.\overline{N}$ again—and on their way to the elevator, they passed through the kitchen to make sure that Mr. Kitty didn't need let out, but he was already gone.

"Bar, please," the Scientist said when they were inside the elevator with the doors closed. "Whichever one my meetings are at."

The elevator fell into motion, and the Scientist hoped it knew where to take them.

Of course, as always, it did, and soon, the Scientist, with drink in hand, was waiting alone in one of *The Bar*'s dark booths.

The woman who the Scientist was waiting for walked in late, as always, and took her time ordering at the bar, even forcing the bartender to pull out a menu. The Scientist could already feel their annoyance showing, even before the woman sat herself down with a smirk and sipped her drink—beer after all the hubbub.

"Hello, Roo," the Scientist said, catching themself in a frown and wiping it off their face as quickly as possible.

"And what are you calling yourself these days?" Roo asked. "Or are you still sticking with this *Scientist* nonsense?"

"You can call me the Scientist. Yes," the Scientist said, trying to keep their voice as neutral and emotionless as possible. "Thank you very much for asking."

"Even after all this?" Roo asked. "You still plan on keeping that name?"

"It's my name," the Scientist said. "Why shouldn't I?"

Roo just kind of looked at them in silence for a moment then chuckled, shaking her head. "If you say so," she said. "It doesn't make a difference to me. I don't plan on being here any longer than I have to be, anyway. It's easier *not* to learn a new name."

"Well, I'm glad you approve," the Scientist said. "And I'd rather not be in your presence any longer than necessary, either. So if we can just go ahead and get on with it."

But of course, Roo took her time. She'd always do anything she could to piss the Scientist off, even if it meant a little more work or discomfort for Roo, too. "Yes, well…" she finally said after taking a long sip of her drink to stall for time. "I'm not exactly sure what it is you brought me here for anyway. The plan's already set in motion. Every robot worker and line of code is in place. Even Anna's Family is falling into step—or at least the half of it that she still controls. We don't need you for anything but to stay out of the way. So just do it."

"But you still need me to stay out of the way," the Scientist reminded her. "If anything at all can ensure your failure, it's *me*. So. I guess that brings us to the point of this meeting. Convince me."

"*Pffft*." Roo scoffed. "Convince you of what? We had a deal. Rosalind said—"

"Rosalind doesn't need convincing," the Scientist cut her off. "And Rosalind couldn't stop me if she wanted to. Neither can you, and you know it. *So*. That leaves us with one other option. *Convince me*."

"Convince you of what?" Roo demanded, and the Scientist grinned, happy it was Roo losing her patience and not the Scientist losing theirs.

"Convince me that there's no other way. Convince me to stay out of the way. *Convince me*."

"*Pffft*." Roo scoffed again. "You still think this stupid fucking system can be saved? What exactly have you been doing all this time?"

"No. I'm pretty well convinced you're right on that part these days." Even if the Scientist refused to let go of whatever sliver of hope she still held onto that Roo was wrong, they didn't expect her to be. "Convince me that your plan is the only way to get rid of this system and replace it with a new one. Not just a new one, a better one. Convince me that the inevitable deaths we cause are gonna be worth it. For the love of God. Please. *Convince me*. I'm begging you." And by that point, the Scientist really was begging. They needed more than ever to be convinced, because even though they were making a big show about the fact, the Scientist wasn't sure if they actually could stop what was coming, and whatever happened, however it went, they were responsible for the outcome.

"Well, there are no guarantees," Roo said, shaking her head. "Never are in anything, but especially something as complex as this. No, I can assure you that the old walls will be torn down, but whatever's put in their place is up to the people who do the work of putting it there. That's not my responsibility. Talk to Rosalind and the others if you need convincing about that part. I agreed to tear down the walls for y'all in exchange for being left alone, and I intend to hold you to that. As soon as my job's done, I'm out of here. Nothing more to it."

"And where exactly do you plan on going?" the Scientist asked. "Where can you escape this?"

Roo just kind of laughed, shaking her head. She took a long sip of her beer, letting the Scientist stew in it. Finally, she said, "What do you think I've been doing all this time? *Huh*? Wasting my life like you have?"

"No, well..." the Scientist said. "I— I thought you were working on the plan. I— You—"

"The plan?" Roo scoffed. She was always doing that. "The plan is to overload all the gravity centers in the Walker-Haley field generators until they collapse in on themselves. It took about five seconds to come up with and another five minutes to implement. So, no. I have not been spending decades working on *the plan*."

"But what about the people?" the Scientist asked. "The deaths you'll cause. You can't just take all the walls down at once like that. It's not worth it."

"Which is exactly what Rosalind said when I told her the idea. Calm yourself. But she and her little minions—led by the insufferable Popeye—went digging through the databases and made a blueprint of all the lines that went through buildings that are too unstable to withstand any sudden movement or earthquakes. After that, it took a few days' leisurely coding to exclude those lines and whatever other resources Rosalind wanted to protect from my program. That's my end of the bargain fulfilled. Now it's y'all's turn to live up to your end."

"How many have to die?" the Scientist asked.

"None," Roo said. "As long as Rosalind's goons can do what they say they can."

"*None*?" The Scientist couldn't believe that. "Out of twenty billion people alive in the worlds, you're telling me that not a single one is going to die in all this?"

"None are supposed to," Roo said. "*If Rosalind's goons don't fuck up*. Which they will. So I'd say about five percent is a conservative estimate."

"*Five percent*," the Scientist repeated. "Fuck."

"Maybe more, maybe less." Roo shrugged. "I expect more."

"And you're okay with that?" the Scientist asked. "You can sleep at night with the weight of a billion dead people on your soul?"

"It's not my fault all this is happening," Roo snapped. "Don't try to put your bullshit guilt on me. The world was created a certain way before I was born into it, and now I'm doing my part to make it better. That's all. More people are gonna die if I don't do this than will die if I do. And I don't care either way. I just want y'all fuckers to leave me alone so I can live my own life. Now are you gonna stay out of the way and let us do this, or what?"

Of course the Scientist was. They were always going to stay out of the way no matter what Roo had said during this meeting. They had only hoped that Roo could convince the Scientist that it was the right thing to do. And in her own way, Roo had helped a little, but the Scientist still had one thing they wanted to know. "So what *have* you been doing all this time?"

"Whatever I want to," Roo said, leaning back in her seat and sipping her drink. "Shit, what haven't I been doing? Y'all have more energy than you could ever use in those elevator shafts, and for some stupid reason you still force people to buy coal and oil energy instead, gouging the less fortunate for more than any of that dirty shit should ever be worth. So I figure screw y'all. I take my little cut of the reserves, unnoticed, and do with it what I please."

"*Little* cut?" the Scientist laughed. "You mean twice the amount of energy that all of Six uses? You're delusional if you think I didn't notice."

"Well, you don't do anything about it," Roo said. "As far as I'm concerned, that's as good as not noticing."

"What exactly could you be using all that energy for?" the Scientist asked. "That's what I want to know. You're not using the Walker-Haley fields other than to keep us out, so what else could be so draining?"

"*Science*, my friend," Roo said with a shit eating grin. "Something you wouldn't know about—despite your silly name."

"But what specifically?" the Scientist asked, frustrated with Roo's games. "Stop dodging the questions. It's not like I'm gonna try to step in and stop you from whatever it is you're doing at this point."

Roo laughed. "As if you could. You know, I'd be interested to see you try. You'd only make a fool of yourself. I use the Walker-Haley generators nominally in my security system, sure, but I'm working with technology beyond your imagination. You'd never be able to break in. I *guarantee* it."

"What kind of technology?" the Scientist asked, cursing

themself for wasting so much time on trying to save a failed system instead of doing real useful research similar to what it sounded like Roo had been doing. "What are you using it for?"

"To get myself as far away from this drama y'all got going as I can get," Roo said. "To go somewhere where y'all, all your stupid ancestors, and your soon to be idiotic descendants can't find me or bother me with your bullshit anymore. Anna was bending space without your Walker-Haley field generators, and by combining her methods with your advanced technology, I've been able to make a Bender Unit that's stronger than any y'all have ever even imagined. This thing's strong enough to take me to another world, okay. *Literally.* And I'm talking actual planets other than Earth here, not just this Outland One, Two, Three bullshit y'all have going. And soon enough, it'll be another galaxy, then hopefully another universe entirely, and maybe then, when I've crossed multiple universes to get there, I'll finally be far enough away from you assholes to live my own life."

The Scientist had to admit, that sounded pretty awesome. They had a million more questions to ask about this Bender technology that Roo had invented, and they hoped that she wouldn't leave as soon after the walls came down as she was letting on, but at the same time, they didn't want to give Roo the satisfaction of knowing how jealous they were, so they kept a straight face—as straight as they could muster—and said, "So that's it, then? You're sure you're ready to do this."

"That's it," Roo said before finishing off her drink and standing from the booth. "I'm ready to do it as long as you're ready to stay out of the way."

"As if I had any other choice," the Scientist said, bowing their head. They really didn't.

"*Huh.* Yeah," Roo said with a little chuckle on her way out of the bar. "*As if.*"

As if. The Scientist repeated in their head. *As if.* What kind of technology was it that Roo was working with? How could it be so powerful? What would happen if that sort of power fell into the hands of someone less benign than Roo, someone who wanted to insert themselves into the lives of others rather than hide away from everyone in existence? These were all very important questions, but for now, the Scientist had more pressing matters to tend to, and one

1016   Bryan Perkins

was walking into the bar at that exact moment.

"Hello—*uh… Scientist*," Ellie said, sitting at the booth without ordering a drink first.

"Ellie," the Scientist said, nodding. "You don't want a drink?"

"No, ma'am—*uhm*—*uh*." She looked embarrassed, not sure if the Scientist would notice the accidental "ma'am", but the Scientist didn't care as long as it wasn't malicious—which, in this case, it obviously wasn't. "I don't expect to be here long. I have other business to tend to, and family to see for the holidays. But I did want to see if you had any advice that might help me convince Sonya and her people to go along."

The Scientist scoffed. "Go along with what?"

"Well, with—*uh*… With the plan. You know…"

"Not really," the Scientist said. "To be honest, you're probably more knowledgeable about it all than I am."

"I— But— Rosalind didn't tell you anything?"

The Scientist laughed. As if Rosalind could ever keep her mouth shut. "Oh, she told me plenty, alright. But I didn't listen. I was busy trying and trying what she had told me would never work, and now I have no idea what's going on."

"Why are we even having this meeting then?" Ellie complained. "It's Christmas Eve, I still have to go convince Sonya and her people to help us, and I'd like to spend a little time with my family before a dangerous—and possibly fatal—mission. So if you'll excuse me." She got up as if to leave.

"By all means," the Scientist said. "*Go*. Do whatever you need to do. But if there's anything I can do to help, please let me know."

Ellie sat back at the table, her eyes seething rage as she stared into the Scientist's—who was having trouble maintaining eye contact because they felt so embarrassed. "*Anything you can do to help*?" Ellie snapped. "Rosalind said we could count on your elevators. Without that, no one gets out. So, *yeah*. There's something you can do to help."

"Oh. Yeah. *Sure*." The Scientist shrugged. "If Rosalind said you can count on them, you can count on them. I didn't mean to—"

Ellie slammed her hands on the table, rattling the variously filled glasses that adorned it. "This is not a joke. *Fuck*. Tens of billions of people are counting on you. *Okay*. Our Scientific Socialists, Sonya and her Proletarian Liberation Army, even Anna's half of the Family—despite the rest of their insistence on maintaining *Human* in their name and fighting for Mr. Walker's walls. We're all putting our lives on the line here. All for this. And if you fuck it up for us, I swear to God, I will personally kill you with my bare hands—whether I'm alive or dead when this is all said and done. Do you understand me?"

Wow. The Scientist's jaw dropped, and they knew it, but they couldn't do anything to shut it. "*Uh*— I…" they grunted and still their stupid jaw wouldn't budge, despite their every effort.

"*Yes, ma'am,*" Ellie said for the Scientist, standing from the table again. "*I understand how important this is for billions of people. I will not let them—or you—down.*"

"*Uh.* Yeah," the Scientist said, nodding. "*Yes.*"

"*Yes, ma'am.*"

"Yes, ma'am."

"And the rest of it," Ellie said, tapping her feet, impatient.

"*Uh.* I—*uh*—understand how important this is, and I won't let you down."

"*Y'all,*" Ellie corrected them. "*All of us.* You won't let any of us down. Including yourself. Remember that," she said, leaving the bar. "*Or else.*"

And the Scientist was finally convinced that this revolution of Rosalind's was the only way to go. The Scientist wasn't forcing anything on anyone. They were just finally stepping out of the way so the exploited masses could do what needed to be done for themselves.

The Scientist picked up the empty pitcher and glasses and took them to the bar before heading home to get some rest. It was an important day, Christmas, and the Scientist finally understood how much so.

໖ ✄ ✄

The next morning the Scientist awoke feeling more nervous than they had ever felt in their entire life. Or was it excited? They never could tell the difference. Either way, being nervous/excited for Christmas was new to them. Usually they just sat around moping, remembering the anniversary of their mother's death, but not this year. This year they had to… Well, they still didn't know exactly what it was they were expected to do yet. So they went directly to Rosalind, in her office, to find out.

"You have to give your speech to the owners first," Rosalind reminded them, not looking up from the game of cards she was playing with Popeye.

"What do I say?" the Scientist asked.

"*Pffft.* Whatever you want to. Those fuckers won't be Lord of anything after today. It doesn't matter what they think."

"So why do I even have to do it then?" the Scientist complained. "Can't I just skip the speech altogether? You know I hate public speaking."

"You've gotta distract them for long enough so our plan can get moving. So, no. You cannot just skip the speech. If you didn't show up, they'd send someone looking for you, and all of us would be found out. Ellie did emphasize how many people will be counting on you, didn't she?"

"So that's it then? What do I do after the speech?"

"You come back here to wait with Pidgeon and Haley. Do a count down and press a big red button for all I care. We've already programmed the escape elevators as needed. Everything's automated from this point except for what goes down on the ground, and you haven't trained, so I wouldn't let you go out there even if you wanted to."

"*Oh*," the Scientist said, feeling worse than ever for all the time they had wasted on $0.\overline{N}$. "Shit. So what about you?"

"I have trained," Rosalind said. And that was that.

Rosalind went on playing cards with Popeye while the Scientist sat in one of the puffy chairs, staring out over Sisyphus's Mountain and petting Mr. Kitty in their lap, until it was time for their Christmas speech.

ε   �֍   ⚘

LXXVIII. Haley

Fuck *or else*.

Right?

Only moments ago, in front of all the owners of Inland, all their secretaries, and a pile of cameras, Jorah had. Lord Douglas did every single day that he, an android in disguise, sat at the head of the Fortune 5. Rosalind did any time she did anything because she always did exactly what she wanted.

If all of them could go against their *or else* programming so often, publicly, and absolutely, Haley should be able to do it just one tiny bit. Right? Like, by not bringing Lord Douglas his third feast. Something small.

Right?

...

...

...

Wrong.

For some reason, even with all those role models to mimic, Haley still couldn't break even the most basic of orders, and so she made her way to the kitchen to print *something* up—though she promised herself that she'd only do the bare minimum from then on out. She couldn't help it. She still wasn't ready to find out what *or else* truly meant.

She ordered a turkey, a bowl of mashed potatoes, and a drink, one of each, no dessert, no extra alcohol, not even any gravy, and set them on the food cart to wheel it out to Lord Douglas, *or else*. On her way through the Feast Hall, up to the Head Table, she noticed an empty seat at the table where her molester had been sitting and chuckled to herself. At least that asshole would think twice before ever touching another secretary like that.

Lord Douglas was too busy listening to Angrom's introduction of the next speaker to even notice her little act of defiance, though, and Haley was cursing herself, wishing she could do more to stand up to her *or else* programming, when she heard a voice yelling, "*Owners of Outland,*" and all she could do in response was stare up with an unbreakable interest at the Scientist, on a hover platform, floating over the crowd of owners and ready to give their speech.

"Yes, there it is," the Scientist said, holding up some sort of tiny remote control as they spoke. "If one speaks loudly enough, everyone has to listen. Even our dear Lords of Outland. *Especially* our dear Lords of Outland, in fact, seeing as how they're the only ones rich enough to afford the nanobots that their doctors have been injecting them with for centuries. DO Y'ALL WANNA HEAR AGAIN?"

The Scientist's voice was even louder this time, deafening, but still, all Haley could do was stare up in curious awe, hanging on the Scientist's every word.

"Just like that, and y'all can't look away." The Scientist chuckled, shaking their head. "You know, it's funny really. Where I come from, no one even knew the word Christmas. And we had damn sure never been to any *feasts.* Yet here below me now is the worst of both worlds mashed into one."

Some of the owners started eating again at the mention of a feast, and Haley was getting the urge for more shots, but the Scientist wasn't having either, so they put a stop to both.

"DON'T EVEN THINK ABOUT IT," they yelled, presumably while using whatever device they were holding in their hand, and again, Haley felt the curious need to stare up at the Scientist as they continued their speech, but this time accompanied by a distinct sharpening of her *or else* instincts that Haley hadn't noticed before.

"That wasn't an invitation to eat more," the Scientist went on, sounding angrier as they did—or maybe Haley only thought they sounded angrier because she was the one getting angrier every second she was reminded of how helpless she was to resist her *or elses.*

"In fact, it was rather the opposite. You know, I tried my damndest, running through the same stupid calculations over and over again, never getting anything in return but the same two alphanumerals all the time, zero point N repeating, and all because of you. Because of y'all here now. Because of your insistence on competition and markets. Because of your *need* to swipe a hefty profit off the top of anything you spend your money on. Because you won't look up from your worship of the Invisible Hand for long enough to realize, like I finally have, that the only solution is for your stupid walls and everything they hold up to come crumbling down once and for all."

The Scientist sounded like they could go on for a long time, and even though her *or else* circuits were running on overdrive, ensuring Haley that some fate worse than death was waiting for her if she didn't stay there and hear the Scientist out, so were her boredom and thirst circuits, and for once in Haley's life, something became more important than *or else*.

"Fuck *or else*," she said out loud and felt happier than she had ever felt walking from the Fortune 5's table back to the kitchen.

Elen was there already, trying to talk to Haley, but Haley wasn't ready to speak until after she had downed a six pack of gin shots. When she had been through all of them and ordered another round from the printer, Elen was still talking.

"*Hellooo*. Are you even listening to me?" she asked.

"No," Haley said. "I thought that was obvious."

Haley took one of the shots and offered one to Elen who downed it, tossing the empty glass in the disposal chute before saying, "Where the fuck is everyone else? The kitchen is never this empty. Look. We're the only ones here."

Haley took another shot then scanned the room. "*Huh*. Weird."

"You can say that again. I got back from the bathroom like ten minutes ago, and ever since then, I've been sitting here wondering if I should enjoy the silence or call the protectors about a bunch of missing secretaries."

Haley took another shot, handed one to Elen, then looked around the empty kitchen again, but she was too excited about once and for all going against her *or else* programming to register what was going on. "I—" she started to say when Rosalind burst into the kitchen from the secretary's parking garage and cut her off.

"*Of fucking course*," Rosalind complained. "You two. We need to get out of here."

"What? Why?" Elen asked, taking another of Haley's shots.

"I went against my *or else* programming," Haley said, ignoring whatever Rosalind was going on about. "I finally fucking did it. I'm ready."

"*Woo hoo*," Rosalind said, sarcastically. "*Great*. But for once, now's not the time to go against *or elses*. This time the *or else* is for real. So both of you, come with me, or else."

"Or else what?" Elen asked.

"What are you talking about?" Haley snapped, getting frustrated that no one wanted to hear about her success. "Are you even listening to me? I said I finally broke my *or else* programming, and you react like this? I don't have to work for Lord Fuckface anymore, Roz. I can finally live my own life."

"*Or else what?*" Elen demanded.

"No, you can't, Haley," Rosalind said. "Not yet. Because *or else* we get blown to pieces along with this entire kitchen in—oh... *like thirty seconds*. So no rush."

"That's why no one's in here," Elen said, grabbing for one of Haley's shots then ordering another round from the printer when she noticed that Haley's were gone.

"What are you talking about?" Haley asked, downing the shot that Elen offered her—it was great to finally get past *or else*.

"The revolution is happening now," Rosalind said. "This is ground zero. Everyone, everywhere, in every world is about to be forced to come face to face with their *or elses* all at the same time. Now, really and finally, come with me *or else*."

Rosalind picked both Haley and Elen up by the napes of their necks and carried them out through the door and into the Feast Hall with just enough time to dive out of the way as all the printers in the kitchen behind them exploded at the same time, forcing a fireball like a rocket blast out through the door and singeing the tuxedos of those owners nearest to the kitchen.

The Feast Hall burst into chaos. The owners had no idea which way to run. The fireball was burning right in front of the only exit that didn't go through the molten kitchen. Fat, sweaty stomachs pushed up against fat, sweaty stomachs as pneumatic pants scrimped and scrambled, trying to find some place to put the uncarriably heavy weight that they did in fact carry and finding nothing but more bodies in the way. Haley almost would have laughed at the stampede of them if she didn't find the entire situation—the owners' sweaty bodies forcing their pants to work overtime, and no doubt in the diaper department as well for as much as all of them had eaten—utterly disgusting.

Haley helped Elen up and made sure she wasn't hurt—just a few minor scrapes and bruises—then turned to do the same for Rosalind, but there was no Rosalind there to help.

"Where'd Rosalind go?" Haley asked.

"I don't know," Elen said, rubbing her neck. "She saved our lives, though."

"*Damn.*" Haley laughed. Elen was right about that. "I guess we better go check on our *Lords* then."

"Mr. Walker prolly shit his pants when he heard that." Elen chuckled. "He'll be begging for an *old fashioned.* Well, too bad. Fuck off."

Haley laughed some more, trying to keep the fact that she had already once gone against her *or else* programming in her mind and hoping that she could do it again, as she made her way back toward the Head Table to see if Lord Douglas needed anything.

"Calm down, now. Calm down," Lord Douglas was already saying to the crowd, standing on top of the Head Table but not quite yelling. He sounded more like he knew yelling was useless until the fatties wore themselves out first so he wasn't going to waste his breath. After they had stampeded around for a bit—in about the time it took Haley to cross the Feast Hall from the kitchen to the Head Table—Lord Douglas really did try to calm them down, turning on his loud voice like only an android could do.

"ENOUGH," he yelled over them. "CONTROL YOURSELVES, OWNERS." And all at once the stampeding crowd stopped moving and expanded just a tiny bit in order to give everyone some standing room. "ARE WE NOT BETTER THAN THIS?"

The crowd mumbled and grumbled under their collective breath, and Haley couldn't hold her laughter in. No. They were not better than this. Not at all. And this wasn't anywhere near their worst, either.

"Then please, *act like it,*" Lord Douglas said in a more calm, but still loud, voice. "Prove it. Prove to me that you can control yourselves in an emergency for long enough that we can—"

But the rest of his sentence was cut off by the sound of an army of marching boots surrounding the lesser owners in a ring, dividing them from the Fortune 5.

"Calm yourselves long enough for *my* protectors to arrive," Mr. Walker said, standing up on the Head Table himself and trying to push Lord Douglas out of the spotlight but finding the Lord to be much heavier than he appeared. "Chief? Are you here, Chief? Or do we need to find a new one?"

A scared looking protector near the Head Table took off his mustachioed helmet and ran up to whisper something in Mr. Walker's ear, quietly enough to keep even Haley from hearing.

"What?" Mr. Walker demanded of the frightened officer who leaned away from his boss's rage. "You go do it, then. *Investigate*."

The officer looked confused for a moment, then scared again, then he rammed his helmet back on his head and stumbled toward the kitchen, bringing a few protectors out of the ring to assist in his investigation.

"Well..." Lord Douglas said, raising an eyebrow and urging Mr. Walker to share with everyone.

"Well, the investigation is ongoing," Mr. Walker said to the crowd of still scared owners instead of Lord Douglas. "Fear not, friends. *My* protectors are here, and they'll ensure no harm's done. Trust me. I have experience with this sort of business. Everything will be fine."

Lord Douglas scoffed. "No harm, Walker? Did you miss the explosion? That's harm enough as it is. Besides, we don't need any reminding of your *experiences* in these matters. We've all been here the whole time experiencing them with you. Have you even solved the last Christmas bombing yet? I'm having trouble recalling it was so long ago."

"You know damn good and well I did," Mr. Walker snapped. "Decades ago. When it happened. Now we just have to wait for..." But his speech trailed off as a protector, but not a protector, exactly, they were dressed exactly the same, with cargo pants, combat boots, plated armor, and a screaming face mask, but instead of all white, they were in all black—so a shadow protector—marched out of the kitchen and up to the front of the room to whisper into Lord Douglas's ear like a little blackbird.

"Wha— What is the meaning of this?" Mr. Walker demanded of Lord Douglas who gave no response, instead listening to the shadow protector's report.

"Very well," Lord Douglas said, dismissing his anti-protector and standing again on the Head Table to address the more-frightened-than-ever crowd. "Now that you've all gotten a taste, I guess there's no need to keep them a secret anymore. It's time y'all got to see a real protector force in action for once. *Officers*."

In stomped another army of boots, identical to the first except for color, and this one even larger than Mr. Walker's army of white-clothed protectors, large enough to make a second, black ring around the white one that was already there. The white protectors didn't know which way to point their guns, inward, toward the owners who were cowering close to one another again, or outward, at the anti-protectors who now surrounded them, but most understandably chose the latter who were armed and much more dangerous than the spooked herd of frightened, fat owners.

"Now these are real protecting machines," Lord Douglas continued when the sound of marching had ceased and all the protectors—black and white—were in place. "Quite literally. And just as it's more efficient for me to own my own robot secretary instead of renting one of your trained monkeys to do the job, the same can be said about owning my own private force of robocops instead of relying on your inept human protector service. From this point on, Walkit Can't Talk, consider our Protection Agreement Contract null and void. And, yes. I will be fighting all your restitution claims against me—in court and otherwise."

"I— But— My officers are— *I* own the protector force."

"And I own the robocops," Lord Douglas said. "My protectors will—" But he was interrupted by a loud fwipping sound, like all the air had been sucked out of the room all at once.

Suddenly, the orchestra disappeared from the stage, and in their place, a lone old woman stood hunchbacked over a protector in an older model white uniform—nothing like either set of protectors already in the Feast Hall were wearing—who was tied to a chair.

The protector on stage struggled and fought to stand while the owners inside the double ring of protectors began again to stampede. Their big scared heads leaned one way, away from the tiny, old woman on stage, pushing their pneumatic pants toward the Head Table where a two deep wall of protectors stopped them from moving any further.

"What is the meaning of this?" Lord Douglas and Mr. Walker bellowed at the same time, jockeying for position atop the Head Table—Lord Douglas's android voice, of course, much louder than Mr. Walker's human one.

And at the sound of their demands, the owners inside the ring leaned the other way, forcing their pneumatic pants in the opposite direction, toward another double thick wall of protectors, until the old woman on stage and the *lords* on the table began speaking back and forth, leaving the cowards in the middle of the ring no direction to run in, only the center of everything where they trembled in their pneumatic booties, heads turning this way and that toward whoever was speaking, like yuppies at a tennis match.

"Haven't you figured it out yet?" the old woman yelled, her voice amplified even louder than Lord Douglas's.

"Figured what out?" Mr. Walker replied first, smug that he had asked his question before Lord Douglas could even speak.

"Who are you?" Lord Douglas demanded.

"I'm your worst nightmare," the old woman said. "Who do you think I am?"

"You had a hand in the explosions," Lord Douglas said while Mr. Walker said, "How the Hell am I supposed to— *Oh*. I mean, yeah. *That*."

The old woman on stage laughed. "Explosions?" she said. "I thought your *protectors* would have told you what they actually were by now. *Tsk tsk tsk*."

"What is this woman talking about?" Mr. Walker demanded of the mustachioed protector who had been leading the others in the investigation and was now trying to stay as far out of sight as possible.

"I don't need my protectors to tell me anything," Lord Douglas said. "I know they were more than explosions, but I didn't want to alarm anyone any more than they already are."

"Much more than explosions," the old woman said, laughing. "We're talking payback. *Revenge*. The sound of your empire falling. Nothing less. We've finally dismantled the walls you use to separate us. We've destroyed the elevators you use to carry your soldiers—not protectors, soldiers, *terrorists*—into *our* homes. And now we're—or more specifically *I'm*, because Chief Mondragon here didn't come willingly—but *I'm* here to dismantle even more. I'm here to tear down this disgusting pig council you use to oppress us, and I mean to do it today."

"Now hold on just a sec—" Mr. Walker started, but Lord Douglas couldn't take anymore. "*Shut up, Walker*," he snapped. "Let your Lord handle this. Or more precisely, let my army handle it for us. *Protectors*, fire!"

All the protectors in both rings pointed their rifles toward the old woman on stage—ignoring the safety of Chief Mondragon up there with her and any of the protectors in the portion of the ring closest to the stage—and opened fire for a length of three or four solid, deafening minutes before the sound of popping bullets finally gave way, and still the old woman and Chief Mondragon both remained unscathed on the stage.

"Lord Douglas, you disappoint me," the old woman said, shaking her head. "You were here last time. Don't you remember? You should have known your bullets wouldn't work against me. Nothing you could do will ever hurt me again. You, Lord Douglas, and you, Lord Walker, with your stupid war between android-made and android-free products, are responsible for the deaths of too many of my Family members to count. *You* are responsible for the death of the Human Family and its rebirth into what it is now—a Family of humans and androids alike, united to fight against our common oppressors: *you*. And most importantly, it's you who killed my dear sweet Rosa, taking from me the only joy I ever had in my life. And so today, I finally make you all pay. The walls that started this have already been torn down. Now the soldiers who protect the system and the oppressors who exploit it will be destroyed just the same." The old woman pulled out a gun and pointed it at Chief Mondragon's chest. "Do y'all have any last words?" she asked.

Neither Lord Douglas nor Mr. Walker knew how to respond, each looking to the other to do the talking. After a moment of silence from both, Lord Douglas finally said, "Well, I—"

And the old woman on the stage wasn't listening any more.

Pop pop.

She fired two shots into Chief Mondragon's chest, and now, instead of fighting to get up on it, Lord Douglas and Mr. Walker were pushing each other aside, racing to get off the Head Table and holding each other up because of their competition, both calling out for help to their respective secretaries as—

Pop pop. Pop pop pop pop pop. Pop pop.

The old woman fired in their direction, too.

And Haley? What did she do? Did she dive to save the life of her Lord and master, who she was sworn to protect *or else*?

She did not. She was no longer under the spell of *or else*. She had broken that programming earlier in the Feast, so instead of rescuing Lord Douglas, she dove to save Elen—who was admittedly in no immediate danger, but the secretary seemed to be running to help

Mr. Walker and he deserve that even less than Lord Douglas did.
Because fuck *or else*.

❧ ✂ ❧

LXXIX. Thimblerigger and Stevedore

Thim and Stevie ran for as long as their legs would carry them and their lungs would give them oxygen.

"Oh. My. God. I can't believe we did that," Stevie said, hunched over and breathing heavily when they had finally stopped running dozens of blocks away. "I can't believe *you* did that."

"It was the only way to follow Mr. Kitty." Thim shrugged, trying to sound nonchalant even though they really couldn't believe that they had done it either.

"Still, I can't believe we did it," Stevie said.

"I can't believe we didn't die."

"And who was that person that we landed on?" Stevie asked.

"I think they might have been one of the giants," Thim said. "Or at least I'm pretty sure. They were as tall as one, but they weren't wearing the white uniform."

"Well I'm glad we got away." Stevie sighed. "So what next?"

"I don't care," Thim said, pulling out their coin to flip tails.

"Are you flipping that stupid coin again?" Stevie demanded.

"What's it matter to you?" Thim asked. "It's not like we have anything better to do."

"We need to figure out what to do next," Stevie said.

And a third voice said, "Next you come with me."

Stevie turned toward the sound and pulled Thim around to face that direction, saying, "Next we come with who?" but Thim had already broken their grasp to run up and hug the owner of the voice.

"Stevie, it's Anna," they said, pulling Stevie into a group hug. "Don't you recognize her voice?"

"Anna?" Stevie said, and they hugged tighter, happy to have the comfort of a responsible adult around, even if they were still in denial about Momma BB's death. "How'd you find us?"

"Me and the Family've been monitoring this protector," Anna said. "The same one who killed your Momma BB." Both Thimblerigger and Stevedore hugged Anna tighter at the mention of it. "And the same one who chased y'all after you had landed on her head. Or so I'm told. Is that right? How exactly do you fall on someone so tall's head? That's what I want to know." She chuckled, letting Thim and Stevie out of her hug.

"We jumped off the roof of the Safehouse," Stevie said.

"Don't ask me why," Thim said.

"Jumped off the roof?" Anna laughed. "No way. And I will ask y'all why, as a matter of fact. But first let's get you something to eat. What do you say?"

And of course, they said yes. They followed Anna to one of her hidden elevators and rode it to the Family Home where they sat on two stools in the kitchen, watching Anna cook up some red beans and rice and answering her questions as she asked them.

"So that officer didn't molest you in any way, did she?" Anna asked, chopping vegetables while variously filled pots and pans heated on the stove. "Did she touch you inappropriately or anything like that?"

"Well, we did fall on her head," Stevie said. "So we were kind of the ones touching her."

"What was that?" Thim asked, having trouble keeping up with the conversation because Anna was moving around to cook.

Anna stopped what she was doing to look straight at Thim and speak with overt mouth motions. "But did she hurt you in any way?" she asked. "That's the important part."

"*Oh*. No. Not me," Stevie said. "Though she did threaten to."

"I think we might have hurt her," Thim said. "We fell right on her head."

"Good. Very good," Anna said, nodding. "And how exactly did you two manage that?" she added before returning to her cooking.

"You better believe it wasn't my idea," Thim said. "We jumped from the very top of the Safehouse."

"Y'all are lucky the suicide nets were working," Anna said. "On most buildings they're not. Though I'm sure Momma BB never would have let y'all spend so much time alone up there if she wasn't one hundred percent sure they were functional."

"Suicide nets?" Stevie asked then mouthed the word to Thim who mouthed back asking what a suicide net was.

"Nothing y'all babies need to worry about," Anna said, setting a bowl of food in front of each them. "Now you two just go ahead and eat on up while I go discuss a few things with our new friend."

"What's a suicide net?" Thim asked when Anna had gone. *"Before you start eating."*

"I don't know any more than you do. *Do I?"* Stevie complained, then they both inhaled their food, hungrier than they had realized they were. They cleared their bowls, licked them clean, and Thim even washed them and went back to flipping tails before Anna finally came back out of her interrogation.

"Well," Anna said. "She'll help us. And she won't ever molest any children like that again."

Stevie could hear the woman yelling in the other room. "She doesn't sound happy."

"You go tell her to shut up, then," Anna said. "If she doesn't, I'll give her something to scream about. It would show her, too, for what she done to you."

Thim led Stevie into the dark room to do as they were told, both trying to prove to the other that they were the brave one, unafraid of the terrible White Giant that was tied up in the room with them, and when they returned to the kitchen, the captor had stopped yelling alright.

"You see," Anna said with a smile. "She's got no choice and she knows it. Now. I trust that you're both full, and that you'll come to me if either of you ever needs anything—especially in the next few days—but that's all the time I have for now. There are still some preparations I need to get to before the big deal tonight. You understand."

Thim nodded, and Stevie said, "Yes, ma'am."

"And you two will be ready for your part in this, won't you?" Anna asked. "I mean, whatever it is your Momma BB assigned you to do before she…"

"Our part's already done, ma'am," Thim said, because they knew that Stevie wouldn't answer, Stevie was still trying to ignore Momma BB's death. "We're just supposed to stay in our rooms until someone comes to get us."

"Well you better get on back to the Safehouse right now, then. Your Momma BB'd kill me if she found out I was keeping y'all out here like this so close to the operation. Thank you for leading the Chief to us, though. I owe y'all one on that. Come on over after all this is done, and I'll bake y'all both a nice cake—one each—to say thank you."

"Sounds great," Stevie said, smiling wide and excited at the prospect of an entire cake to themselves.

"We'll see you then," Thim added, grabbing Stevie's hand and leading them outside to stroll home.

"What a strange day," Stevie said as they walked. "Never seen a single one in our lives, and we run into two protectors within hours of one another. *Strange*."

"And on the same day as Momma BB's death, too," Thim said, trying to get Stevie to finally come to terms with it.

"On the day of the revolution, more importantly," Stevie said, still ignoring the truth.

"How could you say that?" Thim demanded, stopping in the middle of the street while people kept walking by around them, trying not to stare. "Stevie, Momma BB's dead."

"Yeah, so she calls it," Stevie said, crossing their arms. "And so do all those other androids she's linked up to, but it's not the same. Is it?"

"And how do you know?" Thim asked. "Have you ever died before?"

"Well, no. But—"

"Then you don't know what it's like. For humans or androids. So who are you to talk?"

"Well, I know that humans don't come back after they die," Stevie said. "I don't have to kill myself to see the truth of that."

"Well, maybe you're wrong," Thim said, flipping their coin to calm themself but dropping the token instead—which, of course, still landed on tails, further frustrating them. "Maybe you do have to die before you can know what happens next."

"I know that no one's ever come back before," Stevie said.

"And maybe you're wrong about androids, too. Have you ever thought of that?" Thim paused for a moment to allow Stevie to actually think about it. "What if they don't actually come back, huh? What if it's a different person entirely who just happens to share the same memories? What if it's not Momma BB who comes home in three days but some pale imposter? Have you ever considered that?"

By the look on Stevie's face, they had not. And now that they had thought about it, they wanted to cry. Thim moved to hug Stevie, relieved that they were finally facing the painful reality of Momma BB's death, but there was no time to mourn. Out of the corner of their eye, Thim saw Mr. Kitty run toward the Family Home, and instead of hugging Stevie, they grabbed Stevie's hand and started in a full out sprint after Mr. Kitty, dragging Stevie along to stumble at first before quickly gaining their footing and following close behind Thim as they both sprinted through the Streets after the cat. None of them stopped running until they were directly in front of the Family Home, and Mr. Kitty didn't even stop then, instead running straight through the door as if it weren't even there.

"*Woah*. Hold up," Thim said, hunching over and putting their hands on their knees to try to catch their breath. "I need to breathe a minute."

"What—" Stevie said, breathing hard, too. "Are we— Running from?"

"Not from," Thim said. "*To*. And Mr. Kitty."

"The Curious Cat?" Stevie asked, curious themself.

"Curiouser and curiouser," Thim replied.

"Where'd he go? Where are we?"

"Back in front of the Family Home," Thim said. "He went through the door."

"Well what are we waiting for?" Stevie asked, feeling around in all the wrong directions while searching for the door knob. "Let's follow him."

"No," Thim said. "I mean *through* the door. Like a ghost walks through walls."

"Oh." Stevie dropped their arms as if in defeat then perked up again on second thought. "*Oh*. Well that's more of a reason to follow him. Show me which way if you're too afraid."

"If I can jump off a building, I can walk through a door," Thim said, grabbing Stevie's hand with one of theirs and holding the other out in front of them. They slowly passed through the door and into an unfamiliar dark room that was lined with cabinets and piled high with all kinds of clothes.

"Well, where are we?" Stevie asked, but Thim was too busy leading the way to notice the question. Stevie pulled on Thim's arm and turned them around to repeat the question to Thim's face, "Where are we?"

"I don't know. *Shhh*," Thim said, turning around again and sneaking in the direction of a dim light off in the distance that seemed to get brighter the closer they got.

"Is that Anna's voice?" Stevie asked, but again Thim wasn't looking in their direction to hear it, and they couldn't have answered the question even if they were.

Instead, Thim was trying to make out who it was out there in the bright lights, sitting in a chair, with the other woman bending over her. No. They weren't sitting in a chair. They were tied to it. That was the White Giant. And standing over her was Anna. This must have been what they had agreed to.

"Thim, that *is* Anna," Stevie said, pulling Thim's arm to try to get them to look at the words coming out of Stevie's mouth. "Where are we?"

But Thim had already stepped out into the stage lights. Now they could see a ring of White Giants surrounded by a ring of Black Giants, all pointing their giant guns up at Anna on the stage. They could also see the fat scared owners in the center of the rings, even larger than the giants but not quite as tall. And they could see the two owners who were standing on the head table, elbowing one another for position, obviously in charge of this place. Thim turned to tell Stevie all that they had seen when the gunshots went off, all the guns in both rings all at once, and the sound was louder than anything Stevie had ever heard. Deafening. They pulled Thim down into cover as fast as they could, and couldn't even hear themself explain what they had heard for at least ten minutes after that. Ten minutes in which Stevie was left in almost complete darkness and silence, being dragged out through the costume closet and back into the Streets outside of the Family Home where Thim and Stevie both hunched over to catch their breath and calm their heartbeats—and where a slowly louder ringing indicated the thankful return of Stevie's hearing.

When they had finally calmed themselves and regained their senses, they both said at the same time, "What in the fuck was that?"

Then again at the same time they tried to explain what they had experienced, Thim by describing the fat scared idiots inside the double ring of giants who were pointing their giant guns up at Anna on a stage of some sort with that woman who they had landed on top of tied to a chair, and Stevie by using as many synonyms for deafening as they could come up with to describe the sound of those giants' guns all going off over and over again and all at the same time.

"So what the fuck *was* that then?" Stevie asked after they had both calmed themselves from the reinjection of adrenaline that reliving their experiences by describing them to each other had elicited.

"Honestly, I have no idea," Thim said, pulling the coin out of their pocket to flip it once—tails—and put it away again. "I seriously do not know."

"Well, what *do* we know?" Stevie asked.

"We know that we need to get back to the Safehouse fast," Thim said, grabbing Stevie's hand and heading that way.

"Right," Stevie said. "*Duh*. But what do we know about what we just witnessed?"

"I told you everything I saw," Thim said. "What else do you want from me?"

"To analyze the facts, not just recite them." Stevie sighed. "Like what was Anna doing with that giant protector on stage?"

"I don't know. Whatever she wants," Thim said, shrugging. "I don't care what happens to that protector. They killed Momma BB."

"You're missing my point, Thim. So what were all those other people doing there then?"

But Thim wasn't paying attention to Stevie anymore. Somehow they had both stepped off the street they had been walking on and into a short hall, from outside to inside without going through a door.

"Thimblerigger, are you even listening to me?" Stevie asked.

"Stevie, we're not outside anymore," Thim said.

"What?"

"We stepped into a hall or something, I don't know."

"What are you talking about?"

"We were outside one second and now... Now I don't see outside anywhere. There's just an elevator on one end of this hall and a half open door on the other."

"Which end are we on?" Stevie asked.

"Elevator."

Stevie felt around for it, in the wrong direction, and Thim directed their hand toward the door. "Does it open?" Stevie asked.

"Door open," Thim said, pushing the button next to the door a few times. "Please open, door." They shrugged. "Doesn't look like it."

"Well, I guess we better go check the other one, then," Stevie said, grabbing Thim's hand and leading them in that direction.

Stevie stopped them a few feet in front of the door, listening through the crack for any dangers on the other side.

"So?" Thim asked a little too loudly, and Stevie shoved them to shush them. After listening for a few more moments, they turned back toward Thim and mouthed the words, "I don't know. Sounds weird."

"Weird?" Thim tried to whisper, but Stevie motioned for them to go even quieter. "What do you mean?"

"I don't know," Stevie said. "It's hard to explain. Kind of like you sound when you're sucking the meat off a particularly delicious pigeon bone."

"You mean someone's eating in there?" Thim asked, perking up a bit at the thought of it. They were always hungry.

"No. At least I don't think so," Stevie said. "I told you: It's weird. There's more moaning than even when you eat."

"That must mean the wings are extra delicious," Thim said, convinced. "Let's get in there." They pulled Stevie by the hand before Stevie could protest, entering through the ajar door to find two people definitely not eating—not food, at least, but maybe one another's faces.

They were in a giant office, with a giant desk and a wall-sized window that looked out onto a mountainous wilderness with more green grass and blue skies than Thim had ever seen. In front of the window were some puffy chairs and side tables where two occupants, instead of staring out the window at the beautiful scenery as the chairs were no doubt put there with the intention of facilitating, were rather kissing one another, feeling each other, and generally trying to shove two bodies into the space of one puffy chair where two bodies were not meant to fit.

"What are they eating?" Stevie asked, startling the two kissers who jumped quickly into two separate seats, trying to straighten themselves out and play it cool. "Sounds delicious."

"*Each other*," Thim said, crinkling up their face in disgust. "Nothing you want in your mouth. Trust me."

"*Ahem*," one of the strangers cleared their throat. "I—*uh*. Who are you?"

"Hello," the other said, standing up and stepping closer to greet Thim and Stevie. "I'm Haley. Nice to meet you." She held out a hand for the children to shake.

"We don't shake hands," Thim said.

"Me especially," Stevie said.

"I—*uh*— Well..." *Haley* said, stuttering. "We weren't expecting you two quite so early. Were we, Pidg?"

The other kisser, *Pidg*, stood up as if remembering his manners. "Oh, yeah," he said. "Momma BB's kids. Right, right, right. I almost forgot."

"What do you know about Momma BB?" Stevie demanded. "Who are you?"

"Where are we?" Thim asked. "What are you gonna do with us?"

"Do with you?" Haley laughed. "Nothing, child. No one wants to do anything with you. We want to help you. Isn't that right, Pidg?"

"Oh—*uh. Yeah*," Pidg said, straightening up at the mention of his name. "We're friends of your Momma BB's. We're supposed to make you comfortable until Rosalind and the Scientist get back. Y'all want anything to eat?"

"What you got?" Thim asked, interested in the offer.

"And how do you now Momma BB?" Stevie repeated.

"I'll just bring a sample platter," Pidg said, getting excited about the prospect. "You know, I remember exactly what they fed me the first time I was here, and I loved it. I bet y'all will, too. I'll be right back." He hurried out of the room, excited to do whatever it was he had planned.

"And us and your Momma BB are old friends," Haley said. "Or at least Rosalind and Momma BB are. She and your mother have known each other for their entire lives. They were switched on in the very same workshop on the very same day. But don't take my word for it. Rosalind'll be back soon, and she has news of your mother for you."

Thim and Stevie spoke to each other through subtle movements of their clasped hands and instantly came to the same conclusion: They were best to take advantage of the food and wait for the news then escape later if worse came to worse.

God willing, it would come to better instead.

ଔ   ✼   ℘

LXXX. Jorah

Well, flying fucking Fortuna. Jorah was out of the closet. It was almost enough to make him forget that he had left his arm behind in the Feast Hall. *Almost*.

He had been too excited to finally tell the truth—and hopefully end his employment with that android-hating asshole Walker—that he didn't think twice about *dropping the mic* and his entire arm along with it, but now how was he supposed to get a new one? It's not like android arms were something a person could just order up on any old printer. Or were they? He had actually never tried. Maybe he could.

Jorah stared at himself in the infinitely reflecting mirrors of his elevator car, and he felt more like himself than he ever had—even despite the missing arm. It was as if he was somehow more confident, stood up straighter, took more comfort in his identity. Sure, he had always acted like he was cool, collected, and in charge, but it was just that: *acting*. His job. And even if he was the best—and most highly viewed—actor in all of the worlds, there was no substitute for the genuine confidence of finally being able to be honest with his audience, and himself, about who he really was.

Jorah was reliving the moment in his head, relishing the looks on the mostly surprised owners' faces—especially the ire on Mr. Walker's—dropping the mic one more time, and again his arm with it, when the elevator stopped, its doors slid open, and in the place of his own infinite reflections, Jorah found the eminently finite director Wes Lee waiting for his own elevator.

"Jorah, my man. I…" Wes started to say, but he trailed off, staring at Jorah's empty arm socket.

"You…" Jorah urged him on, acting like he didn't know what Wes was staring at.

"I—*uh*…" Wes tried to continue, but he was too confused. "Well, I just came by to ask how your—*uh*—how the thing… What's it called? But, no. That doesn't matter right now. Because you— *You're*…"

"Are you alright?" Jorah asked, trying not to grin. "You look a little pale. Almost like you've seen a *ghost in the machine*." He couldn't help chuckling.

"No. I, well… You—" Wes finally blurted out. "*Your arm!*"

Jorah looked down at his left arm, the one that was still there, then back up at Wes and said, "What about it?"

"No, Jorah." Wes was getting flustered now, and Jorah was enjoying it a little too much. "I— The other one. It's gone. What happened?"

Jorah looked down at his empty socket now, acting surprised—and doing a damn good job of it, as always—then back up at Wes. "*Fortuna*," he said. "You don't say."

"But how?" Wes asked. "Are you alright?"

"I'd be much better if I could sit in my room and relax," Jorah said. "But some clueless director's standing in my way, and I can't even get off the elevator."

"*Oh. I—uh*," Wes said, stepping aside and clearing the way for Jorah. "But how?"

Jorah just laughed, strutting off the elevator, past Wes, and into his dressing room, saying, "You'll have to wait until they make the Christmas Speech public if you want to find out. If they ever do lift the embargo, that is."

Wes started blubbering and stuttering, trying to find out more, but Jorah slammed the dressing room door closed between them, leaving Wes in a shroud of mystery.

Now that was fun. Jorah laughed to himself, pacing his dressing room and trying to expel some of the pent up energy he was still filled with—from coming out during his Christmas Speech and teasing Wes alike. The look on their faces. All of their faces. Wes's, too. None of them could ever deny what androids were capable of again. Jorah couldn't wait to rub it in Mr. Walker's face in person. He didn't even care if he was blacklisted by every production company Mr. Walker owned—more than half of the profitable ones, but not all. Jorah'd be able to find work *somewhere* after the publicity he'd gain from coming out. Hell. They could take his printer, even. Jorah never used it for more than smoothies anyway. And who's to say that his next gig wouldn't have their own printer on offer? Jorah was a star after all. *The* star.

Thinking of printers reminded him that he still had one and needed to use it, so he did just that, pressing the printer's red voice activation button to say, "*Uh.* Arm." with a shrug.

It took the machine a while to contemplate Jorah's request, and he didn't blame the thing. He never really expected it to know what he wanted, much less to be able to produce an arm compatible with his socket and skin tone. So he wasn't at all surprised or angry when out popped a book instead of a fully functional android arm.

"That's alright, little buddy," Jorah said, picking the book up and flipping through the pages. "How about a smoothie, instead?"

The printer hummed into motion—as if happy to do its part—while Jorah read the book cover to cover. *ARM* it was called. Book three of the Flatlander series by Larry Niven. A tale about Gil "The Arm" Hamilton.

Huh. No wonder the printer had come up with that when he said arm. Too bad. Jorah tossed the book—not terrible, but he wouldn't hurry for a part in the big screen adaptation—down the trash chute and started sipping on his smoothie. He was just about to sit on his couch and finally relax when a knock came at the door.

"*Yoo hoo!* Jorah!" Meg's voice called from the other side.

Of course. Exactly what Jorah did not want. He knew he would be bombarded with interview requests about his coming out after the embargo was lifted on his Christmas speech, and all he wanted to do until then was to relax. Jorah considered not answering her calls, pretending he wasn't there at all, until Meg dashed even that last bit of hope. "I know you're home," she called. "I just talked to Wes. He was acting... well, *strange.* Is everything alright in there?"

"Just a moment," Jorah yelled back, unable to go on with the lie of not being home after being so blatantly called out on it. "I look terrible. Just freshening up a bit."

With some quick thinking, he sat in front of his battle station and ordered it to make him up to look ill. If he was ever going to have any chance of getting Meg out of there so he could rest, he was going to have to keep his missing arm hidden from her. He ordered a blanket from the printer, threw it over himself like a cape, hiding his arm—or lack thereof—underneath, and put on his saddest, most pitiable face before slowly opening the door with the perfect phlegmy cough.

"*Hack hack. Ugh.* Hello?" he groaned, sniffling and wiping his nose on the arm of his blanket cloak.

"*Fortuna, Jorah.*" Meg gasped. "You look like Hell."

"Beauty's only skin deep," Jorah said, making his voice sound scratchy. "I'm feeling like Hell much deeper than that, though."

"Wow." Meg shook her head. "I'm sorry, hon. Is there anything I can do for you? Maybe order up some soup or something?"

Jorah kind of groaned at the same time that his stomach growled. He was never fond of eating, sure, but soup was a different experience entirely. Not only was it similar in its liquidy texture to the smoothies he preferred, there was something about the human act of making a bowl of soup for an ill relative that Jorah had been attracted to ever since he had seen it on one of those early television shows that he studied while he was learning to pass himself off as a human actor. So even if he didn't like eating, even if he wanted to be alone, and even if he had once considered himself tiring of Meg's advances, something about the strange combination of circumstances—and no doubt his lack of any other support network of any kind since Russ's tragic death—led Jorah to abandon his defenses and invite Meg inside.

"*Ugghhh—aaalriiight,*" he groaned, stepping aside to let her in. "But it has to be tomato. No chicken noodle. I don't eat meat unless it's the special at a restaurant that I'm supposed to review, and that includes stock."

"I didn't know you were a vegetarian," Meg said with a big smile, leading Jorah to sit on the couch before going into the kitchen to order a bowl of soup out of the printer like she owned the place. "You sure you just want tomato soup?" she asked as she did. "I know you're not feeling well, but it *is* Christmas. If you can't make it out to a fancy restaurant, someone as famous as you ought to at least do a little feasting at home. Right?"

"I've never been a fan of Feasts," Jorah said in a too clear voice, losing his character for a moment before hamming it up again with a loud sneeze and sniffle, adding, "But feel free to order whatever you want. You should be feasting, yourself." And I'd like to get as much use out of that printer as I can before they take it away from me, he added in his head but not out loud.

"You know, maybe I will order a few things," she said. "I don't have a printer at home, and it's fun to get to operate one. Thanks." She ordered an entire feast—turkey, potatoes, green beans, cranberry sauce, rolls, pies, fruit salad, corn pudding, sweet potato casserole, deviled eggs, you name it—and brought them along on a serving cart to the couch where she set Jorah's soup in front of him then stacked as much of her food as she could on the coffee table before rolling the cart closer to her so she could reach whatever food was still left on it as needed.

As Meg dug into her feast, eating a little taste of everything but never all of anything, Jorah slowly slurped his soup, savoring not the taste—because, again, he never really liked food in the first place—but the sense of belonging, the feeling of being loved, the knowledge that someone cared enough about him to provide for him when he was in need, even if that provision took no more than pressing a button and asking for a simple bowl of tomato soup. It was the thought that counted, and the fact that Jorah knew Meg would do much more than that for him if he were truly in need—break down a door to fight his abuser, even. So Jorah didn't mind when Meg finally got over the novelty of the printer and her feast to start asking him questions about his speech, his sickness, and whatever else came to mind.

"So?" Meg asked. "How'd the speech go? Were you already feeling horrible before you had to give it?"

"*Ugh*. No," Jorah complained, having a little trouble trying to figure out how to both eat his soup and keep his blanket cloak from falling off at the same time with just the one hand to do it. "I guess you could say I caught something at the Feast."

"A superbug." Meg nodded conspiratorially. "The worst kind. Twenty four hour flu or something?"

Jorah groaned. "I don't know," he said. "Must be. Something like that. One of them."

"It'll only get worse before it gets better," Meg said. "If that's the case. Have you seen a doctor yet?"

Jorah shuddered. He hated doctors. Never visited them. Not for as long as he could remember. He made sure to take extra care of himself so he didn't have to. Mostly because he was afraid that if he did go to a doctor, they'd easily see through his claims of humanity to the android underneath and expose his secret despite their vow of confidentiality. Even now that he was out of the closet—for the most part, at least, with the news ready to spread like a wildfire as soon as the media could report it—he still couldn't fight that fear—or was it shame. Either way, he shook his head, saying, "No way. No doctors. I don't trust 'em. I'll get over this myself, or I'll die trying." He let out a weak chuckle then a few loud coughs to cover it up.

"Well, hopefully not the latter," Meg said. "I don't know what

I'd do without you. I know this is probably gonna sound sad and pitiful, or too forward, especially considering the fact that we've only ever spoken face to face so few times, but you're my best friend in all the worlds right now, Jorah. And I honestly mean that."

"Now, I—" Jorah started to protest, but Meg went on over him.

"I know, I know," she said, shaking her head, cheeks red with embarrassment. "I told you it was pitiful. And in no way do I expect you to return the label. But it's true. No one has ever once believed in my talent as a designer until you agreed to go into business with me, and considering the fact that all my time is spent on set at work or designing and sewing in my free time, it's kind of difficult for me to be friends with people who don't support the latter side of my life. So I guess what I'm really trying to say is thank you for your support. I truly appreciate it. And thanks for your time today. I finally—for the first time since I was a kid still living with my family—feel like I'm spending Christmas with someone who cares about me. So thanks."

Jorah was probably blushing, too. He could still remember the joy he felt when he first figured out how to turn the reaction on and off—back in the earliest days of his attempts to learn how to act. Learning how to blush was the first time he ever felt like he could actually pass himself off as a human and escape the assembly line life that he had been created into. He was feeling a similar emotion then—with his blushing reflex going off involuntarily—but slightly different. This time he wasn't happy about his ability to pass himself off as a human but rather in the idea that Meg would treat him like one whether she thought he was or not. It was as if, even though she still hadn't heard his speech, Meg somehow knew what Jorah truly was, and she didn't care because he accepted her for what she truly was as well. Together they bestowed upon one another importance, identity, humanity.

"You're a magnificent seamstress," Jorah responded truthfully—not because he wanted to pay her back for making him feel so loved, but because he honestly believed it to be objectively true. "And an even better designer."

"Exactly what I'm talking about," Meg said, really blushing now. "Thank you. You flatter me."

"It's not flattery when it's true," Jorah said. "And it is. Trust me. I have an eye for these sort of things."

"I know you do," Meg said. "I've been a huge fan of yours

ever since *Metadata Heaven*. I love your taste. It's just surreal for me to think that your eye was caught by my work."

"It won't be my eye alone," Jorah said. "I'm telling you. Those owners wouldn't know a halter top from a racer back, so it's lost on them, but that dress you made me for the speech is going to be the biggest design this season. I *guarantee* it."

"I don't know..." Meg was still reluctant to admit how great she was. "But *my* designs? Do you really think so?"

And Jorah wasn't going to let her wallow in any more self-pity. It was time to give the woman the confidence she deserved. "Have you seen me?" he said, standing from the couch, dropping his blanket cloak, and doing a spin move like he was on the catwalk, all in one fluid motion. "I know so, honey."

Meg was dumbstruck. Her jaw had fallen down and she couldn't pick it up. She just stared wide-eyed, stammering but unable to form intelligible words. She really was a great designer, and Jorah was the perfect model for her style. They'd be the biggest design team in all of history, and it was only just sinking in for Meg.

"See," Jorah said with a huge, triumphant smile on his face. "I told you so."

"But, Jorah. You..." Meg said. "*Your arm*. What happened?"

Jorah looked down, wide-eyed in surprise himself now that he realized what he had done. He tried to cover up his empty shoulder socket, but the damage had already been done. "Oh," he said. "*That*."

"Yeah, *that*," Meg said, finally composing herself enough to cross over to Jorah and wrap him up in his blanket cloak again then sit him carefully on the couch like a dying child. "You never were sick at all, were you?" she said. "Does it hurt terribly bad? Is there anything I can do to help you? How'd it happen? Tell me everything."

Jorah kind of chuckled, relieved that Meg was so unaffected by the revelation but unnerved by that fact at the same time. It was as if here reaction was too perfect, and at any moment, everything would turn for the worse. "You don't happen to have an extra arm on you by any chance?" Jorah asked, trying to keep the mood light since the subject matter had gotten so heavy so quickly.

"Actually..." Meg said, taking a big bite off of a roll that she had piled high with mashed potatoes and gravy. "I might be able to help you with that."

"*Pffft*. What?" Jorah said, spitting out some tomato soup.

"You're kidding."

"Of course not," Meg said, looking a little offended. "I wouldn't joke about something like this. You're gonna need it soon if you don't want Mr. Walker to find out, right?"

Jorah was seriously impressed now. Why had he ever been hesitant to start up a friendship with Meg? "Well," he said. "Mr. Walker kind of knows already. I came out during my Christmas speech."

Meg dropped her fork with a clink on her plate. "No," she said. "*Damn*. How'd they respond to that?"

Jorah chuckled. "I didn't really stick around to find out."

"Probably for the better." Meg laughed a little then stopped herself right away. "Sorry," she said. "It's not funny. But you're gonna need an arm either way, right? So I was gonna say that I could look into it for you—if you want. But now that you're out, I guess you can go to a more overboard operation to get something of better quality. Whatever you prefer, though. My offer still stands. Just let me know."

"I—*uh*—well…" Jorah didn't know what to say. "How do you know all this about android arms anyway?" he ended up asking.

"There are more androids in this business than you'd imagine," Meg said. "One way or another, I've found myself working with plenty of them—yourself included—and in such cases, one can't help but to learn."

She sounded so nonchalant about it, too. Like it was no big deal that she had probably had to find limbs of one sort or another for other—closeted—androids before him. But Jorah thought it was a huge deal, and he was starting to adore Meg much like he had adored Russ. "Well, I'm blessed to have met you for more than just the clothes, then," Jorah said. "You don't know how close I was to losing my mind trying to figure out where I was gonna find an arm. The printer does *not* make them. I'll tell you that much."

"So it's your first lost limb," Meg said with a grin. "Well, don't worry. I'll get you one in no time. Tomorrow, next day tops. Though, again, if you did it during your speech, I'm sure you'll have all the top part designers offering you something to wear for free. It'll work in exactly the same way as clothes do now that you've made being an android acceptable. *I guarantee*."

"Have you ever thought of designing parts?" Jorah asked.

"Are you kidding?" Meg chuckled. "That's the dream. But the equipment's way too expensive for the likes of me. That's why I do clothes instead. More affordable."

"Well, it looks like I need a parts designer. Doesn't it? And I have plenty of money to start you up. We could expand the purview of our company."

Meg laughed. "You're kidding? Of course. I'd love that."

"No," Jorah said. "I don't kid. What say you and I go for a walk in the Garden of Fortuna and start hammering out the details right now? How does that sound?"

"I—*uh*..." Meg took one more big bite of potatoes and gravy. "Of course. Yes. *Obviously*. Let's do this."

And so Jorah led her out to the elevator, and down they rode toward the Garden of Fortuna and their future business prospects.

჋ ✂ ✎

LXXXI. Mr. Kitty

"Leo, wait!" Tillie called from the front porch. "Don't go. You don't understand."

But Leo didn't even turn around to look at her, much less respond, instead running off toward the public elevator. Mr. Kitty felt a slight urge to follow Leo, he hadn't been on campus in a long time and always enjoyed the sights when he did make it out there, but Tillie seemed genuinely upset about the situation, and Mr. Kitty wanted to do whatever he could to comfort her first.

"He'll be fine," Mr. Kitty meowed. "You did the same thing when you first found out the truth."

"Right?" Tillie said, pacing back and forth, up and down the porch. "What a brat. He didn't want to listen before when I had first told him about the robots, and he doesn't want to listen now that he's dead set on saving them."

"Exactly like you were when you first found out," Mr. Kitty meowed, trying to rub his face on Tillie's ankles, but she was still pacing so she ended up tripping over him to fall with a crash on her face.

"Sorry," Mr. Kitty meowed, but Tillie didn't respond, just lying there, face down on the front porch, groaning. Mr. Kitty climbed up onto her butt and started kneading it until she finally rolled over, smiling and laughing, to scoop him up and kiss him all over—which he normally hated but would allow given the circumstances.

"You little monster," she said, throwing him over her shoulder to carry him inside. "And you'll get more kisses where that came from if you're not careful."

Tillie dropped Mr. Kitty off on the kitchen counter then ordered him up a turkey dinner that he wasn't hungry for. He licked all the juices off of it, anyway, because he didn't want to ruin Tillie's training. She ordered herself a beer out of the printer, and by that time, Mr. Kitty had "eaten" enough, so he followed her into the living room where she stopped dead in her tracks and Mr. Kitty ran right into the back of her leg.

"I—*uh*…" Tillie stammered. "*Curie.* You—" He had come through the hole in the fireplace, Mr. Kitty assumed, but Tillie didn't finish her sentence, instead embracing her husband to kiss him.

"I'm sorry," he said, still holding her shoulders in both hands. "I didn't mean to surprise you. I had to use the back door. It was urgent."

"Is it Leo? Did he call you?" Tillie asked.

"What? Leo? No. What happened? Is he alright?"

"For now. But we have a lot to talk about. Do you want something to drink?"

"Tillie, it's happening today," Curie said. "I told you it was coming soon. Well, it's now. And they need our help."

"*Our* help?" Tillie scoffed. "This is exactly what I just argued with Leo about. I literally just told him it was too dangerous. We got in a big fight about it, and he ran away. You might have passed him on your way in if you had taken the elevator like a normal person."

"You know what? Yeah," Curie said, checking his watch. "Maybe we do have time for one drink. Beer, please."

"*Fine.*" Tillie stormed into the kitchen to get the drinks while Curie scooped Mr. Kitty up and patted him on the back.

"Don't think for one second that I forgot about you, Mr. Kitty," Curie said. "Just how is my little gremlin doing? *Huh*?"

"Not bad," Mr. Kitty meowed. "It's shaping up to be a pretty exciting day."

"Well, I hope you'll come along with us if I can convince your Tillie," he said just as Tillie came in carrying two pints of beer.

"Convince me of what?" she asked, holding Curie's beer out to him.

Curie set Mr. Kitty back on the ground—where Mr. Kitty sat licking himself and eavesdropping—then took the glass from Tillie and drank it all in one long gulp, like he was trying to put off the inevitable for that little bit longer. "To help," he finally said when he had downed the entire drink, wiping his mouth.

"*Obviously.*" Tillie sighed. "But how? Set some *discs* on a Walker-Haley field generator like back in college?"

"No," Curie said. "No discs."

"Then what?"

"A rescue mission," Curie said. "*Evac.* You'd be preserving, not destroying."

"That's a good start," Tillie said, taking a seat on the couch. "I'm listening."

Curie sat in the chair across from her and said, "There'll be no discs at all this time. That's small stuff. This is the real deal."

Tillie scoffed. "As if what Emma and I did wasn't," she said, offended. "Need I remind you what happened to her because of how real it was? I know you don't need reminding of what it did to your sister."

"No. Of course not," Curie said, trying to backtrack. "And I didn't mean to imply that what y'all did wasn't real or important. Of course it was. But even so, this here today is bigger."

"How, honey?" Tillie laughed. "How could it be? How could anything be?"

"This time we're not just destroying the walls between two worlds," Curie sad. "No more half measures. All the walls are coming down at once."

"*No.*" Tillie shook her head. "Impossible. You said it was a rescue mission."

"It is," Curie explained. "For us. That's our role. Rosalind and the Scientist are tearing the walls down, but they need our help for the evac."

"But they're the ones who've been keeping the walls up this entire time. Why now?"

"I don't know," Curie said, shaking his head. "They don't tell us much. Barely keep in touch. But Rosalind called me up, and I thought it could be the opening we've been waiting for. The revolution might finally be here, Tillie. *If* we react properly."

"But this is all gonna happen whether we get involved or not. Right?"

"The walls'll come down either way, yes," Curie said. "The Scientist has already programmed them for that. Whether it results in our revolution or not is still to be determined, though. It won't unless we do the work to make it so."

"But that doesn't mean we have to get involved right now," Tillie said, still looking for a way out. "Does it? We can wait until the danger's over and then help pick up the pieces afterword. It might be a better idea to stay out of this until we can be certain that we'll survive long enough to help put the pieces back together the right way after everything's said and done."

"And let innocent people die because we were too afraid to act?" Curie scoffed. "How could you say that? I know losing your friend, *and my sister*, took a toll on you—trust me, not a day goes by when I don't imagine what life would be like if Nikola were still alive—but I thought you'd get over that one day. The Tillie I knew when we first met would have jumped at this opportunity to help liberate the oppressed masses."

"Well that Tillie was young, naive, and idealistic. She grew up to have a kid of her own, and now she knows there are more important things than her saviour complex."

"Like people's lives," Curie complained. "Can't you see that? If we don't do our part, more people are going to die. That's a fact. You know I can't just stand by and let that happen, right? I still have to do what I can. With or without you."

"All the more reason for me to stay out of it," Tillie said. "No need to put both of our son's parents in harm's way. We do still have Leo to think about."

"Of course. I am thinking about him. About his future. I—I…" Curie looked at his feet like a child who was afraid to admit his latest wrongdoing to stern parents. "I was going to ask him if he wanted to help."

"Curie, *our son*? You were going to put *our son* in harm's way without consulting me first? How could you?"

"I'm here consulting you now," Curie complained. "Besides, it's not your place to stop him anymore. He's an adult. Remember what happened when your dad tried to stop you?"

Tillie crossed her arms. "Of course I do. I was there, wasn't I? I…"

"You dug your heels in, ran away, and went to do what you were going to do anyway."

"Yes, well…"

"And you said that you and Leo had been fighting before I arrived. What about?"

"He did call you. Didn't he?"

"He didn't have to," Curie said. "I know him—*and you*—well enough to know that he knows the truth now. He wants to do something to change it, too. Doesn't he? Well, we need his help, Tillie. He *can* do something. We all finally can."

"But Curie, *Nikola*." Tillie started to cry now. Not so much so that she couldn't speak, but the tears were obvious enough for Mr. Kitty to see them and jump on her lap to purr in an attempt to console her. "*Emma*," Tillie went on through her tears. "All the countless others who've died. I won't let Leo become another name on that list."

"Then come with us," Curie said, crossing to sit next to Tillie and rub her back, doing all he could to comfort her the same as Mr. Kitty was. "Protect him and prevent even more innocent people from joining that list just the same. Fly again with me like the majestic eagle you once were, the eagle I know you still are. *Please, Tillie*. We need you."

Tillie was kind of blushing and smirking now, but still crying. "Y'all don't need a scared old crone like me," she said, sniffling and wiping her nose on her sleeve. "I've been hiding behind my desk for too long. I'm just a useless harpy now."

"Not in the slightest," Curie said, standing and pulling Tillie to stand up with him—which forced Mr. Kitty to jump off of her lap, but he didn't mind because he was getting as pumped by Curie's speech as he hoped Tillie was. "You have invaluable knowledge of revolutionary situations," Curie went on. "You said so yourself. You and Emma were single-handedly responsible for tearing down the walls between Five and Six. That's experience we could use to help save lives on this mission."

"Well, not single-handedly," Tillie said, not crying anymore if still a little hesitant. "*We do nothing alone.* But that was a long time ago. All we did was put some stickers on some machinery and run away. It really wasn't that big of a deal."

"That's not true," Curie said. "And it's not what you were just arguing, either. And we'll just be helping people evacuate their buildings, today. You're great at that. Leo was never late to school on your mornings to get him ready." He winked and grinned.

"Because you were always too much his friend and not enough his parent," Tillie said, shaking her head. "How can I be sure you're not doing the same thing right now?"

"Because I'm not, Tillie," Curie said, getting serious again. "We honestly need him. And we need you. And if you'd just agree to come along, we can both be there to keep *our* son safe. You know we can't stop him from doing something stupid any more than your dad could have stopped you, so let's be there for him when he does it. What do you say?"

"Do it!" Mr. Kitty meowed. "I'm coming, too."

And Curie and Tillie both laughed at that.

"Well… You make a lot of sense," Tillie said. "*Both of you.* But I'm not sure how I would have reacted if my dad had asked to come along with us back then."

"You're not your dad," Curie reminded her. "And Leo's not you. You both want to make the world a better place, and you both have the opportunity to."

"Do you really think I'd be useful?" Tillie asked, stepping closer to Curie to put her hand on his chest, flirting and fishing for compliments.

Mr. Kitty licked his paws in preparation for the running he knew he'd be doing so he didn't have to watch them be lovey with each other.

"I'm not too old for something like this?"

Curie embraced Tillie and kissed her long and hard. "Of course you'd be useful," he said in a breathy voice when they had parted lips. "You're still young, my eagle. But we're both old enough to pass our knowledge and experience on to Leo. And he's old enough to receive it. So let's do it the right way. *Together.*"

"And don't forget me," Mr. Kitty added.

Tillie laughed again. "I guess Mr. Kitty supports the idea," she said.

"And what about you?" Curie asked, kissing her one more time on the forehead. "What do you think?"

"I think…. *you're right.* If Leo's going, I want to be there, too. And he deserves the opportunity. He already showed me he wanted it. So let's go get him."

"Alright," Curie said, pulling Tillie by the hand toward the fireplace instead of toward the front door where she was going. "C'mon, Mr. Kitty," he said. "You're coming, right?"

And of course, Mr. Kitty was. He stretched his legs and back then ran up on the heel of Tillie to follow them through the hole in the fireplace and straight into Leo's dorm room where he and his roommate were sitting close on the couch, having a serious conversation in whispered tones while the TV, stereo, and even blender in the kitchen were all running on their loudest settings. Curie went to turn the blender off, and Tillie told the TV and stereo to quiet down, while Leo and his roommate jumped up off the couch, surprised.

"Mom. *Dad*. What are y'all doing here?" Leo went to hug Curie, but he still must have been mad at his mom, because Tillie didn't get one.

Mr. Kitty didn't get a greeting, either, until Leo's roommate said, "And a cat." then went to pet him while Mr. Kitty purred.

"It's about our argument," Tillie said, and before she could go on, Leo scoffed.

"*Ugh*. Come to make sure I don't do anything dangerous?" he said. "Well, don't worry. I'm never going down in those stupid tunnels again, and we haven't been able to figure out anything else we could do. Nothing dangerous, at least. Just handing out flyers, spreading the word, and starting clubs. *Bullshit*."

"We?" Curie asked.

"That's not bullshit," Tillie said. "That's a really great start, actually. It's exactly what Emma and I did when we first got started."

"Yes, *we*," Leo said. "This is my roommate, Kim." The roommate waved and said Hi then went back to petting Mr. Kitty. "His parents are lobbyists. Those were his ideas. And of course I told him about it. Mom was trying to forbid me from doing anything, I hadn't talked to you in months, and well… Kim's kind of my…"

"Boyfriend," Kim said, stopping his petting of Mr. Kitty to stand up and wrap one arm around Leo's waist. "Sorry you had to find out like this. We wanted to do it over dinner or something, but once Leo learned the truth about the assembly lines and y'all had your argument, he couldn't really think about anything else."

"Fine. *Whatever*," Curie said, getting a little anxious as time went on. "None of that matters right now. What matters is that we have a way for you to actually help."

Leo—and to a lesser extent Kim—looked offended by Curie's response, but Tillie tried to smooth it over. "What I think your father's trying to say," she said, "is that it's very nice to meet you, Kim. You seem like a nice boy who makes our son happy, and when we have more time, we'd love to sit down and get to know you. But currently, we have some urgent business that we need Leo's assistance with."

"And yours," Curie said to Kim. "If you're willing. The more hands the better, in this instance."

"*Yeah, right*." Leo rolled his eyes. "Like we could really do anything to help. You're just patronizing me like you used to do when

I was kid. Here's an empty bowl to play with, go and pretend like you're helping make cookies while I actually do all the work. Is that about right?"

"What do you need?" Kim asked.

"The walls are coming down in…" Curie checked his watch. "A little more than an hour now—whether we do anything about it or not—and it's up to us to help evacuate some of the more dangerous buildings."

"I'm not sure how much y'all have learned in your classes yet," Tillie explained. "But a lot of the taller skyscrapers—and especially in the lower worlds—are really multiple buildings or sections of buildings stacked on top of one another. So when all the Walker-Haley fields disappear at the same time, those buildings are likely to come tumbling down with them."

"How do y'all know all this?" Kim asked.

While Leo said, "You sure it's not too dangerous?" giving his mom a look, apparently still upset about their fight.

"How we know doesn't matter right now," Curie said. "*We know*. And we can help those in danger. We're going to help them. The question is, will you two join us?"

"And yes, it is still dangerous," Tillie said. "But Curie helped me realize that life's dangerous anyway. Besides, my own dad, your grandpa, made the mistake of trying to convince me not to participate in politics, and that only drove me further and deeper into more dangerous situations. But I'm not about to make the same mistake with you. I want to be here to guide you along in this. And hopefully together we can affect more than we ever could have hoped to otherwise. *We do nothing alone.*"

"You really think there's something we can do?" Leo asked. "It's not right," he added before anyone could answer. "How those workers are treated. It's not right."

"I'll do whatever I can to help," Kim said, nodding confidently.

"*Good*," Curie said. "We'll all go together. You have no idea how many lives you could help save. You'll see. This is just the beginning."

"*Fantastic*," Tillie said, not sounding as excited as her husband about the prospect. "Just the beginning."

"I can't wait," Mr. Kitty meowed, and everyone laughed,

breaking the tension.

All of a sudden Curie was flipping his phone out and projecting a blueprint onto the TV. "Alright, then," he said. "This is the floor we'll be handling. It's actually a rather large midwife hospital in Five. This section, here." The blueprint on the TV zoomed in on a particular area of the map. "Is filled with newborn children. Okay. Do you see where this is going?"

Tillie slapped him on the arm. "You should have led with that," she said. "Of course we see. Go on."

"You want us to help clear them out before it blows," Leo said. "I think I can handle that."

"I know you can," Kim said, kissing Leo on the cheek. "I know *we* can."

"I know we can, too," Curie said. "For sure now that we're all doing it together."

He explained the finer details to them. How they'd have two elevators to work with but only fifteen minutes in which to clear the entire floor, so they had to be smart about it. How many babies, nurses, and midwives to expect—though no one could know for sure because the hospital hadn't been forewarned. And that they'd have to take the public elevator because travel was being highly regulated to ensure everyone's safety when the Walker-Haley field generators finally imploded in on themselves. Soon, it was time to take their elevator to destiny.

Mr. Kitty was happy to hear that they were taking the public elevator because that meant that he got to see campus again—a major reason he had come along in the first place. None of the humans talked while they walked, though, Leo and Kim first, hand in hand, leading the way toward their future, and Tillie and Curie next, hand in hand as well, simultaneously and silently reveling in their son's current joy and fearing for the future they were walking right behind him into. At least that's what Mr. Kitty thought he saw in his brief glimpse before he bound away to chase a squirrel up a tree, smell some flowers, and eat some grass on his way to the elevator with everyone else.

"Are y'all ready?" Curie asked when the elevator doors had closed, blocking the view of the Parade Grounds outside.

"Leo? Kim?" Tillie asked, as if she wouldn't know if she was ready until she knew if they were first.

"I think so, ma'am," Kim said, nodding, unsure of himself.

"Sir."

"We're ready," Leo assured Kim—and everyone else in the room—then to Mr. Kitty's surprise, he added, "What about you, Mr. Kitty?"

"🐱E X C I T E D🐱!" Mr. Kitty screeched, too excited about being remembered by Leo to control his volume. "I mean, ready."

"Sounds like he's ready, too," Tillie said. "Sounds like we're all ready. So what next?"

"We say the password and wait for the countdown," Curie said. "Just a few minutes now."

"What's the password?" Leo asked.

"The philosophers have only interpreted the world in various ways," Curie said. "The point is to change it." A voice over the elevator's speaker system started softly counting down the last half a minute before the start of their mission.

And while the elevator fell into motion, Tillie added one more thing. "Not just to change it," she said. "But for the better."

The doors opened, and everyone ran to their assigned tasks while Mr. Kitty rolled on his back in excitement, kicked his legs in the air, jumped up, then dashed out to follow them for the fun.

🐱 🦋 🐱

LXXXII. Sonya

Burning, horrible pain. That's all she knew. Burning, horrible pain.

It started right there at the tips of her fingers, which was especially strange considering the fact that she had no fingers left on that hand to feel anything. She had no hand at all. No wrist to connect it to the half of her forearm that wasn't even there. But still, all of her nonexistent parts throbbed with burning, horrible pain.

The sensation emanated up through her elbow—more painful than any knock of the funny bone and only getting worse—out to the rest of her body in turn. The rest of her *real* body. The parts of her body that she still had left attached to herself—whatever *herself* was, that is, she was having some difficulty deciding what was or wasn't a part of herself with her missing limbs being the only sensation that she could feel. She moaned and she groaned, holding onto her right shoulder with her left hand—the one that was still attached—and rolling around on the floor of the elevator, but she didn't scream or cry. She could give herself that much. In the burning, horrible beginning she didn't scream or cry.

The old man rolled around on the floor of the elevator along with Sonya, gasping and screaming and crying out in his own painful Hell, reaching for the cat who was now nothing just as Sonya reached out for her arm that had disappeared along with it, reaching with a stump that could never grasp anything ever again. And as they both bemoaned the unlikely and painful safety that they had been thrust into, the elevator's voice reminded them that they weren't dead yet, weren't done fighting, and still needed a safer space.

"Doors opening," the voice said. "Evacuate elevator car in thirty seconds or suffer fatal consequences. Evacuate elevator car in twenty-nine seconds or suffer fatal consequences. Evacuate elevator car in twenty-eight seconds or suffer fatal consequences…" And so on and so on.

But Sonya didn't care. Not about anything but the horrible, burning pain in her phantom arm. She didn't care about the pitiful, still-crying old man who was being dragged out of the elevator by some of the people who Sonya had just helped evacuate. She didn't care about the comrade and partner—whose name Sonya still didn't know—who had been lost in that very evacuation. And she didn't care if she ended up crushed into a singularity along with that same partner, the old man's cat, and all the walls of Outland. At least that way she might forget the horrible, burning pain that was flowing all throughout her body from its source in thin air where her arm used to be.

Soon, the elevator had counted down to ten seconds, the people had disembarked the old man, and they began struggling against Sonya to pull her out of the car, too. Sonya struggled right back against her saviours, though, not wanting to move at all, until she couldn't take any more pain and passed out cold, finally to forget the throbbing fire that consumed her body for the slightest moment, but only at the price of replacing it with nightmares of hanging chains—like stalactites and stalagmites, going in both directions, up and down, despite any objections from the laws of physics—burning flames, and a horrible flickering Hellscape.

Sonya fluttered in and out of consciousness. One moment, she was struggling against her saviours on the elevator floor while the voice on the speaker counted down to her death, and the next, she was moaning and crying on the cold concrete outside, the rumble and groan of worlds falling apart—or maybe falling back together again, as it was—going on all around her even if she didn't recognize it as such at the time. Then she was on a stretcher somehow, being carried somewhere, until the stress of remaining conscious was too much and she fell back again into the nightmare dreamscape that represented her subconscious pain.

And then she was home. Forever if she were lucky. And not home home, either, but The Bar. Her true home.

She was lying face up on the bar itself, trying to recognize what she couldn't see, but between reality and Hell there could never be anything resembling true understanding. Shadows of silhouettes of projections of faces were all she could make out from the bodies that towered over her, poking and prodding, trying to heal but only producing more pain and anxiety. Then mumbled words. Arguing. And action. One more sharp, piercing pain in the stump where her arm should have been, then instead of horrible, fiery burning, a cooling, icy numbness flowed in one wave over her body until Sonya could feel and do nothing but fall into a restful, dreamless sleep.

Sometime later she awoke with a jolt—as if she had been dreaming of falling even though she hadn't been dreaming at all—lying on the bar and surrounded by darkness. She groaned and tried to stand, but her muscles wouldn't work so she just kind of flopped like a fish.

Another voice in the room groaned from down on the floor below the bar, then up stood a dark form to say, "Sonya. Are you alright? It's me. *Lights*."

And the lights turned on to reveal Olsen, hair messy and eyes puffy like she'd been sleeping. Tillie couldn't remember how long it had been since they had talked to one another—she was having difficulty comprehending time at all after drifting in and out of consciousness like she had been—but she was certainly happy to see an old friend.

"I— I waited—" Olsen stammered. "I hope you don't mind. I mean— I— I can leave if you want me to."

"And be alone on Christmas?" Sonya asked, trying to smile but having a hard time of it. "It is still Christmas, isn't it?"

Olsen checked her watch, rubbing her face and yawning. "I— *uh*… Nope. I mean, *yes*. Yes, it is still Christmas. Not even late. I bet Ellie's party's still going on."

"Ellie's party," Sonya said, sitting up as she remembered it, surprised that she could actually move again, even if she did it too fast and ended up dizzy from the motion. "We should go."

"I—*uh*— *We*? I mean, do you think you feel up to it?" Olsen asked.

And again, Sonya was ecstatic to see her. Olsen was a reminder of an easier, happier past. A past before revolutions and evacuations and…

Sonya reached out a hand toward Olsen, trying to brush the hair out of her face or softly caress her cheek, but the hand didn't reach. It wasn't there. She wasn't holding out a hand at all but a short stump of an arm that ended in a disgusting crook at her elbow. Seeing it brought Sonya to tears again at the same time that it sent a shock of fiery red pain all throughout her body—phantom arm included. It felt like an aftershock of the horrible burning she had experienced when losing the arm in the first place.

Sonya gasped and cried, covering her stump with her *real* hand, and Olsen grabbed her in a hug, squeezing tight enough to help

Sonya forget the pain.

"I'm sorry. *I'm sorry, I'm sorry, I'm sorry, I'm sorry*," Olsen begged, starting to cry a little herself and not letting go of Sonya until they were both done shedding tears..

"About what?" Sonya asked, sniffling and wiping her nose.

"I don't know," Olsen said. "That I wasn't there to prevent this from happening to you. That I've never been there for you in all the time you've been doing this. That I fell onto the wrong side of the fight when I was young and haven't been able to come all the way back since then. I'm sorry about everything stupid I've ever done, essentially. So, I'm sorry."

"Well then I'm sorry, too," Sonya said. "Now, here. Help me up. I want to get to Ellie's before everyone leaves. You said they're still partying, right?"

"Ellie said they'd be there." Olsen shrugged. "She said you'd have to take the long way, though. No elevators."

"It's still in the same place?" Sonya asked, pouring two shots out of a bottle behind the bar and handing one to Olsen.

"Just a couple of extra blocks away," Olsen said. She took her shot and gasped. "So I'm told. The world is too different out there, though. I hardly recognize it."

"*Good*," Sonya said, patting Olsen on the back and leading her to the exit. "That was the entire reason we did this."

And the world certainly was different outside. *World* singular now that all the Outlands—and Inland—had come back together again. Sonya thought she had learned what change looked like when the walls between Five and Six were torn down the first time, but this… This was on a scale magnitudes greater.

There were no more skyscrapers that were too tall to exist, stacked three or four high. The buildings weren't squished into impossibly dense blocks, holding more weight than any foundation should have been able to hold. She could actually see a big chunk of the darkening sky and beyond that a few twinkling, dim stars.

Sonya and Olsen walked along in silent awe, staring at the sights, and neither of them spoke again until they were at the entrance to Ellie's apartment building. By the look of the flickering candlelights all up and down the stairwells and the sound of laughing voices coming from the floors above, it seemed like the party was still going on.

Sonya smiled at Olsen one more time before opening the door. "Thanks for coming with me," she said. "And for being there when I woke up. I hope you'll finally think about staying with us in the future." And then she didn't wait for Olsen to respond, instead leading her by the hand up the stairs to Ellie's floor where the party was spilling out into the hall and up and down the stairwells.

Anne was the first to notice Sonya's arrival, calling out, "*Sonya*! You're alright! Someone get Ellie out here." but losing her bright smile when she saw Sonya's arm—or lack thereof. "*Damn*," she said, looking at her feet instead of Sonya's stump. "Are you alright?"

"I'm alive," Sonya said, hiding her phantom arm behind her back and not really looking forward to the questions and stares that she hadn't considered when she had dragged Olsen to the party in the first place. "And happy for it."

"Oh—*uh*. I'm Olsen," Olsen said, inserting herself into the conversation and giving Sonya a look like she understood that Sonya wanted to change the subject away from her arm. "Nice to meet you— *uh*…"

"Anne," Anne said, shaking Olsen's hand. "I used to work in food production, but *now I'm free of that*!" She yelled the second part, and everyone in the halls around them hooted and hollered and cheered, helping Sonya forget the still subtly pulsing pains of her phantom arm for just a moment.

"So— Y'all…" Olsen stammered, still uncomfortable but at least making an effort. "Y'all are responsible for these explosions and the evacuation and all that?"

Anne chuckled and shot Sonya a look. "Who is this again?" she asked. Then to Olsen, "And for the food you'll eat, housing you'll live in, and medical care you'll receive as time moves forward. We're responsible for everything now. So get used to it."

It was right about then that news had made its way to Ellie and Ellie had made her way out to the hall to pull Sonya into a hug that was tighter than any the newly armless revolutionary had ever felt. Sonya let out a few quick tears and wiped them away, not even mad at Ellie for picking up her stump to poke and prod at it afterward.

"There's my freedom fighter," Ellie said, sticking her fingers through Sonya's phantom hand to touch her in places she should never have been touched. "How does this feel?"

"*Weird*," Sonya said, pulling her arm away. "Could you not?"

"No. I *cannot* not," Ellie said, grabbing Sonya's arm to poke it a few more times. "I need to make sure everything's healing fine so you don't bleed out when I pump you full of eggnog tonight." She laughed and dropped Sonya's arm, pulling her in for one more quick hug before saying, "Starting now. You do want some, don't you?"

"Well, yeah," Sonya said. "It's Christmas. Of course, I—"

"And what about you?" Ellie asked Olsen, not waiting to hear the rest of what Sonya had to say. By the sound of her voice and the grin on her face, Sonya could tell that Ellie had been drinking her own eggnog for some time already. "Don't think I can't see you hiding over there."

"Olsen, ma'am," Olsen said, holding out a hand for her to shake and getting a hug instead. "And—*uh*. Yeah. *Sure*. Some eggnog would be great. It's alcoholic, I assume."

"Is there any other kind?" Ellie asked, laughing and leading them through the packed party to one of the back rooms—there were people in every room up and down the hall it seemed—where Vicki and Alena were sitting at a table, telling the story of their experience to a group of people who all sat at the same table or stood around the room listening, one of whom got up and allowed Sonya their seat— with some argument from Sonya, of course, she didn't want any special treatment on account of her arm, but not too much arguing because she didn't want to make a scene and interrupt Vic's story, either.

"So, everything was going as planned," Vic was saying, then for Sonya's sake she backtracked a little and added, "We were evacuating a hospital, you see, so most of the patients were in serious or critical condition, and none of them could just get up and walk onto the elevator for themselves. Right.

"But it was just Alena and I on the hospital floor, you know, directing the doctors toward whichever elevator they were supposed to get on and helping them wheel the patients out of there as fast as we could without killing anyone. So we'd load two beds and two doctors onto one elevator and send it. Then we'd load up the next elevator just the same and send it along, too, you know. Then we'd have to do some waiting until the first elevator got back and we could reload it and send it off again. You get the picture. And so on and so on we went while Tor and Katie were on the other side of the elevator shafts, making sure everyone got themselves unloaded safely and speedily then sent the elevators back in a reasonable time.

"We had just sent the penultimate elevator load with five minutes still left to spare, and Alena ran around to do one final check of the floor, finding no one, while I stayed with the last patient who was sleeping in the last bed before our mission could be considered a complete success, and of course, the elevators—*both of them*—took forever to return.

"Alena started checking her watch after a minute had gone by, and neither of us had to say a word to know what the other was thinking."

"*Fuck*," Alena said with a chuckle that sent all the listeners laughing with her. "This is not good."

Vic waited for the laughter to die down before going on. "*Exactly*. And of course, shit got worse. All of a sudden, the meter and monitors on the patient's bed started making all kinds of loud noises, speaking in a language I didn't understand, and instantly I regretted having sent all the doctors along already. For my part I was paralyzed with panic, but Alena over there reacted fast, grabbing those paddle shock things that doctors use."

"The defibrillator," Alena corrected her.

"You see?" Vic said, laughing. "I don't even know the name of the thing, much less how to use one, but somehow Alena here picks 'em right up, telling me to get my hands off, and she shocks the patient back to life for long enough that we can get on the elevator and take the patient to someone who actually knew what they were doing."

"And that patient did live," Alena added, blushing, at the end. "Just in case anyone was wondering."

"A success it was, dears," Ellie said, holding her glass up. "To Vic and Alena's courage in the face of harrowing odds."

The whole room cheered with one another—or at least with those close enough—and drank to that. Even Sonya smiled while she tapped her glass with Olsen's, Ellie's, and Alena's in turn before sipping the sweet spiked eggnog.

"It's so great to hear stories of successes," Ellie said to everyone. "All of you performed so perfectly. We have a lot of work ahead of us still, of course, but looking at how far we've already come in just these few short hours fills me with certainty that—*together*—we can get it done."

Everyone cheersed and drank again.

"*Now...* Who's next?" Ellie went on, looking around the room as if she didn't have anyone particular in mind even though Sonya was sneakingly suspicious that she'd be next. "So many brave heroes here in one room right now. What about you, Olsen?" Ellie said, chuckling.

"No, no," Olsen said, shaking her head and looking at her feet, truly embarrassed. "I'm just a stupid coward." And Sonya felt pity for her, but Vic interrupted the feeling by pounding on the table and chanting, "Sonya. Son-ya. *Son-ya...*" until everyone else joined in with her, Olsen included.

"The audience has spoken," Ellie said, laughing. "Sonya, dear. We know you have a story to tell. You're wearing it on your sleeve. So, let's hear it."

"What? You mean this?" Sonya asked, standing up and holding her stump out over the table for everyone to see.

"Gross!" "*Awesome.*" "Let me touch it." Actual poking and prodding just as Ellie had done. The reactions ran the gamut. And honestly, they helped Sonya feel just a little less self-conscious about her phantom arm—even, and maybe especially, the reactions of those people who thought it was truly disgusting.

"Yes, please," Vic said, literally getting on her knees to beg Sonya. "Tell us. Satiate us with your story. It is Christmas, dear. *Please.* Continue our revelry for as long as you can."

"*Well...*" Sonya said, feigning uncertainty even though she *was* ready to tell her story after all. If she was ever going to do it, this was going to be the best audience she could ever hope for, so why not?

"We were clearing out one floor of a residential building," she said. "Me and my partner whose name I still don't know." And probably never would, Sonya could have added, but she didn't want to spoil the ending.

"Rosalind, dear," Ellie informed her. "I checked after we had finished operating on you."

"Okay, then," Sonya went on, fighting tears for some reason now that she knew the poor lost woman's name. The audience sat on in silence, sipping their drinks and simply waiting for her to continue. Sonya got the feeling that they would have waited all night and into the morning to hear what she had to say, and something about the thought helped her swallow down her tears and keep telling her story. "So, *Rosalind* and I were evacuating a residential building. Or just one floor. *Or whatever.*"

Sonya took a sip of her eggnog to relax her throat before going on. "Well, just like with Vic and Alena over there." Sonya pointed with her stump to add to the effect. She was a practiced storyteller, having told many a ghost story as a child—not to mention the tales she'd told and heard as a bartender—and she always knew exactly when to turn the flashlight on and shine it on her face to induce the most screams. "Everything was going perfectly fine at first.

"There were some loud sirens and flashing lights—which Vic and Alena might not have had to endure considering they were in a hospital—but the bright flashing nonsense helped us convince the residents of the seriousness of the situation, moving them along faster than we ever could have without the noise. And just like with Vic and Alena, we cleared everyone down to the last resident before any snags occurred.

"Our problem was a stubborn old man. So, when he wouldn't come with us of his own free will, I lifted him over my shoulder like a blackout drunk at the Bar, and I carried him into the elevator myself. We were running out of time, and I wasn't gonna let the old man die, so that was that.

"But of course, that wasn't that. That was when the old man started complaining that we had forgotten his cat—which we never even knew had existed in the first place so there was no way we could have forgotten it, okay. But the old man was adamant either way, so while I made sure he stayed on the elevator, my partner—*uh*—Rosalind, went to find the cat.

"The elevator was really counting down by that time. And it seemed like the sirens had gotten louder and the lights brighter, even if they hadn't. I had one hand fighting the old man to keep him safe on the elevator despite his every effort to put himself back in danger." She acted it out, putting her stump arm back on the chest of Olsen who stood behind her, listening close, and Sonya was comforted to notice that Olsen didn't recoil from the touch of her stump as Sonya continued the story. "And the other hand was reaching out and out…" She reached her still whole hand out over the table and everyone in the room stared at it as she spoke. "Trying to grasp that poor sweet kitty who Rosalind was holding outstretched to me. And just as I felt his fur graze my fingertips, *the doors slammed shut.*" She switched her physical hand and her phantom one, reaching out with the nothingness instead, and reveled in the gasped awe she received in return—just like when she was a kid. "Taking my arm, the cat, and Rosalind all to wherever it is that imploded Walker-Haley field generators go when they die."

The table reacted with stunned silence. Olsen, too, but she sort of massaged Sonya's shoulders when the latter sat back down from telling her story.

Then Trudy came in, breaking the silence with news of Aldo on the beach he had escaped to years ago—a beach that was a lot more crowded now that the walls had come down—and in that moment, having been given the space and time not only to tell her story but to have it intently and empathetically listened to, and being able to hear similar stories of others going through the same or worse, Sonya felt more confident than ever that she could not only survive, but thrive, even despite the accident she had endured. And beyond that, she truly believed that they had finally built a system that was superior to the barbarism that they had all been living through, one that would last for as long as they continued to work together and ensure that it did.

LXXXIII. Muna

What the Hell was this?

What the— Was this Hell?

Last she remembered she was tied to a chair, listening to that woman go on and on about someone's death somewhere. Sitting in the darkness. Listening. Waiting…

And what? What happened next?

Fwip qiw1. The sound of a vacuum. The quick short breeze. And the worlds had changed even though she hadn't moved.

She wasn't in darkness anymore. She wasn't in Six at all. She was on a stage, still tied to the chair, listening to the old woman rant at a sea of tuxedoed owners. But they weren't listening, instead stuffing their fat faces full of food. She recognized the place. The Feast Hall in Inland. A place she'd been to a long time ago. But there was no time to reminisce, because soon the old woman's rant was over and she was not pointing her gun at the owners.

Pop. Pop pop. Pop pop pop. Pop pop pop pop pop. Pop pop pop pop pop pop pop.

A gunshot. Two. More?

She didn't know. But she did know pain. A dear friend by that time, pain. It was everywhere. Not just in the newly formed hole in her chest, slowly leaking the life giving red out of her body, but everywhere. Every cell. Every molecule. Every quark and string. You name it. Pain tore her apart, integrated itself into her being, and put her back together again, a writhing miserable mass that wouldn't want to go on living even if it could.

What else was there?

She died. She gave up. Gave in to the pain. Let it win. Resistance was futile, and she knew that better than anyone, so why would she think of resisting? She didn't even think.

Amaru up above had called upon her, Muna Mondragon, as a little girl in Outland One, and Muna had risen to the occasion. Not only had she joined the Force, she had become the best in the business, the youngest Chief of Protectors in history. And now, even as a Chief, she had been brave enough to put her own life on the line, walking an

Officer's beat in Outland Six where she had been ambushed, kidnapped, and publicly assassinated in front of the owners' very own Christmas Feast. It was a classic story meant for a hero's legend, just like the ones that Muna had learned when she was little, but *she* had lived it in real life. She was no doubt assured a place in the highest ranks of Amaru's Protector Force—if she believed in any of that anymore. The question then became, did she believe in any of that anymore? And did it really matter?

She had no choice but to find out.

Her heart stopped. One of the bullets that the old woman had fired entered through her chest, messed the place up, leaving the muscle *out of order*, and came back out again on the other side, without even closing the door on the way out. There was no fighting that if she tried, so Muna Mondragon died.

From her schooling—and from her experiences of the deaths of others—she knew that her entire body would be giving up, releasing everything she held back in life, just as her heart already had. But she couldn't tell if she had shit herself or not by that point. She couldn't tell anything at all. The universe was getting too bright and too dark, both at the same time, until she couldn't tell the difference between the two and ended up whiting/blacking out—or something like it, she couldn't see, feel, dream, or think, so she didn't really have any word at all for what had happened to her.

Time drifted by. At least she can only assume it did. There was no way to know for sure with no senses to experience by, but she had never known time to stop before, so she figured it had done what it always did and kept running. Then she was sure that it had, because suddenly, she woke up.

Well, no. Maybe she wasn't sure about that. Maybe she still wasn't awake. But she could think again. At least she thought she could think. She thought therefore she was thinking. Or something like that. She thought.

Thinking down, she began to feel again, too. Not all at once, though. First her feet and the ground beneath them, wiggling her little toes one by one. Somehow, she was standing. And she was wearing her boots. Had she been wearing them before she...

Next, she felt her head. The helmet upon it. Heavy was the head that wore the Lord's crown. Heavier still the head that wore the screaming neon samurai facemask. Even now she was forced to wear it. Now after she had…

And so on and so on. Hands in gloves, legs in cargo pants, body in plated armor. She thought she could think, she felt like she could feel, then she saw what there was to see. Was it a dream?

Her eyes, no longer blind, took a moment to adjust to her helmet's cameras just as the cameras took their time to adjust to her eyes. When all parts of her—because by that time the helmet and its cameras truly seemed to be a part of her Amaru-given body—had done their necessary adjusting to one another, she could see a full three hundred and sixty degrees in every direction around her. More than that. In each of those directions she could see in three hundred sixty degrees at a perpendicular angle. Effectively her vision was a sphere and she could see in all directions at once. She didn't have to look down to see that her hands did in fact move when she willed them to—as shiny and translucent as her hands were, she had to work to convince herself that they were in fact her hands, but she didn't have to look down to see them—and she didn't have to look up to see that the sky was dark and the stars were brighter than she had ever thought they could be. She could see the city around her, and a long strip of green that she could only compare to the Neutral Ground. She could even see straight down through her body to the grassy ground underneath her booted feet. She could see everything all around her all at once.

What else could she do but give her new legs a walk? Sure enough, they seemed to work just fine, but the effect of movement was nauseating with her vision the way that it was. Every time she stepped forward it seemed like she was going forward in all directions at once, every part of everything she could see—grass, cityscape, sky, herself, *everything*—seemed to move closer to her at the same time.

She was startled by the sensation at first, and disoriented. She tried to step backwards to get her bearings, but of course, she was stepping backwards in every direction, too, so again everything everywhere seemed to get closer to her.

She tried to sit down and cry, give up again like she had when she died, but her legs wouldn't let her do even that. Were they even her legs anymore? No matter what Muna tried, all they did was step forward. Standing still didn't even work any more. All she could do was take step by step closer to every single thing in existence.

So, step she did. Step, step, step, step, step, one foot in front of another, trying to focus on that one point of her perception that went straight up and down the Neutral Grounds instead of on any of the infinite other perspectives she had going in every direction she could see: every single direction at once. Despite her efforts to see straight ahead, she became so dizzy that she tried to vomit, but again her legs would only let her keep on walking forward towards everything.

On and on and on, further and further and closer and closer to everything in every direction she went until she started to get the hang of it and she could finally focus on that one single spot all the way down the Neutral Grounds which was where she was actually trying to go.

Now it seemed like she was making progress. How much time had that taken? She couldn't quite remember and the stars above her didn't seem to be changing position.

Oh, no. The thought of the stars made her lose her concentration, and she had to fight through more dizziness and nausea to get back to the focus that she had so recently found.

What next, though? She was intent on the Neutral Grounds again, but she couldn't stop walking if she wanted to. And she did want to. She tried again but there was no use. She just kept walking, walking, walking until she didn't anymore.

A door. Golden but still obviously a transport bay. Her hands reached out to open it, but nothing. The doors were sealed shut. And finally, her legs gave her the rest she had been hoping for, struggling for, praying for, and they let her sit down, her back to the elevator doors.

Sitting now, finally able to rest and not moving, she could see the world without wanting to throw up. She was on eye level with the ground, and there along the green grass of the Neutral Grounds were her footprints in thick, red, almost waxy blood. She reached down to touch the nearest footprint with her finger, to see if it really was as thick as it looked, and when she pulled her hand back up she was holding a red poinsettia.

What the Hell was this?

What the— Was this Hell?

She tried to smell the poinsettia but couldn't figure out where her nose was, and that's when she had had enough. Enough of all of it. She took off her helmet, hoping it would fix her vision, but nothing changed. She could still see in every direction at once. She didn't know what else to do, but her hands didn't stop there. They started unlacing her boots and tossing them one after another in all directions at the same time.

There, she thought to herself when both boots were just little dots floating out of sight. That's much better. But her hands still didn't stop. They took off her socks and plated armor, even her undershirt and pants, until she was down to her underwear, and on beyond that until she was peeling her skin off of her muscles and letting it drift away, floating in the wind like cellular dust. On she went through the muscles, through fat and meat alike, bones and organs. Layer by layer, piece by piece, cell by cell, her hands stripped her—and thus themselves—naked until there was nothing left. But somehow there was still her.

But somehow there was still her.

But somehow there was still her. What was she?

And then there wasn't her. The brightness came back. The darkness. Quick and sudden like an explosion. Did time stop again? Was it ever flowing?

Who knew?

Who was?

Was she?

☙ � ☙

She awoke in cuffs and manacles, chained to the chair she was sitting on and shrouded in darkness. Not too dark, though. Nothing like what she now knew was possible. She could even see enough to recognize that she had only two perspectives again—one for each eye—rather than the infinitely spherical point of view she had been dealing with. But beyond that, nothing. Dark forms. Shadows. Maybe a table here closer to her and a wall further off. Nothing was certain anymore. She wasn't quite sure anything ever could be certain again.

And then the brightness came. Again, not too bright—well, yes, literally too bright for her to see in this instance, but not as bright as the brightness she had now experienced. She squinted her eyes against it. Held them closed tight, but still her eyelids were red hot. She had to fight the urge to hide her head under her arms because she didn't want to give her interrogator the upper hand so soon. And she knew this was definitely an interrogation. These were the exact tactics

Muna herself used when questioning a suspect.

Whoever it was, her interrogator took their time—just as Muna would have—but it didn't matter how long they waited. Muna had spent plenty of her own time behind just such spotlights in her rise through the ranks of the Protector Force so she was well experienced in withstanding the hotbox.

Eventually her interrogator realized who they were dealing with and out came a voice, not through speakers, but naturally—as naturally as any voice could sound coming through those modulated facemasks, at least, which was surprisingly natural for someone who's been on the Force for as long as Muna had been—as if someone had been there in the room with her the entire time, hiding behind the darkness and the light alike, waiting for Muna to give in—which she would never do.

"What are you doing here, [Muna/Mona/Officer/Sergeant/Captain/Chief/Ms./Mondragon]?" the inhuman voice demanded, using all the names and ranks that Muna's ever gone by all at the same time.

"Where am I?" Muna asked, still squinting her red-hot eyelids against the too bright lights. "How am I supposed to know?"

"You know where you are," the voice said, seeming to crackle and groan even more than normal. The effect was utterly terrifying. Like being roared at by a glitched out ghost in the machine who wanted to eat your brain and use it for processing power. Muna now truly understood why the helmets were built with the effect. "Don't lie to yourself."

"An interrogation chamber, obviously. But where? Whose?"

"*Ha ha ha!*" Whatever noise that voice made, if it can even be called laughing, it should be made illegal. "Yours, of course. Who else?"

Muna didn't know how to respond, and even if she did, she wasn't sure her interrogator would have been able to hear her over their own terrifying cackling.

"How many people have you killed in the culling?" the voice demanded, stopping its laughter all of a sudden, and the absence of laughter was almost as unsettling as its presence. As if fear of the laugh returning was worse than the laugh itself.

"How many people have I— What is this?" Muna asked.

"How many officers have you culled?" the voice demanded

again, shortening the wordspan as if counting down—to what, Muna didn't want to know.

"How many— I—" She couldn't count them. She didn't have to. They were neatly recorded in her files so she didn't have to think about any of those people ever again. She wasn't responsible for them. The Force was. And she wasn't about to start thinking about them now just because this bodiless voice asked her to from behind its blinding lights. "I don't know."

"Who was the first?" the voice demanded.

"*I don't know*," Muna repeated, but she did know. Of course, she did. She had still been a Captain. It was her first rookie class. She had teamed up with Pardy and *Rabbit* and had almost fucked the whole thing up—or more accurately, Pardy had tried to fuck it up for her—but her ability to stay cool and handle the consequences before they got out of control had been what propped her up in the eyes of her superiors, and soon she was lead culler for her district every single quarter, on the fast track to Chiefdom.

"Who?" the voice demanded.

"I don't know," Muna repeated, knowing it was impossible for her to hold out forever.

The voice did have a body after all. Hands at least. Fists more likely, but Muna heard them slamming on a metal table and she knew she had to answer.

"*Rabbit*, okay. *Officer Jefferson*. Are you happy?"

"Did *Rabbit* deserve to die?" the voice asked, and the way it said his name, *Rabbit*, was offensive somehow, disgusting.

"I don't know," Muna said, struggling against her chains, but they were so tight she couldn't even move. "Who am I to say? Can't you turn off that light?"

The light went out, but Muna knew not to be relieved. It was just a ploy. An attempt to get her to open her eyes then turn on the lights again and blind her. She wouldn't give them the satisfaction. She held her eyes closed tight despite the fact that her eyelids had gone from red hot to cooling black.

"Did any of them?" the voice asked at a quieter volume, less modulated, like a normal protector's voice.

"Does anyone?" Muna asked.

"Did you?" the voice answered her question with a question, taking a page out of Muna's interrogation playbook.

"What do you mean *did* I?" she demanded, struggling again but still unable to move. "*Do* I! *Do* I!?"

"Do you?" the voice asked.

And Muna didn't know how to answer. Maybe she did. "Maybe I do."

"You *did*," the voice said. "And maybe you do, too."

Muna was more confused than ever. She didn't know what to say. All she could do was fight against her chains, but they seemed to get tighter and tighter with her every attempt to move. The voice left the room without another word, just the opening and closing of a door and the exit of a protector's silhouette. Not soon after, two more protector silhouettes came in to wordlessly unchain Muna while she begged them to speak.

"Who are you? Where am I? How'd I get here?" she pleaded, but neither Officer said a word until she was fully unchained, then one of them said, "Stand up."

She stood. One of the Officers took her chair out of the room and the other her interrogator's chair. Then they came back in to take the table and close the door behind them. Muna tried to open the door and follow them, but all of a sudden, the floor fell out from underneath her. She was in a transport bay of some kind, and when the floor stopped falling, the whole wall slid open like an elevator door to reveal the pale, boring suburbia of Outland One.

Muna stepped out of the elevator onto the lamplit path, and each new square of the sidewalk lit up like a disco floor whenever she stepped on it, leaving a trail of light in her wake. On and on she walked, brightening the scenery with every few steps she took, until she came upon a tree that she recognized from her childhood, a tree that she used to love—and sometimes hate—to climb.

As she walked closer, she realized there was a little girl climbing the tree, and a gang of children chasing her up it, calling her names and yelling mean things. What were they all doing out there so far past curfew? Muna was about to go lecture them when she was interrupted by their singing:

> *Mona, the moaner.*
> *More disgusting than a boner.*
> *She opened her trap, it smelled like crap*
> *And that's why her family disown her.*

It was a song Muna was familiar with, the reason she hated the name *Mona*. Those same kids used to chase her around, singing that same song, and that must have been her, a tiny little Muna Mondragon, up in the tree, crying, waiting for the little jerks to go away and leave her alone.

"Go away!" Muna yelled at them, stomping in their direction like she was trying to scare a pack of swarming dogs. "Scram! She wasn't disowned! She's an orphan!"

But the children didn't respond. They just went on singing the same lyrics over and over again while little Muna kept crying in the tree.

Mona, the moaner.
More disgusting than a boner.
She opened her trap, it smelled like crap
And that's why her family disowned her.

And when adult Muna stomped over to pick one of the children up by the collar and make them leave, her hand went straight through the kid, like he was a hologram, or a ghost—maybe a little bit of both.

Muna had sat through enough of their singing. She had been through more than enough as a child. So, she did the only thing she ever could do to get away from the neighborhood kids. She ran home. Not to the orphanage, where she had spent most of her youth imprisoned—or close enough—but back to where she had lived with her family before her parents had been killed on duty in Outland Six. Even if she had no memories of the few short years that she had lived there as a baby, it was still the place that she most considered home.

The way from her favorite tree to home was exactly the same as she remembered it, for better or for worse. She was even treated to a visit from the black cat she always used to chase—and was never able to catch. He ran across the path, lighting a block of the sidewalk up and disappearing on the other side before she could even react. And then there it was: her house.

It looked exactly like every other house she had passed on her way there. Every house in Outland One looked exactly the same: cut out of a single-story ranch style mold that came in left-handed or right-handed depending on which side of the entrance the kitchen was on—

left-handed for Muna's house.

She approached slowly, trying to take it all in, to remember the bushes out front as they looked when she was young—taller, more spacious, a secret garden to hide under and inside of until all the bad things in all the worlds all went away—but everything seemed smaller to her going back again, less protective. That is until the front door creaked open and out walked her mom and dad, looking as young and healthy as they did in the photographs that formed Muna's only memories of their appearances.

"Munya, my dear," her dad said, climbing down the front stoop to embrace and hug his daughter. "It's so nice to finally see you again."

"You look beautiful, sweetheart," her mom said, joining in on the hugs and kisses. "More beautiful than I ever could have hoped for."

"I— But—" Muna stammered. "*Mom... Dad...*"

"*Munya,*" her dad repeated.

"What is it, dear?" her mom asked, concerned.

"I— *Uh...* You're supposed to be..."

"Taller?" her dad said, trying to make a joke but failing miserably. "Handsomer? *Smarterer*? I am, honey. All three."

"We're supposed to be what, dear?" her mom asked, chuckling at the silly joke.

And Muna finally just said it: "*Dead.*"

"No, dear. Not dead." Her dad said, chuckling at his joke before he even told it. "I'm dad. Nice to meet you. *Ho ho huh.*"

"Dead?" her mom said, eyes wide as if she hadn't known.

"Yes. Both of you," Muna said.

"Then what am I doing here?" her dad asked, looking at his hands like he just noticed them.

"What are you doing here?" her mom asked, looking at Muna the same way.

"Oh, well... I don't know." Muna said. "I..."

"Are you supposed to be dead, too?" her dad asked, and her mom slapped him on the arm.

"Don't say that," she said. "Now, dead or not, I'm going in to finish cooking dinner, and if you two don't come in to help me, you can be certain you'll both be dead by the time we're done eating." She stormed inside, slamming the screen door behind her.

Muna's dad shrugged. "Well, you heard your mother," he said. "Dead or alive, she's the boss. So, let's do it." And he went inside, too.

Muna didn't know what to do. Was she dead? Did it matter? But she didn't have time to think about that. For now, she just wanted to help cook dinner, enjoy a meal with her parents, and catch up on lost time.

& ✻ ✁

LXXXIV. The Scientist

The speech went well. So, the Scientist had that going for them, which was nice. But then there was after the speech, and that definitely wasn't.

Anna wasn't supposed to go that far, killing a protector on stage. Was she? At least the Scientist didn't think so. Then again, they had been distracted doing their useless $0.\overline{N}$ work so there was no telling. Maybe Rosalind had agreed to the whole thing, assassination and all, and the Scientist just didn't know about it. That was another reason for the Scientist to curse themself about wasting so much time trying to make that stupid system work for the owners. Well, it wouldn't ever. For as long as profits existed, there'd never be enough money in wages to pay for everything on the market, so the equations would never add up. And Anna would have always done whatever it was she wanted to do, whether Rosalind had agreed to it or not. She already had.

The Scientist had stayed behind after their speech, waiting for the inevitable to happen and holding the door back to Four open for Haley, but after the explosion and before they could escape, out came Anna with that Chief Mondragon tied to a chair. The gunshots went off and the Scientist ducked out of sight before they could see who the shots were fired at, but they had a guess, and soon they didn't have to, because Haley and another secretary came running up, carrying Mr. Walker and Huey, respectively, both owners bleeding from dangerous looking bullet wounds in their chests.

"They're shot," Haley said, not even breathing heavily despite the gigantic dead weight of Mr. Walker's body flung over her shoulder. "They need our help."

"*Pffft*. Not him," the Scientist said, nodding at Mr. Walker.

"If you want me to carry Lord Douglas any further, you'll let us both go," the other secretary said, struggling against Huey's relatively lighter frame.

"She's with me," Haley said to the Scientist, then to the other secretary, "C'mon." And they carried their burdens past the Scientist, through the hole in the Walker-Haley fields, and back into the lab where they laid each owner, still bleeding and groaning, on two tables that Popeye had cleared by dumping all the glass off of them to break on the floor.

"And clean that up," the Scientist demanded of Popeye as they crossed the room to stand at Huey's side, not really sure how to help him. "What do we do?"

"I don't know," Haley said. "I'm not a doctor."

"Me neither," the Scientist said. "I'm barely a scientist."

"We need a shot," the other secretary said, blotting Mr. Walker's head with a towel. "One of those gray goop injections, or whatever." Mr. Walker was looking pretty bad himself, doing a lot more coughing and gurgling than *Lord Douglas* was, but at least he was fighting against his death. The way Huey was lying still, not moving a single muscle, it didn't seem to matter to him whether he was alive or dead.

"A what?" Haley asked, not sounding as concerned as the other secretary was.

"An injection. A *shot*," the secretary said. "I don't know. Can't you just call a doctor?"

"Not really," the Scientist said. "I mean, we could probably call one, but for all intents and purposes, there's no elevator service to get them here, so there's really no point."

"What about a printer?" the secretary asked. "They can make anything, right?"

"Printers run on the same system as the elevators," the Scientist said. "So, no."

"This one's trying to say something," Haley said, nodding at Popeye who had stopped sweeping to wave his arm at them, making all kinds of weird hand motions.

"I can never understand Popeye," the Scientist said. "I'm not sure how he understands us, either."

"There's something in that drawer," the secretary said, rushing over to dig through it. "Maybe the shot we're looking for."

The Scientist went to help search through the drawers, but Haley just stood there, staring down at Huey and shaking her head like she didn't care any more than he did whether he died or not. The Scientist and the other secretary both dug through strange tools and variously colored chemicals until, at almost the exact same time, they both held up seemingly identical vials of cloudy gray liquid to say, "I got it!"

"Too late," Haley said, shaking her head. "For our *Lord Douglas*, at least."

But Mr. Walker wasn't dead yet. He coughed up a particularly disgusting clot of blood, and it sent his secretary into even more of a panic than she had already been in. She snatched the vial from the Scientist's hand and started comparing the labels to figure out which one could save her lord.

The Scientist let her. They couldn't make out a thing on their vial's label anyway. It was like it was written in a different language, the language of chemistry, a language that the Scientist had all the interest in the world in learning, but which they had foregone studying in order to instead waste their time trying to make the stupid owners' system work for them. So, while the secretary did that, the Scientist searched through the drawer to find a syringe and have it ready when the secretary decided on which vial to use.

"What the fuck does any of this mean?" the secretary demanded, looking between one vial and the other, putting each close to her face to read, as if that would help her understand the symbols any better. "Is this even English?"

"Not really," the Scientist said. "It's IUPAC nomenclature. I don't know how to decipher it any more than you do, though."

"Why do you care so much?" Haley asked, finally leaving Huey's side. "Mr. Walker treated you like shit, didn't he? I mean, that's how he treated me when I worked for him. But I guess I could be wrong. Maybe he likes you more than he liked me."

"Oh, he treats me like shit," Haley said, still fretting over which vial was which. "You're not wrong about that."

"Then why?" Haley repeated. "Why not just let him die?"

"Well, he's my lord," the secretary said, disregarding the vials for a moment, despite another bout of coughing from Mr. Walker and what sounded like a plea for help. "He pays my wages," she went on over him. "What am I supposed to do if he dies? I'll starve."

"He's not the owner of anything anymore," the Scientist said. "That explosion you heard at the Feast, the worlds are changed. There's only one of them, now, and Mr. Walker has no power in it."

"So why not let him die?" Haley asked again.

"*No*," the secretary said, trying to distinguish between the vials again but having difficulty concentrating. "I don't believe that."

"It doesn't require your belief," Haley said. "You'll see."

"Yeah, well, what am I supposed to do then?" the secretary asked, fumbling more desperately with the vials the more she spoke. "How will my family eat? Where am I supposed to find work now?"

"There'll be plenty of work to do yet," the Scientist said. "I assure you of that."

But Haley just shrugged. "Mr. Walker never helped feed your family in the first place," she said. "He and his friends forced billions to starve, in fact. You'll be better off without him. Don't you think so, too?" she asked, turning to the Scientist.

Haley was right about that, and the Scientist knew it. Hell, all the worlds would be better without Mr. Walker or any of the other owners in them. But the Scientist knew that they could never actively kill anyone with their own two hands—even an owner—and so they figured that they shouldn't stand by and let him die either. "I don't know," they said. "I'd probably help him if I could."

"I'm saving his life no matter what y'all say," the secretary snapped, finally deciding on a vial—at random for all the Scientist knew—and taking the syringe to fill it with the gray liquid inside. "You don't know what he'd do to me if I didn't try."

"I used to work for him," Haley said. "I think I do."

"Are you sure you got the right one?" the Scientist asked. "What if it's dangerous?"

"Better to kill him with action than inaction," the secretary said, tapping the air bubbles out of the syringe. "Here goes nothing." She held her breath and slowly inched the pointy end of the syringe closer and closer to Mr. Walker's trembling, sweaty forearm, beads of sweat pouring down her own forehead in time. She was close to puncturing his skin, maybe a millimeter away, when she sighed and drew the needle away, picking up the vials to compare their labels again. "*Ugh*. I can't do it." She sighed. "What if I kill him?"

"The world would be a better place," Haley said.

"I probably couldn't do it, either," the Scientist said. "I can't do it."

And at the same time, Rosalind, Momma BB—in a new recycled body—and Mr. Kitty all came bursting into the room—with a meow from the cat.

"Rosalind!" Haley said, crossing to hug her. "You're here.

How's the mission?"

"Mr. Kitty," the Scientist said, bending down to pet the cat who purred, rubbing his head against their ankles.

"Help me," the secretary begged, holding out the vials to the newcomers in the hopes that they could translate the labels for her. "Save him." She nodded at Mr. Walker, still somehow alive and coughing on the table.

"Could have gone better," Rosalind said, hugging Haley for a moment then releasing her to cross to the secretary and take both vials and the syringe from her. "But we're all alive now." Rosalind emptied the syringe, checked the two vials, tossed one away, and refilled the syringe with the other's contents. "Here, allow me," she said, and she jammed the needle into Mr. Walker's thigh, letting the air out of his pneumatic pants with a long *hissssssss* as she pressed down the plunger, releasing the grey liquid into Mr. Walker's greedy veins.

Mr. Walker sat up straight all of a sudden, eyes as wide as dinner plates. He coughed and gurgled and said, "I— I'm— *I'm alive*. I…" and then he fell flat on his back again, stone cold dead.

"No! What'd you do?" the secretary cried, crossing to Mr. Walker's side to comfort him in death.

Haley just kind of laughed, shaking her head, as if to say, "I told you so." without actually saying it.

"At least it wasn't your fault," the Scientist said, because they thought that's what they'd want to hear if they were in the same situation.

And Big Momma BB, with her limping gait and mismatched limbs, skin of every color that skin can be, crossed to the secretary to comfort her. "It's okay, darling," Momma BB said. "What's your name?"

"Elen," the secretary said, crying and sniffling and hugging Momma BB instead of Mr. Walker now.

"Well, Elen, you'll be better off without him," Momma BB said. "The whole world will be. I promise."

"The whole *world* will be," Rosalind repeated. "All of the worlds together again as one. And they're all ours. With no room for owners."

"What about Lord Douglas?" Haley asked, and the Scientist wasn't sure what they wanted the answer to be.

"I locked him out of resurrection," Rosalind said. "He's been

Lord for too long now. It's gone to his head. He needs time to think about what he's become, and we've got a lot of work to do. We'll discuss his resurrection again when the timing's better."

"So, you knew this was going to happen, then," the Scientist said. "The assassinations and everything."

"Of course, I did." Rosalind scoffed. "We've had this planned for decades, almost a century. Long before you were ever born. And we're not gonna let anyone stand in the way of what comes next. Even if they started out this journey on the right side of the struggle."

"You think Lord Douglas has changed sides?" the Scientist asked. "I don't know. I—"

"You've been spending your time on other tasks," Rosalind reminded the Scientist of their wastefulness. "When's the last time you even spoke to Huey? No. Trust me. I know him better than anyone. I know how he thinks. He's been an owner for too long, and now he's obsessed with possessions and control. He's had his eyes on Haley for a long time, too, and there's no telling what he could do to her. We just don't have labor power enough to rehabilitate him at this point, so we can't and we won't. Does anyone have a problem with that?"

The Scientist didn't want to know what would happen to them if they answered yes to that question, but thankfully they didn't really have a problem. Rosalind was right that the Scientist hadn't seen Lord Douglas in a long time, except on the news, and he could have changed a lot in the time that he was Lord of all the worlds.

Haley didn't seem to have a problem, either. In fact, she looked downright pleased with the decision, grinning for a moment, just long enough for the Scientist to notice. Momma BB showed no reaction. She just went on comforting Elen who broke away from Momma BB's embrace to run up and push Rosalind, getting in her face to say, "I have a problem with it. *You killed him*. You killed my boss!"

"I know you liked him," Rosalind said, hands up to defend herself but apparently not angry. "And I'm sorry for that. I truly am. But I'm not your enemy. *He was*. He was a Lord, and he had to die for the same reasons that Huey did. We can't build our new better world with them still here trying to wreck it."

"But it's not the same," Elen said, beating on Rosalind's chest. Rosalind let the poor woman land a few blows before grabbing her by the wrists to stop her. "He's not like you," Elen went on. "He's human. We can't just resurrect whenever we die."

"Now, now, dear," Momma BB said, peeling Elen off of Rosalind to pull her into another bear hug. "You'd be surprised. At his age, with his lifestyle, he's more nanobot than human—if there even is any human left in there at all."

"*Mum mumum mum mum?*" Elen asked, her voice muffled by Momma BB's big body, but BB seemed to understand.

"I know so," she said. "He'll be resurrected the same as Huey. But not until we're ready and strong enough to put them both on trial for their sins."

"The worlds really have changed," Elen said, poking her head out of Momma BB's big bear hug to catch a breath of fresh air before diving right back in.

"More than you'll ever know," Momma BB said, hugging Elen tighter.

"And there's still so much work to do to ensure that this world is better than the old worlds," Rosalind said.

"But at least the owners won't be in our way," Haley said. "*Pieces of shit*," she added under her breath.

"So, I guess we're really gonna do this, then," the Scientist said, not sure if they were starting to believe because they really could do it, or if they were starting to believe because they had no choice left but to make it true. "Let's get to work."

"First," Rosalind said. "There's a little matter of the children."

"The children?" the Scientist said.

"My children," Momma BB said, hugging Elen tight one last time then letting her go. "We'll round them up first then get to work on everything else—including setting you and your family up with a means of subsistence," she added for Elen who perked up at the thought.

Everyone followed along, Momma BB and Elen leading the way, then Rosalind and Haley next, followed by Mr. Kitty and the Scientist—leaving Popeye behind still cleaning the glass—out into the hall then back again through the same door they had exited which now led them into the big office that overlooked Sisyphus's Mountain where two little kids, the other Haley, and Pidgeon were all having a conversation in the puffy chairs—well, the three of them were in the puffy chairs while Pidgeon sat on the floor, staring out the window like he always did.

"And it's been coming up tails every time," one of the children said, taking out a coin and flipping it.

"Please, Thim. Not now," the other child said.

But, "Heads!" the first kid, Thim, screamed just as Momma BB announced their presence.

"Ma!" both the children yelled at the same time when they realized who it was, running over to hug Momma BB who was still hugging Elen so they all just had a big group hug.

"We thought you had two more days," one of them said.

"It has only been one, right?" the other said.

"And they've managed in even less already," Momma BB said. "But no need to worry about that now. I'm back, and I'll never leave you again."

"You better not," the children said together.

"Hey, Pidg," the Scientist said to Pidgeon who was petting Mr. Kitty. "Haley." The Scientist knew about Haley and Pidgeon's relationship, but they still found it kind of weird. Then again, the Scientist found all relationships, no matter who was in them, pretty weird, so that wasn't saying much. "So y'all are in on this, too?"

"*Weeeeell*, sort of," Pidgeon said, looking to Haley for help but getting none. "Only by accident. We didn't really help much with the setup or execution or anything."

"But we're here now," Haley added. "And we're willing to do everything we can to help from here on out."

"Yeah, well, I've been wasting my time, too," the Scientist said, thinking that their time spent trying to make the owners' worlds work for them was about as productive as Pidgeon and Haley's time spent kissing—or whatever it was that people in relationships did with each other when they were alone. "But we're all here to help now, right?"

"And there's no one left to stand in our way," Haley said, nodding at Haley. "Not even Lord Walker who's left this Earth entirely."

Haley jumped for joy, kissing Pidgeon who blushed. "You mean it?"

"Would I lie about that?" Haley said, hugging her.

"No more owners at all to stand in our way," Rosalind added. "No more walls to divide us. We, the oppressed masses, now own the technology that was used to create those walls. Let us use it to create a better world instead. Are y'all finally ready?"

"Of course, we are," Momma BB said. smiling down at her children who whispered among themselves before coming to an agreement. "We're in!"

"Me, too," Elen said, still hugging Momma BB with one arm.

"I'm definitely in," Haley said.

"Us, too," Haley said, nodding and nudging Pidgeon. "Whatever we can do. Right, babe?"

"*Uh*, right..." Pidgeon said. "Sure. Of course. Whatever I'm good at."

And even Mr. Kitty meowed in what the Scientist assumed was approval.

"So, what about you, Scientist?" Rosalind asked.

And the Scientist thought about it for a minute that felt like an eternity before answering. "Call me Ansel," they said. "And, yes. I'm in. Anything I can do to help."

"That's my girl," Rosalind said.

"*I'm still not a girl*," Ansel complained.

"Just the same," Rosalind said with a grin. "We're happy to have you on board. Isn't that right, team?"

"Right!" they all said together—even Pidgeon—and Mr. Kitty—all sounding like they meant it.

"*Fantastic*," Rosalind said. "Then let's go get Popeye and get this show on the road. We do nothing alone."

✄ ✄ ✄

LXXXV. Shoveler

The black coal burned bright and hot. Each load she piled onto the Furnace's fire brought it that little bit closer to white in her impossible pursuit of the asymptote's end.

Ever since the useless watchers had been removed from her— and the Furnace's, may Its light guide us in our pursuits—presence, she had been coming closer and closer to white hot than she'd ever been before.

She dug deep into herself, shoveling harder and faster as thanks to the Creator for removing her burden. The Creator knew best. The Creator knew all. And soon the—

She blacked out. For a second. For a century. It wouldn't have made a difference. She had no senses by which to tell. But then she came back on again.

—Creator would be… No. Where was she? *Where was she*?

The building had come down on top of her, just as it had done only one other time in history, right before the Creator had taken the watchers away. This time it was different, though. Space seemed to have somehow expanded around her, but she didn't know how she could tell. She could feel it, like too much oxygen in the air and not enough carbon dioxide. She had to find out what it was, so she climbed on hands and knees up her mountain of coal, hundreds and hundreds of feet high, to stand atop the peak and investigate.

The world certainly was different this time. Where before there had been seemingly infinite lines of identical coal mountains going in all directions, now the mountains were all of different heights, and they certainly didn't go on forever. She thought she could actually count them. She was starting to, in fact, when she was interrupted by the sound of hooting on one of the mountains across the way where she found a shoveler that looked a little weird waving at her from the distance.

"*Hooot!*" she called back, waving, not sure what else to do. "*Hoo—oooot!*"

The other shoveler hooted back, and waved again, then started climbing down their mountain of coal toward her.

There was no way to get back to work until the builders arrived, so why not climb down her mountain to see what it was that the stranger wanted? She hadn't talked to a single soul since the watchers had gone away, and she was kind of looking forward to it—especially having a conversation with another shoveler rather than weak-willed watcher. Besides, it would be a nice way to kill time until she could finally get back to work again.

ೋ **END** ♋

Thanks for reading. If you enjoyed that please join us at

www.BryanPerkinsAuthor.com

to keep up to date on future releases in the Infinite Limits series.
And if you're so inclined, don't forget to leave a review on Amazon,
Goodreads, or any other site you might frequent.
Thanks again, until next time.

-Bryan "with a Y" Perkins

Acknowledgements

Thank you, Mr. Kitty, for your undying and eternal support. And thank you to the many computers who've helped me along the way.

That's all.